Also by Joe Moore

Believe Again,
The North Pole Chronicles

1st in The Santa Claus Trilogy

Faith, Hope & Reindeer

2nd in The Santa Claus Trilogy

Return of the Birds

Santa's Elf Series

Santa's World,
Introducing Santa's Elf Series

Jamie Hardrock, Chief Mining Elf

Shelley Wrapitup, Master Design Elf

GLACIERS MELT

&

MOUNTAINS SMOKE

By Joe Moore

Published by The North Pole Press

Published by The North Pole Press

Smoky Mountains, Tennessee
ISBN13:978-0978712952

Cover design by Mary Moore
Photos by Mary Moore and Terry Ann Fritchman
Copyright © 2014 by Joe Moore

Library of Congress Catalog #2013900359

Information about and for this book may be obtained through
contacting North Pole Press at: Info@thenorthpolepress.com.
Printed in the United States of America

Dedication

There have been many people that have walked the path with us through all our trials and celebrations. Some have left us at crossroads to decide paths for ourselves. Some have disappeared right about the time we needed them most. And two have held our hands and sometimes helped carry us through some of the darkest periods of our lives, and never gave up hope on us, even when we couldn't see the path ourselves any longer.

These two people have done more than any friend or any relative would ever do, because they believed in us, and believed that helping us was their purpose. So this book is lovingly dedicated to Terry Ann and Randy Fritchman. Without them not only would the North Pole have been lost, but Santa and Mary Claus with it. Thank you for helping us make the transition to a better Santa's World.

Acknowledgments:

As no man is an island, so too, does any author write a book in a vacuum. The inspiration and pure physical toil of this book is the result of several people and a few timely suggestions. Much of the research done on the melting ice cap comes from various sources through the Internet. Many hard working scientists and even NASA have contributed to understanding much of what was put forth here. And while some of this book is pure fiction, unfortunately much of the polar ice disappearing is not, and we are looking at the total dissolution of the North Pole as early as in our lifetime and certainly within our children's.

This book is not written to cause alarm, or to put forth the concerns of global warming, or to point fingers or make accusations. This book is written to continue legends that will shortly be called into question by our children's children about what happened to Santa and Mrs. Claus, the elves, reindeer, etc. It is meant to carry on traditions that I still feel are needed to fuel our children's imagination, and to keep the teachings of Santa Claus before us. Because they are as much needed today as in any time before.

I wish to thank several people starting with my editor and friend, Tracy Lewis Shepard who has taken this journey with me through the entire trilogy and whose help and guidance has been invaluable. What she has done for me of her own volition I can never repay.

There are a few fellow professional Santa Clauses that I also wish to thank, but will not divulge their names, so as not to cause retribution to them or their reputations. They have assisted in helping me sort through the sordid, and sometimes sad state of affairs that continues amongst far too many men that don the red suit. Too many parents have too many terrible stories and as a professional Santa, I apologize for the actions of so many, but their control is not within mine.

All I can say is that I know many wonderful, genuine fellows who make it their life's work to bring happiness and joy to children and families. I am proud to be associated with these fine gentlemen and their Mrs. Clauses. It is unfortunate as in all things in life, that the few spoil it for the many. One can only hope that they eventually see the error of their ways, or get tired of trying to harm others in word and deed.

Beyond those mentioned above, I save the very best for last. She truly is the quintessential Mrs. Claus and loves so many purely and simply, especially me. She is my closest friend and my constant companion. Without you my dear Mary, I would not enjoy the blessings I have received as life would not hold the meaning it does for me. Thank you for everything and for loving me so completely, as I do you.

Scan code

and get your

FREE Color Digital Copy

of *Glaciers Melt & Mountains Smoke*

Table Of Contents

PART ONE:

THE DISCOVERY

Life is what happens to you

while you're busy

making other plans.

— John Lennon

CHAPTER 1

WATER, WATER, EVERYWHERE

Jamie Hardrock stood looking at the wall before him. "It looks like it is alive," he commented as much to himself as the person next to him. "It seems to be moving back there. Perhaps you should stand back."

The younger man moved away without another word. He had brought this strange sight to his superior as he should, but he wasn't anxious to see what might lie beyond.

Jamie stood before the wall and picked up his heavy double pick. His muscular physique had wielded this tool millions of times over his 300 plus years. He took aim and firmly, but gently, struck the top of the wall

Immediately the ice at the top began to crack and rivulets of water flowed toward the floor. The crack began spreading in all directions and Jamie yelled, "Get everyone out – NOW!" As he got his own feet moving, he heard the rumbling and cracking behind him and felt sick to his stomach.

He and the other miner caught up to the others and Jamie just kept yelling, "Get out! Get out now!" They sprinted up the shaft toward the opening but were quite a ways from the opening when they heard a large boom and then the sound of a torrent of water coming rushing toward them. The water overtook them and soon the band of miners were swept away like logs in a flume. They were banging against the walls uncontrolled as they went rolled in the freezing water.

It spat them out of the mouth of the cave and the water flowed through the streets of the village. It began to taper off, but looked as if someone was draining a fire hydrant.

Jamie picked himself up, coughed out some water and shivered a bit, "Is everyone alright?"

"I think Whistler has a broken arm, and a few of us are pretty banged up, but other than that everyone seems okay," replied one of his crew bosses.

"Get him over to the infirmary. I need to report this at once," said Jamie, "This may have more serious implications than a flooded mine."

The younger miner that had been standing by him also coughed out water and replied, "You'd best get out of those wet clothes first before hypothermia sets in. Otherwise you'll be at the health center, too. That water is only 29° Fahrenheit."

Jamie nodded and walked off toward the Woodlands.

A half hour later he knocked on the door of the Kringle's home. The lovely Mrs. Kringle opened the door and said, "Hello Jamie, this is a surprise. Won't you come in?" Jamie's height was about two thirds of the lady before him and he tried to muster a smile.

"I'm afraid this is not a social call and I need to see both of you right away," Jamie said solemnly.

"I'll go get Nick. Why don't you wait in the study?" As Mary placed her hand on his back to lead him and she said, "Are you wet?"

He chuckled and said, "Only my hair and beard, I

changed before coming. This is what we need to talk about."

"I'll get him and we'll be right in. Can I get you something warm to drink?" Mary now was concerned about both her guest and his news.

"Ah, no thanks, I had water before I came by. I'm fine right now." He moved to the room she indicated.

Mary walked to the workshop where her husband was working on a variety of projects and said to him, "Nick we have a visitor and it seems important. Could you please join us?"

As Nick rose he asked, "What's up?" He moved to Mary, and as was his custom, he gave her a little peck.

"Jamie is here and he's soaking wet, and I don't think it's from a shower," she said softly.

"Oh not again," Nick said in exasperation.

"I'm afraid so, but this is the first time it has involved the mines," she responded.

They both hurried to the study to hear Jamie's report.

Jamie stood when they walked in and Nick motioned him to sit down and be comfortable. As Nick looked him over he could see the beginnings of a couple bruises on Jamie's face and arms. And indeed he still looked water logged even in his dry clothes.

"Are you okay Jamie?" Nick asked concerned.

"I got a little banged up, and Whistler broke his arm, but we'll live," said Jamie.

"Okay, let's hear it," said Nick fearing the news but needing it nonetheless.

"We were working in the new shaft that is heading

east. Jinxy came up to me and said he had come against a strange looking sight and was afraid to go any further without my permission. When I came to the spot I could see it moving behind the wall, so I gave it a little tap toward the top to see how bad it might be, and the whole thing gave way." Jamie shivered again as he finished.

"Has it stopped?" asked Mary.

"I'm not sure," replied Jamie. "The water was flowing when I left but not as fast or much. I'm afraid either way, it is what we have feared. I believe the whole North Pole is melting."

Nick raised his hands. "Now hang on a second, Jamie. We don't know that for certain. Could it be that this was an isolated pocket?"

"We've never come across one before." Jamie shook his head. "And there is no reason to think this would have been one, and in the middle of winter as well. That water was below freezing and it should have been frozen, but it was anything but. Plus if you add this to some of the other goings on, it seems to point to the fact that this whole area is becoming unstable."

Several buildings over the last year had begun to have foundation issues, and a few had started to list a bit. They knew that the North Pole was losing its ice shelf at an alarming rate, but each winter the Pole had refrozen and they hadn't developed a problem. Until now. Many articles written from the States and Britain had spread the word that the ice shelf was less than 50% of what it had been in the past, and they were saying that the North Pole would be ice free within another decade or so.

This was extremely bad news for the residents of the North Pole, as there was nothing below the ice but ocean. Though the elves had brought tons of dirt, sand and other materials up in order to grow trees, plants and the like, it certainly wasn't enough to keep the village from being swallowed whole and disappearing forever beneath the surface.

The protective dome couldn't keep the ice from melting underneath their feet. Santa Claus had a big problem and the elf before him now proved how serious it was becoming.

He looked up at Mary. As the Chief Elf Organizer or CEO, it was her responsibility to keep the village and villagers safe. She looked at Nick and said, "We will have to reconvene the Council, right away."

Nick nodded his head and said, "We also need to bring in anyone who could advise us further." He suggested elves like Topo Geosphere, who was their primary geologist, and Whitey Slippenfall, who was in charge of the town structures and security be brought in. Whitey was already a member of the Council and would be there anyway.

Mary said, "I'll set up a meeting for the earliest possible time this week. Although I am not sure what can be done to hold back Mother Nature."

"I think the crux of the meeting will be more as to what alternatives we can come up with," said the current Santa Claus, "Aeon Millennium hinted that someday the North Pole, such as it is, might have to move."

"How and where would we move?" asked Jamie. "We have been here for hundreds of years, and our longevity is tied to the magnetism of the North Pole."

"These are questions and discussions for the Council," answered Nick. "And as always, with the combined intelligence of everyone we will figure out the answers."

Jamie correctly assumed that Nick did not wish to discuss the topic further right now, so he excused himself from the Kringles.

CHAPTER 2

SHAKE, RATTLE AND FLOW

In another part of the North Pole Whitey Slippenfall was dealing with a different problem. "What happened in here?" he asked as he surveyed the damage in Egrid Shortpockets' Light Shoppe.

Egrid steadied himself against one wall and said in a shaken voice, "The whole building starting rocking back and forth like I was in some crazy fun-house! The lights fell everywhere and it sounded like firecrackers going off at my feet."

Egrid, afraid to move an inch because the house was so wobbly, clung to a shelf with one hand, his other plastered to the wall. "I think it happened to Priscilla's house, too," he nodded toward Priscilla Huffenpuff's Ornament Shop and home next to his. "She wasn't home when it happened, but I heard some loud crashes coming from there."

Whitey said "I think it is okay now. You can move out of your corner."

Egrid looked unsure and said, "What if it starts again?"

"I don't think that shelf is going to hold you if it does," answered Whitey. "Best you move outdoors for a little bit until I can check this out."

Whitey looked in and around the structure and was relieved to see it wasn't permanently damaged. He walked over to Priscilla's home and called her name. There was no answer so he walked through the shop door. Sure enough, shattered glass lay all over the floor and most of the normally full shelves looked empty.

Whitey moved through the building making sure Priscilla wasn't injured and laying somewhere in need of help. He found nothing but more broken ornaments and personal belongings strewn across the floor. He noticed a structure crack in the back of the house and didn't like the way it extended up the corner of the wall. *That's a load-bearing wall,* he thought to himself, *Not good, not good at all.*

Whitey was aptly named, as he sported a full head of white hair that looked as white and big as a snow bank. He had piercing green eyes, and was taller than most in his village. Whitey was the protector of the North Pole. He handled the defenses and also the security within the Pole. Very rarely did anything untoward happen in the village, but if it did, Whitey was called to the scene. His keen senses were known throughout the village, and he had a great capacity for sensing what was right from wrong.

He moved to the outside. He looked down to see another crack in the ice that ran through the back of the house and off toward the hills behind the house. When he returned to Egrid's, he found the same thing going in the opposite direction from the farthest corner of that home.

He had seen these cracks before in various places around the village. More often than not, they were associated with damage at or near any buildings close to them. This had happened too often in recent days. He had not witnessed the events, but the results were always the same. Damage, and lots of it. The worst so far had been at Britney Clearwaters' plant. Britney was in charge of the water flow through the North Pole. She and her staff controlled the amount of melt and the treatment of the water for purity, for the entire village.

A few weeks ago her plant experienced what was at first thought to be an earthquake. The pipes broke lose and water tanks ruptured. There remained a few places that were not getting any normal flow of water, still. And though no damage was done by the flooding, it was a major disruption that hadn't been fully repaired yet.

Whitey scratched his head and wondered why this was happening now. After centuries of peaceful existence in the farthest reaches of the world, away from tallfolk and their endless conflicts, now their peaceful village seemed to be cracking right under their feet. *And how can we stop it?* he asked himself.

CHAPTER 3

ROUND ONE

Mary Claus, as Mrs. Santa was more often called, had put the word out to the Council Elders that a meeting was needed to discuss the disturbing happenings throughout the North Pole. In addition to the elders she also requested Topo, Forrest Hedemup, Bilge Seaseeker, Frosty Evergreen, Jackson Killowatt's son, Sparky Terrawatt, and a few others who had helped in the past on particularly thorny issues to be present. She set the meeting for Thursday and asked the invitees to 'study up' on the situation at the Pole and bring ideas and recommendations.

On Thursday, the Council chambers were filled with elves, charts, reports and papers of various kinds. The Council took their seats, and as was the custom, the president, who was the reigning Santa Claus, brought the gavel down and brought the meeting to order.

Many changes had taken place during the several hundred years of the village's existence, though the Council structure had changed little. Santa and Mrs. Claus headed the central positions, exactly as Nick's parents had done when Kristopher Kringle was the Santa Claus. The Council members were made up of Ella Communicado, the communications director of the North Pole, Freida Cutinglass, the Chief Decorator of the village, Jackson Killowatt, who is in charge of the power supplies to the village, Alfie Newsworthy, the

Pole's historian and record keeper, Keeney Eagleye, who is in charge of the Hall of Records and the Naughty/Nice list, Willie Movinmuch, who developed and takes care of transportation to and in the North Pole, Denny Sweetooth, the North Pole's baker, chef and dearest friend to the Kringles, Whitey Slipenfall, who is in charge of the town structures and security and finally, Britney Clearwater, who manages the vast water flow in the North Pole.

Nick opened the meeting stating that obviously something serious was happening to their beloved North Pole Village and the situation needed to be addressed. He asked Whitey to give a report on some of the goings on, in case anyone in the room was unaware of the problems that had ensued. Of course they knew about the incidences, but kept silent during the report anyway.

Whitey explained the problems and damage to the Water Department, the Light Shoppe and Ornament Shop and others. He spoke of the cracks and residual damage after the events. Afterward, Mary Claus spoke of the near disaster at the mine, and that water was flowing from the shaft and freezing into large areas around the base of the village.

"Obviously we have a problem, and we need to figure out what is happening," Santa said. "What we need now is to understand how, and if, we can remedy the situation. We have invited many of you here to help resolve this. Before we discuss ideas and suggestions, I would like to hear from our resident scientists, Bilge Seaseeker and Topo Geosphere, about what is taking place in the Pole. Bilge would you begin?"

Bilge Seaseeker stood about three and half feet, and was fully six inches shorter than most of the elves. He had a studious face and pitch black hair that he wore in bowl cut around his head. He wasn't quite as round as Denny, but because he was so short, he looked it. His voice was somewhat harsh and scratchy and he was hard to understand under the best of times. He came to the center of the room and looked up at the Council dais. The local oceanographer cleared his throat and said, "It has been written by many scientists from several nations that, and I quote, 'Arctic variability is dominated by multi-decadal fluctuations. Incomplete sampling of these fluctuations results in highly variable arctic surface-air temperature (SAT) trends. Modulated by multi-decadal variability, SAT trends are often amplified relative to northern-hemispheric trends, but over the 125-year record we identify periods when arctic SAT trends were smaller or of opposite sign than northern-hemispheric trends. Arctic and northern-hemispheric air-temperature trends during the 20th century (when multi-decadal variability had little net effect on computed trends) are similar, and do not support the predicted polar amplification of global warming. The possible moderating role of sea ice cannot be conclusively identified with existing data. If long-term trends are accepted as a valid measure of climate change, then the SAT and ice data do not support the proposed polar amplification of global warming. Intrinsic arctic variability obscures long-term changes, limiting our ability to identify complex feedbacks in the arctic climate system.' End quote. So there you have it,"

Bilge Seaseeker concluded.

Everyone from the Council, and most of the gallery, stared blankly at Bilge. After several moments of silence, Freida Cutinglass finally asked "Did he say something? Does any of that mean something?"

Ella and many others laughed and she looked to Topo, "Topo dear, would you mind explaining to the crowd what Bilge just said?"

Topo Geosphere stood alongside Bilge. When the two were together you couldn't help but picture a shorter version of Laurel and Hardy. Topo stood a full foot taller than Bilge and was much slimmer. He wore his black hair down over his forehead and combed to the side. His wire rimmed glasses were almost invisible in front of his hazel eyes. He looked to be in his forties, though he was 254 on his next birthday in May.

He answered, "Yes, putting it in more easily understood layman's terms, the hubbub about global warming that we keep hearing about is not the only situation causing our current problem. He stated that the changes to the Pole may be a usual trend in the earth's normal history.

"For instance, the Earth has several poles, not just two. It has a geographic North Pole, where we are, and a geographic South Pole. These points generally mark the Earth's axis of rotation. But as most everyone knows, the Earth also has magnetic North and South Poles, based on the planet's magnetic field. When you use a compass, it points to the magnetic, not the geographic, North Pole. The Earth's magnetic poles move. The magnetic North Pole can move in loops of up to 50 miles or 80 kilometers per day. And its actual location, or average, of these loops, moves at approximately 25 miles each year. In the last 150 years, the pole has wandered a total of about 685 miles or 1102 kilometers. Of course the magnetic South Pole moves in a similar fashion.

"The poles can actually switch places. Scientists have discovered this by examining rocks on the ocean floor that retain traces of the field, similar to a recording on a magnetic tape. They estimate that the last time the poles switched was 780,000 years ago, and it's happened about 400 times in 330 million history of the Earth. Each reversal takes a thousand years or so to complete, and it takes longer for the shift to take effect at the equator than at the poles. The field has weakened about 10% in the last 150 years. Some scientists think this is a sign of a flip in progress."

"So are you telling us that the magnetic north is flipping and that this is causing our problem?" asked Keeney Eagleye.

"Actually no, what I am saying is that it is possible that the North Pole is undergoing a usual shift as has happened throughout its history," replied Topo. "We think what is taking place is not so much global warming as polar warming."

"So in other words, we are seeing a historical trend and we are melting up here?" Denny asked incredulously.

"That's about the size of it, except that it is accelerating at a more rapid rate than we first thought. This is primarily because the more ice that melts, the less the Arctic can reflect the sunlight as the ocean is darker and therefore absorbs heat," replied Topo.

"How serious is this and is there anything we can do about it ourselves?" asked Mary.

Topo looked at Bilge who tilted his head and shrugged. He shuffled his feet a moment clearly thinking of his answer and looked at the Council saying, "I don't wish to beat about the bush, and what I am about to say is not an alarmist speaking, but a realist, and this is sincere speech. I have conferred with Bilge and many others within the tallfolk communities. And I guess there is only one way to put this...in the next year or less we will become the new Atlantis, only our village will sink to the bottom of the Arctic Ocean."

The room exploded into discussions about how quickly they could move, and complaints of the idea of losing their entire home, shops and more. Nick and Mary looked at each other and allowed the news to settle into their minds.

Nick finally banged the gavel several times to bring quiet to the chamber. He looked at Topo and said in a soft voice, "Not to shoot the messenger, but when were you going to let us in on this news?"

Bilge stepped forward and said, "We only recently realized that the ice decrease and the SAT was happening at an accelerated velocity which contradicted original theory. It was perceived that another multi-decadal event would take place prior to having to determine any nomadic activity..."

"English..." Keeney fairly yelled at the scholar.

Topo again answered, "We first thought we might

have at least a decade or two, but it is melting and growing warmer far more quickly than we had thought. We only verified the time frame we are actually working with when you called the Council meeting."

Another explosion of voices took place and again Nick banged his gavel to bring the roar of the crowd to silence. When there was peace once more Nick asked, "So as we are to understand it, we have a year to relocate the entire North Pole Village to a more stable area?"

Topo looked down at the floor and Bilge looked anywhere but at any of the council members. "Well?" pressed Nick.

"Maybe less," replied Topo, "perhaps only 6 to 9 months."

Nick fell back in his seat, stunned. How could he oversee the move of a village that had been standing for centuries in so short a time? And move it to where? Anywhere they would try to locate would draw an enormous amount of attention and of course would expose them to the rest of the world.

He asked the question that was on everyone's mind, if not the most immediate problem before them. "Topo, do we know how this will effect our longevity and what might happen to us once we leave the close confines of the magnetic pole?'

Everyone's breath caught as they stared at Topo. Topo only shook his head and said, "No."

The whole room seemed to release a collective gasp and whispers ensued where there were loud voices before.

Santa said in as chipper a voice as he could muster, "First things first, we need to decide where we would like to move the village. We need to get the assistance of anyone we can throughout the world to help us accomplish this feat. I would like to begin by suggesting we contact everyone who could help us that has been invited to the North Pole previously. We helped many of these people in the past and now it is time they help us if possible."

"I second that motion," said Denny looking as serious as Nick had ever seen the elf, "and I move for a vote."

The motion was passed unanimously and Nick said, "Okay, that's done. Ella would you please work with Keeney to get the word out as soon as possible?" Ella nodded.

"Now, are there any other suggestions that should be addressed immediately?" questioned Santa.

"Should we discuss where we are going to move to and how?" asked Whitey.

"I think we should take a day to digest the news we have received and reconvene tomorrow, for two reasons. I suspect we need to let others know about our situation, and secondly, I believe we will have a clearer idea and more practical thoughts after we have had a moment to formulate some possibilities in our mind," said Mary.

"I agree with our CEO," said Santa using Mary's official title. "I think we are too close to this news to discuss it with any rationality now. But I wish to emphasize the following, every year we pull off miracles and every year we accomplish more in a month than a host of companies or countries could achieve in a year or longer. This news is dire, we can overcome this problem as we have so many in the past. I know Aeon had alluded to the fact that eventually we would have to move the North Pole, so in a way, I guess I knew this was coming. But as is his way, he never provided me answers as to how to accomplish such a monumental task."

"So now it is up to us," Nick continued. "And we will find that path and complete this undertaking. I ask you to remain as upbeat as possible and think seriously only of solutions rather than consequences. I also invite any interested party from our village, or outside it, to help us fulfill this quest. With that, I order this Council adjourned until 9:00 tomorrow morning." And Santa brought down the gavel once more.

Chapter 4

Where, Oh Where?

The rest of the day the Kringles discussed the possibilities of where and how to move the North Pole or more accurately the village.

"I need to look at Aeon's book and see if he gives me any type of hint," said Nick.

"Don't you think you would have noticed something before if he said you would have to move the North Pole?" asked Mary.

"Dad said he mentioned something to him when he last saw Aeon," Nick said, "Or should I say the second to last time he saw him."

Aeon Millennium had been the resident expert on time and time travel when Nick's father Kris Kringle was Santa Claus. Aeon had come to Nick once and told him that he would eventually take Nick's parents to another dimension or 'existence' when a certain time came. That time had come a few years back and both Nick and Mary missed them greatly. Unlike others who suddenly disappeared without a word, Kris and Annie were allowed to say their goodbyes to Nick and Mary.

Kris told Nick 'that there is nothing left for me to show you, and in fact you have outdone my abilities and I am extremely proud of you.' Annie had said much the same to Mary, but added "You are the daughter I only wish I could have had since a child, but I am honored to have been your 'Mom' for so many years."

With that the three of them disappeared into their new existence. Nick now ached to ask his father what he thought he should do.

Many years before Aeon had left Nick a book with instruction for some key things Nick needed to learn, events that would occur and schematics for much of the technology that was in place at the village today. But Nick hadn't referred to the book for a couple of years, as he had come to the end and their were no more secrets to be gained from it.

Nick rose from his chair and went to the study. Behind a series of books about history he found the book from Aeon that he had hidden. He started in the beginning where Aeon told the purpose of the book and about the time continuum that he now used regularly and especially on Christmas Eve. He skimmed past the parts of instruction and the schematics that remained in the book, as he had taken copies of the pages rather than tear them out as he had done with the first couple inventions.

But look as he might he did not see anything regarding moving, or changing the North Pole or the village's location. He did find one cryptic comment that Aeon had written that gave him pause. He remembered trying to understand what the old wizard was trying to tell him when he first came across the passage, but couldn't make heads or tails from it. It simply read, *There will come a time when you don't know where to go. Return to the first place you visited with your father before the error, and follow your heart and direction upon that place.*

As Nick read this now, it made no more sense to him than it did then. He and his father had visited the world together and often. He could not remember a time when they visited anywhere 'in error' and they had made several trips together on Christmas Eve, but never got lost or ended up somewhere they didn't intend.

Nick closed the book as Mary came in and saw the disappointment on his face. "No luck?" she asked.

Nick shook his head and said, "Nothing. No mention of the North Pole really, only a few events that have come to pass and predictions that already happened."

"Seems we are on our own," Mary said in an excited voice, "You know it only makes sense that this should happen with you. Your father will always be the Santa Claus of the North Pole, and though you have been Santa for many decades, I think a new 'North Pole' should be developed by you and your family."

Nick shrugged, "I'd rather leave the status quo alone, but since I do not have a choice unless we can put water wings under the entire village, we need to come up with somewhere else."

Mary laughed at his comment and said, "It is nice to see your sense of humor hasn't left you entirely. How about I make us a nice cup of tea and we can talk about the 'where' as we drink it."

"How about a cup of cocoa?" said Nick hopefully. Mary had been trying to get Nick to cut down on his consumption of cocoa, including asking his chief cocoa elf, Coco Nicenhot, not to cater to her husband's whims so frequently.

"Let's compromise." Mary chuckled. "Tea now, cocoa when we come up with a solution. This will give you more incentive."

Nick always knew when he lost a battle with his wife, and always gave up before it could be a problem. He shook his head and said, "At least there's hope."

He took the large globe from one of the tables in his office and followed his wife to their more comfortable study.

After she brought them some hot orange pekoe tea, Mary said, "Okay you are the world traveler, where would you like to move to?"

Nick snickered and said, "You forget my dear wife, most places I have only seen briefly, at night, and I was working. I can't vouch for what they may be like to live at."

"At least we don't have to worry about the weather. Assuming we will build another dome wherever we end up, we can choose what ever type of environment we wish."

"True." Nick pondered a moment and said. "It might be nice to pick a more suitable place to get supplies in and out of."

The two began looking at the globe and talked about many possibilities, each with their own unique set of advantages and challenges. They were at it several hours, and they narrowed down or eliminated many places, but there were far too many left to make a decision quickly. They decided they would make a shorter list and take it before the Council and see if anyone else had come up with the same locations the next morning.

CHAPTER 5

ROUND TWO

The next morning Nick and Mary woke to a particularly bright sunny day. Though this was only February, and the true sun would not be seen for another month, the artificial light in the dome was particularly brilliant this day.

"Wow! The gang must have really wanted to wake us up. I think they have the brightness setting at maximum," commented Nick.

"Perhaps they want us to know that brighter days are ahead," said Mary smiling. "Personally, I think it is wonderful and will thank them for it."

After dressing and having breakfast they walked toward the Council chambers. As they got closer, the crowd swelled until the Kringles were having difficulty making their way to the building. The word had spread throughout the North Pole about the situation and everyone wanted to hear answers and know what to do.

When the Kringles finally made it to the door, Whitey opened it and let them escape the throng. "They began coming at six this morning. I had a feeling this was going to happen so I came early. I have spent the last three hours trying to keep them out."

Nick looked at the crowd's worried faces and considered the situation. He said, "Since this affects every being in the North Pole, I suppose we should let them in."

"There's not enough room in here," Whitey protested. "We couldn't possibly fit them all."

"Let's fit as many as possible, especially those who were here so early, as they are the most anxious I would guess. For the rest, have Ion Crosswire set up a speaker system to broadcast our discussions outside."

"I'll get right on it," agreed Whitey.

"Whitey, we will need you in the chambers, designate this to one of your helpers," said Mary with a determined voice. "They can take care of this and we don't want you getting caught up in crowd control."

Whitey nodded and simply said, "Will do."

The Kringles moved into the inner sanctum of the chamber and Nick announced to the others already there, "It seems we will have visitors this morning."

Jackson was a medium sized elf with brown hair that fell to his shoulder in a flip and a very bushy mustache. When he spoke you couldn't help look at his mouth because of all the hair over it. He asked, "Do you think this wise? I am not sure a lot of what will be discussed should be 'open to the public'."

Mary chimed in, "Since this affects everyone's future, I believe they have a right to hear what we have to say. Besides, what if one of them has a better thought than us? I'd hate to miss that opportunity. I believe Nick can keep the crowd orderly."

"And if I can't I will simply clear the chambers and we can continue," said Nick.

Jackson shrugged and a couple other members shook their heads. Denny laughed and said, "Then let the craziness begin!'"

Mary and Nick took their places in the dais and the crowd lead by Whitey Slippenfall noisily began to shuffle into the chambers.

As the chamber filled, in walked a rather nerdy looking elf with thick black framed glasses, wrinkled clothes and spiked style but mussed hair. His head was as round as an orange but he had an bright intelligence in his eyes and a pleasant demeanor. He walked up and around the dais to Santa's chair and leaned forward on the immense desk before him.

"Good morning, Ion" said Nick.

"Good morning your Majesty," Ion said.

"I really wish you wouldn't call me that," Nick growled. "You and I have known each other for nearly a century and worked on numerous projects together."

"Okay, sorry. Good morning Santa," Ion said with a grin.

"Better, but Nick would do fine," Nick retorted.

"I respect both the position and the man. So 'Santa' is as casual as it will ever get for me," replied Ion, "Okay you're completely set up. Press this button here if you wish to mute the Council's conversation or any part of it, and push it again when you want everyone to hear."

"Where are the microphones?" asked Nick.

Ion smirked and then said, "Already set into the dais. We did this a few years back when we figured the need would present itself one day."

"Oh, one of those slow days when you ran out of other things to tinker with?" Nick said with a smile.

Ion shrugged, "Remember anything you say after I

push this button will be heard throughout the North Pole."

"Wait," Nick grabbed Ion's arm. "Throughout the village? Are you serious?"

"Santa you know I am always serious and, yes, you are piped into the same system that I set up for Carol Joynote when we decided to pipe music throughout the village," answered Ion. "I am sure that everyone will wish to hear these proceedings, and it will prevent, or at least minimize, incorrect information and rumors. Also Ella has it patched into her information counsel so that the distribution establishments will also be hearing this. So I guess you could say you are worldwide. Ready?" Ion held his finger over the button.

Santa nodded nervously, and as Ion pushed the button, Santa said in a much louder voice than he intended, "Will everyone take their seats?" He lowered his own volume and continued, "Considering the gravity of our discussions, I have arranged it for everyone to hear the Council and our deliberations today. I have allowed an open forum, but I emphasize, at the first sign of disruption I will clear the chamber and discontinue the broadcast."

Nick hated sounding so abrupt, but there was a lot to be done and far less time than he would have desired to do it in. He was Santa Claus, but in times like this, he was also the leader of the village and everyone would look to him for answers.

He brought down the gavel and announced that the Council meeting come to order.

As the silence finally became complete he opened

with these remarks. "As is obvious, the village has heard the problem that lies before us. For the benefit of those who may not know the entire story or, worse yet, is under misguided information, I will explain the problem, and I won't mince words." He paused.

"It has been learned that though we knew the North Pole icecap was melting more each year, it is now certain that our village is in danger of this continued melting. Regardless of the reasons behind it, our village is in danger of sinking into the Arctic Ocean and in a relatively short time.

"Rather than attempt to find a way to stay on a literal sinking ship, we need to determine, first, where to move the village and second, how. In other words, what is the most expeditious way to do this quickly. I have allowed everyone both here in the village and elsewhere in our world to hear our thoughts with the hope that as in the past, the combined thinking and the overall brilliance of our residents will produce a plan and the results to accomplish this before it is too late.

"Now that I have put forth sincere speech to explain our predicament, I will ask that we hear from members of the Council first, and then I will open it up to the gallery."

Nick leaned back and looked toward the other Council members. After several moments, Alfie Newsworthy, the historian for the elves, leaned forward in his chair cleared his throat and said, "Mr. President, in numerous discussions I have had with the other Council members and lay people, it has been pretty firmly decided that everyone will follow our Santa Claus and CEO to whatever location they feel most strongly about."

Nick looked incredulously at Alfie and the gallery before him. Many in the crowd were nodding their heads and whispering to their neighbors.

"Well I must say," Nick said after making several incomprehensible noises, "I am honored at the loyalty and support that you have put forth. But I would also like to hear some ideas from others on what might determine a practical location so that we may make a proper decision."

Jackson took the floor and stated, "Since we need to leave the magnetic pole, I will need to redesign some of our power to thermal from magnetic which will continue to use Britney's water supply as before, so we will need to make certain that a good water supply is included in the location."

Britney said, "And if we move anywhere away from an ice pack, we will have to figure the additional resources we will need to supply water to the village, in addition to our increased power supply needs."

"Has anyone thought about moving to the South Pole?" asked Freida Cutinglass.

"The problem I see with that is setting up a reasonable supply route," stated Nick, "No continent touches Antarctica so it would be difficult to set up rail and road service to bring in and distribute products as efficiently as we do here. Also, there exists some potential melting problems there as well. However, at least there is solid ground underneath the ice there."

Mary jumped in saying, "And could you imagine

inviting other folks to the South Pole. I could picture their reaction for a free trip to lower Argentina." Several people chuckled and Denny laughed out loud.

A hand came up slowly from the gallery in front of them. It belonged to Stacy Buttons, the chief doll maker to the North Pole, and Nick recognized her at once, "Yes Stacy?"

Stacy stood and said in a soft voice, "Begging the Council's pardon, but if we have pretty much anywhere in the world to choose from, could we please pick a place that has more colors than white?"

The whole room exploded in cheers, laughter and comments.

"Wherever we pick," Mary chortled. "It will certainly have land underneath it." And the room erupted again.

Nick let the disruption continue for a few moments more as he thought it did much to relieve the tension in the room. He finally brought the gavel to life and called for order.

The room settled down and Nick said, "Okay, note made, more than one color." The room chuckled again, but kept its order.

Other issues were brought up and it was decided the next location should be a country that was primarily Christian in its populace. It should also contain no civil unrest or be anywhere near in danger of an uprising. It should be democratic or parliamentary in its political structure, and as mentioned earlier, easily accessible to move goods and supplies including people. When the original North Pole was established this last issue was not as important to the village as it was today.

As Whitey was responsible for the North Pole's security including its dome, Nick asked him, "Are we able to set up the dome anywhere we desire, or are there any parameters we should be aware of, or need to take into consideration?"

Whitey shook his head and said, "As you already know we have placed domes all over the south in all our distribution points. We can build a protection and camouflage dome pretty much anywhere we have the room. It is also possible that depending where we choose to move, it may not need to be as large an area as we have here. We don't need to rely nearly as much on our forest as we did when the village was first established."

"Assuming that we could tap into more natural resources other than magnetic, how much area would we need?" asked Mary.

"Assuming an adequate water source along with the probability of utilizing solar, which we are unable to use now for six months of the year, and the wind generation we were beginning to install up here, possible natural gas resources, and adding how close we are on cold fusion from one of our inventor/scientists in the south, I would estimate 3 to 5 square miles," finished Whitey.

"That's about 67 to 85% less than we have today," said Nick in astonishment.

"Yes, but initially we needed more area to build much of what we didn't have," said Whitey. "Topo, Bilge, Britney and I went over the numbers yesterday. We have accomplished much in the last 300 years." He chuckled.

"That puts a whole new spin on this," Nick sighed. "I was trying to figure out an area more than three times that size. I could only come up with the Australian Outback, the Brazilian Rainforest or the Sahara Desert."

Denny said, "Uh, none of those places sound too desirable for me, especially with those snakes in Australia and Brazil."

"That is the first bit of good news I've heard in the last 24 hours or more," said Nick, "Mary and I can prepare a short list of ideas and present it to the Council next week if that's agreeable."

"So moved," said Britney.

"Seconded," said Jackson.

"Moved and seconded, all in favor say 'Aye'," said Nick. The Council members agreed verbally. "Any opposed?" asked Nick to a silent room. "Okay, next order of business, and again I speak to those of you who were not in this room yesterday. It was decided that in order to take on this monumental task we would need the help of every elf and tallfolk possible. We voted unanimously to bring many of the people we have brought here in the past to assist us, especially given the short duration we have to accomplish this.

"We need to alert Christel Bunkinstyle and the other innkeepers that they will have full inns, and we need to make the Rooming House and both Bunkhouses available for elves and tallfolk alike," continued Nick.

"Perhaps we could convert one of the manufacturing areas into a makeshift bunkhouse as well," Mary spoke up. "It won't be the most comfortable, but it may serve the purpose."

"Good idea," Nick smiled at his wife. "Speaking of,

we will have to ship everything we can to the southern centers. We will have to miniaturize everything feasible and ship it quickly. I will have both our boys, Kristopher and Michael, assist in the organizing and movement of each manufacturing area. Each elf shall be responsible for organizing and packing their own shop. We will help with any miniaturization of your goods and belongings for transport to the new area."

"May I make another suggestion, Santa?" asked Keeney.

"Please...," said Nick.

"I think it might be a good idea to contact Cory Peters and ask him to contact Santas that might be of particular use on helping us at either end of this relocation," said Keeney.

Cory Peters and his wife, Katy, were tallfolk that ran a bed and breakfast. Attached to it was a school that taught the top men seeking to portray Santa Claus around the world. He had been teaching many years now and had a large number of Santa 'Ambassadors' as the North Pole called them. They helped Santa obtain children's wishes, and they did charitable acts across the various countries in the name of Santa Claus.

"An excellent idea," said Nick enthusiastically. "Ella will you see to that?"

"Of course, Santa," replied Ella.

"Any other ideas or thoughts?" asked Nick.

Another hand rose from the gallery and Nick acknowledged the elf by name, "Yes, Ramsey?"

Ramsey Hampton was one of the balloonists and an artisan in ice sculpture. He stood taller than most around the Pole and he looked like a sailor with a tight physique that was almost as muscular as Jamie Hardrock and Forrest Heademup. He looked at the Council and spoke clearly, though you could hear the concern in his voice, "Do we know what may happen to us physically if we leave the North Pole? I have always been told it was the magnetic properties of the North Pole that allowed us to live so much longer than tallfolk."

Nick looked at Ramsey with equal concern and said, "Frankly, no. We are not sure what will happen to us and if we will age more quickly, or not at all. I have thought much on this, and I will remind you that many elves have lived for decades in the south, and they have not aged any faster than any elf in the North Pole. I am hoping we will find ourselves in a similar fashion. But in truth, I do not think we know for sure what may happen. We will have to take our chances."

Ramsey nodded and retook his seat. Many mini-discussions ensued after Nick's answer and he let them, as he knew everyone was anxious about their future prospects, and no more so than he and Mary. Considering they were tallfolk and Nick was pushing two hundred and Mary nearly one hundred they wondered if they would follow Nick's parents footsteps and live many more centuries or revert to a more 'normal' lifespan of tallfolk in the south.

Death was a rare occurrence in the North Pole. Many elves were over three hundred years old and some were in their 4th century. Kris' parents were over three hundred when Aeon came to collect them, and because of the Pole, they had never known a sick day in their lives.

In fact, Nick had never experienced illness since the day he was born, and Mary was young enough when she came to live at the top of the world with Nick, that except for illnesses she had as a child, she also had not been sick and commented often about it during their years together.

Nick knew this was a source of concern particularly to Mary. Many times she talked about losing friends like the Handlers who had begun Mattel, and many others like them. A few of the first people they had invited to North Pole had passed on, and Mary wished she could have prevented their demise.

This was the one thing that concerned Nick more than the rest. He was particularly worried about he and Mary's two sons that were both in their thirties now. Like Nick, neither Kristopher or Michael had seen a single sick day.

Would that radically change now? In the North Pole, there were no food allergies, diseases, or excessive weight gain - with rare exceptions, like Denny Sweetooth. Nick thought it was only that Denny was as short as he was round, and he'd probably came to the Pole that way, though he never asked.

The meeting returned to near silence and Nick asked for other questions. Most that followed were more individual or personal in nature, and the Council did its best to answer them as seriously as they were asked, Nick saw all were becoming tired and that continuing this would probably not accomplish anything of great value.

He called for adjournment and the motion was immediately agreed to by the Council members.

As Mary and Nick walked back toward their woodland home Nick looked to his wife and saw that one tear had fallen and another following.

"What's wrong my love?" he asked with concern.

"I was thinking about our beautiful home," she sniffed and wiped the second tear away. "It is so wonderful, and it is more than I ever would have dreamed of when I was living in California. And to imagine it sinking below the waves with its beautiful woodwork and designs breaks my heart."

Nick thought for a moment and said, "If I remember, my parents said that the elves built them that house in a few months. As we know, they have only gotten better at what they do over the last century, so it is entirely possible they can make us a more beautiful edifice on this next go around."

"Nick, when the elves built your parents house, our house, it was at a time when much of the rest of the village was already in place," Mary said sadly. "Now they will have to build everything at once and so many needs must come before our own, like manufacturing centers and the dozens of shops, the inns, the eateries, and..."

"Whoa there my dear wife." Nick waved his hands to slow her down. "Yes, these things must come to pass, but there are actually many more elves than when the village was first established, and we now are working with the people of the south, who will also lend a hand," said the exasperated Santa Claus. "Maybe we will have more makeshift structures at first, but in my heart I believe you and I will have many years ahead of us to rebuild to the splendor of this home. And this time it will have your touches to it rather than my parents."

"Our touches, you mean, and I have never complained once about any part of that house, and would probably do most things exactly the same," protested Mary.

"Even so," continued Nick, "you have mentioned a few things you would change if you had the chance to do it over. And now here's your chance."

Mary moved closer to Nick and took his arm as they walked. After a few moments she looked down and asked Nick softly, "Do you think we will really have 'many years ahead of us'?"

Nick pondered the question as he had done so many times recently. He looked directly into Mary's eyes and said as softly, "I truly believe that yes, we will. I do not know how or why, but I believe God isn't finished with us yet. But if He were, I could never be happier about the life I have lived with you and our two sons. So I would go with a smile on my face, but my gut tells me that it is not yet."

"I believe you are right," said Mary in a hushed tone. "I also don't think our time is over. I do worry about us not being together, though."

"Ho, ho, HO, Mary Kringle!" Nick fairly boomed. "You forget what I keep telling you. If you ever leave me I am going with you! And we will be together until the very end of time. Aeon knew I needed to find you to

fulfill my destiny. I showed you the passage in the book
he left for me."

Mary smiled and nodded her head. "I remember, I
just wanted to make certain you weren't getting tired of
me."

"You are not that lucky, my dear lady," and Nick
gave Mary a kiss on the lips. "Whatever we will face
ahead of us, we will face it together."

Their home was in sight and they saw Kristopher
standing at the front door waiting for them.

Their eldest son, Kristopher, stood a full two inches
above Nick and was stocky, but not overweight. He had
his father's and grandfather's facial features of a more
round face with high cheekbones that were nearly
always rosy in hue. He sported a closely copped beard
that was beginning to show gray streaks. His hair was
also like his father's and had been solidly white for the
last decade. Now at thirty-five, Mary could see how he
resembled his father when she first met him in
California. He was named after his grandfather, whom
they both resembled. Kristopher Nicholas Kringle was
the first Santa Claus of the North Pole that the elves
sought to be the gift-giver for the world.

Kristopher asked, "How did it go?"

Nick looked quizzically at Kristopher and asked,
"You didn't listen to it?"

"Of course I did," replied Kristopher. "But I wasn't
there to see the mood of the crowd or the reactions of
the Council. It sounded calm enough, though I imagine
you could cut the tension with a knife."

"I was more than a little concerned when Mom and I

got to the chambers and saw the crowd," mused Nick. "But I think they mostly wanted more information, or to determine the truth of what they heard, and were not there to cause problems."

"They wanted to see what the plan was, eh?" said Kristopher.

"Pretty much, yeah," replied Nick.

"So what is it – the plan I mean?" asked Kristopher.

"Could we go in and sit down, first?" Mary said tiredly. "I think your father and I are beat."

"I'm sorry," Kristopher said. "I was anxious to hear. Michael expected you would both be exhausted and he is working in the kitchen on lunch for us."

With that Kristopher stepped away from the door and let his parents pass through the entry. As they walked in a wonderful smell filled the air reminiscent of garlic and other spices. They followed the smell to the connected kitchen and family room at the back of the house. As they stepped in they saw their younger son, Michael, standing over a cutting board, chopping green onions.

Michael looked up briefly and then returned to his duties. In a blur of words he said, "Hi. Boy, you both look wore out. I thought you might be in the mood for cedar-planked salmon with my avocado relish."

Like Nick, Michael enjoyed being in the kitchen more than anywhere else. Michael, Nick, Denny and Pierre would spend hours working on a variety of culinary delights, to the enjoyment of everyone they served. Unlike Nick though, Michael also spent a good deal of time baking with his mother, so he was more proficient in both the cooking and baking arena than Nick, which didn't disappoint Nick in the least.

Michael was his fathers height but looked more like Mary. He had her deeper green eyes and more strawberry blond hair. His hair was cut short, in what Kristopher called the "businessman's haircut" and he sported no facial hair. Michael often commented that he didn't have the "caveman gene" that his father and brother had. Mary had named him Michael Joseph after her grandfather, and Nick had always liked the name. Both boys were good looking, but truth be told, most thought Michael was more fair-haired and better looking than Kristopher.

Mary answered Michael, saying the meal sounded delicious, and that after a little rest she would be more than ready to enjoy her son's efforts.

Nick and Mary plopped into the comfortable armchairs and sighed deeply.

"So where are we moving to?" Kristopher immediately questioned.

"What? Oh Kristopher," Nick said with a sigh. "We don't know yet, and we are too tired to discuss it now."

"Not a clue, eh?" prodded Kristopher. "I heard you talking about Brazil, Africa and Australia. Were you serious?"

"Mom and I couldn't be serious about any place, until we heard what was needed," said Nick tiredly. "Now really, give us a little quiet time to gather ourselves, and we can talk more about this later."

"Seriously, bro," Michael said, "Give them some time. Maybe they will ask our opinion if we let them be."

Mary laughed and said, "Oh, is that so?"

"Hey, we figured you have already wrestled with this, so you might want our opinions or at least suggestions," said Michael jovially.

"We shall see...later," Mary said the last word on that subject for the time being.

CHAPTER 4

A TOWERING SITUATION

As the Kringles were settling into their family room in the woodlands, Whitey Slippenfall was summoned to the visiting center. He met Fergie Keepitneat at the Reindeer Inn.

"What's up?" Whitey asked,

"We heard a loud crack a little ago," said Fergie, "And it has been followed by a sound like rolling thunder several times since then."

"Can you figure out where it is coming from?' queried Whitey.

"Near as any of us can tell, we believe it is around the lower tower of the gondola," replied the Innkeeper.

The gondola was fairly close to the Inn, so it made sense that if it was having issues, the elves at the Inn would hear it first. A long, low rumble shook the Inn and everyone in it.

"Kinda like that," said Fergie.

"How many times has that happened?" asked Whitey.

"Gunther," Fergie yelled toward the back. "What is that, four?"

A voice came from the rear of the Inn, "I make it five in the last hour and a quarter."

"All right, I'll go take a look," said Whitey. "Do me a favor and call Willie Movinmuch and ask him to come down here as quickly as he can."

Willie was the transportation chief of the North Pole. If anything flew, rode on wheels or floated on water, it was under Willie's purview. And though the gondola did none of these, technically it was Willie's responsibility, and he would know more about its inner workings than anyone else. Fergie contacted Ella who connected with Willie.

Like the rest of the elf nation, Willie had listened to the meeting, so when he heard he was needed by the gondola, 'Pronto', as Ella said, he could guess why.

The greatest weight stress in the North Pole would be either the train station, especially when a train was there, or the gondola. And both of those were in the Visiting Center.

He jumped aboard his snowmobile and gunned the engine to life. *Thank goodness this isn't happening at a time when we have visitors in the station or running around the village*, Willie thought to himself.

A few minutes later he pulled up to Whitey as another rumbling began. He could see the cables and one of the cars swaying and moving as the ice around their feet shook. It nearly knocked Whitey over and it was only because Willie was still on the snowmobile that he, himself didn't fall.

This tremor lasted a little longer than the last Whitey thought, and by now the cables were lashing about.

"That's not good," Willie said when the shaking finally ended.

"So what do you think?" asked Whitey.

"I think we should shut down the gondola and

remove the cars from it to reduce the stress before the whole thing falls down or worse," stated Willie.

Whitey was walking around the base of the gondola tower. "I don't see any cracks around here like I have at some of the houses and shops in the village," he said.

"That may not mean anything," puzzled Willie, "It could be deeper, and that only causes me more concern. It may give way underneath and the whole thing come crashing down."

"Do you think it might fall over and hit the Inn or another structure?" asked Whitey.

"Let's hope not. If we can reduce the weight and certainly not use the thing, we can eliminate the danger. Then let the whole place go swimming," grumbled Willie.

"That's quite an attitude you got there Mr. Transportation," Whitey looked at Willie with a raised eyebrow.

"Are you kidding me?" Willie snarled. "You should be in charge of trying to keep everything moving when the temperature rarely reaches 40 degrees. For centuries now I have fought constant freezing and maintenance on every machine up here from aircraft to snowmobiles. I would dearly love to move to a warmer climate, so I could deal with different problems and do so without wearing gloves."

"Sorry, I didn't realize it was so rough," Whitey said, genuinely feeling bad for the elf, "We best get a team down here quickly and begin dismantling this monster before it does some serious damage."

Whitey nodded, "I'll get my guys down here and we

will start on the gondola cars and cables."

"I'll call some people to begin taking apart the tower," added Whitey. And they both walked off talking into their radios.

Chapter 7

Eagle River Trouble

Ella Communicado was talking to Cory Peters and was apprising him of the situation. She asked Cory about the idea of having the Santas help out. She was remembering what a handsome man he was as she spoke to him. He had a chiseled face that looked as strong as the rest of his body. He spent several years in the Navy and was one of those who had developed his muscles while on active duty and had not lost the strength he gained.

"I can think of several that would drop everything for the chance of meeting Nick, either again or for the first time, as he skips some years due to other commitments," said Cory. "The problem is, that since we do not know where the village is moving to, I can't guess how many I can get. Unfortunately many won't travel to or from foreign countries."

"I understand," said Ella, "But any help will be appreciated."

"Do you need assistance at the village or where you are moving to?" inquired Cory.

"I haven't spoken to the Kringles regarding details, yet," she replied, "but my guess is they are needed more at the sight we will be moving to. Especially as I am certain we have a lot of excavating and building to do once we arrive, wherever that is."

"Actually, I need to come up and see Nick about another problem we are having down here," Cory stood to his full 6'3" frame and began pacing while he spoke with Ella.

"Good heavens," exclaimed Ella, "You aren't having geo problems also, are you?"

"No, nothing like that, this is more public relations related and personal for Nick," he answered.

"Uh, this may not be the best time," Ella stated. "I believe Santa and Mary have their hands full and don't have a lot of time to spare on other matters, right now."

"And believe me when I say, I wouldn't ask if this was not an urgent matter. The truth is, I was going to call him this week to set an appointment," Cory said.

"Could this be handled by a conference call or something?" Ella questioned.

"This is of such importance that I think a face-to-face is necessary," insisted Cory, "Besides we will need a little time to come up with a planned response and strategy."

"Wow, that serious?" Ella asked, astonished. There had never been an incident involving the Eagle River, Wisconsin school in the past. What could have happened to cause Cory such concern, and especially now?

"Yes, I'm afraid it is," said Cory. He had never sounded so dejected to Ella before in their conversations.

Ella was known for being able to put thought into "sincere speech" as elves called complete truth. A pleasant looking woman with dark hair and dark mysterious hazel eyes to match, she was one of the more desirable ladies of the North Pole, and was often sought after by the single men of the village.

What made Ella important (and feared by less sincere men) was her ability to see through to the truth, or make sense of any garbled discussion, and put it into words that everyone could grasp. There are some that just have a difficult time talking with others. Ella could understand what they meant and spoke their thoughts in a concise manner. So Ella knew that Cory was sincere and needed an audience with Santa.

"Alright," said Ella. "I will inform Santa that he needs to make some time for you, but you will have to come here, as I am sure he won't be planning any stops in Eagle River any time soon."

"Understood." Cory sighed with relief and said, "I'll start planning the trip, may I presume that you will arrange the last leg from Fairbanks as you always do?"

"Yes" responded Ella. "But don't make any plane reservations until I speak with Santa first."

"You have my word," said Cory. "But do please talk to him with haste. This is something that I think the longer it festers, the worse it will be to try and correct it. If it can be corrected."

"Don't worry, Cory," said Ella. "I am sure he will want to know immediately whether he can count on the support from the ambassadors or not."

"Very well," said Cory, "Thanks for helping me out with this, Ella. It may not be quite as serious as your problem, but it is a close second. I am extremely sorry about your situation, and I can't begin to imagine what the overall mood is there."

"You might say 'guarded' for now. I think a good

many of us are too much in shock to react to the news, yet," she explained, "But I am hoping that when they do, it will be constructive as it has been in the past and that we will put our efforts into the task. Anyway, I need to go. I will take your opinions and request to Santa tonight if I can, or first thing tomorrow for sure."

"Many thanks Ella." Cory smiled, "It will be good to see you again, regardless the reason for it."

"You too, Cory. Goodnight." She smiled in return.

"Goodnight." As Cory hung up the phone, Katy entered and asked, "Did you tell her the problem?"

Cory shook his head, "I didn't want to say anything to anyone, not until I talk with Nick directly. Besides they have a situation they need to handle themselves."

Cory relayed the information Ella gave him.

Katy looked astonished and said, "Move the whole North Pole? Is that possible in so short a time?"

"I would have to say if it were anywhere but the North Pole, then probably not, but considering the miracles they pull off everyday as due course, not to mention Christmas Eve, then I would say if it is possible to be done, it will be accomplished by the elves and Santa Claus," said Cory hopefully.

"What do you think Santa will do with the problem down here?" she asked returning to her original subject.

"I really have no idea." He sighed. "I have been trying to figure a way to countermand what is going on, but it gets worse. And now this..." Cory bowed and shook his head.

"You have done what you could, Cory," she said sympathetically. "Santa will know how to set the problem right, and you will meet him soon enough and begin a tactical game plan after you do. Considering what else he is dealing with, he may rely on you to carry it through."

"And I will do it," he said. "Consider what we have accomplished before. When we were helping those poor women escape from their despicable lifestyle, and we ran the shelter for abused women and children. I think whatever Nick needs me to do, I will be happy to do it. Look at all he has given us."

"No question," agreed Katy, "and I know you will be able to do whatever he needs you to. But let's put it aside until you hear back from the North Pole and go have dinner. I fixed one of your favorites."

They walked to the other end of the bed and breakfast their heads full and their stomachs empty.

Chapter 8

Epiphany

As Katy and Cory were settling down to dinner, the Kringles were doing the same at the North Pole. Nick did a blessing asking for guidance and help for the mighty task ahead and passed the feast Michael had prepared for them.

Kristopher was a man on a mission. He had done some traveling in the past few years and had some definitive ideas about where to relocate the village. He was doing his best to lobby his ideas to his parents.

"I have given this some serious thought," he said, waving his fork about. "There are many wonderful areas that we might consider moving to, and I have prepared a short list of places you might consider."

Nick realized that Kristopher was like a dog with a bone. He decided he might as well hear him out. He looked over to Mary, who shrugged at him and gave her head a little shake. She had realized as Nick had, that there would be no stopping Kristopher.

With a sigh Nick said, "All right, let's hear it."

Kristopher smiled and said, "Okay, I'll start at the top with my first pick. Why not move to Southern California where Mom is from?"

"Earthquakes," Mary said without emphasis.

"Population," chimed Nick.

"Crime," Michael joined in.

"Brush fires," answered Mary.

"Mudslides," fired Nick.

"Traffic," said Michael. "Although they have some really fine restaurants."

At that Nick and Mary both laughed, "Dear Michael, always thinking with your stomach," Mary said laughing.

"Not stomach, taste buds!" Michael exclaimed, "Can I help it you both have taught me to love the taste of so many foods?"

Kristopher was not amused and said, "Now wait a minute, I am trying to be serious here and I think you should take my suggestions seriously."

Nick looked at his older son and said, "We do take you and your ideas seriously. But there are many reasons, as we have stated, why Southern California wouldn't work."

"If we build a dome, we will not have to concern ourselves with brush fires or mudslides," argued Kristopher.

"That still leaves earthquakes, and our dome will not protect us from that, as it won't keep this village from sinking," explained Nick. "Plus the population of Southern California is so large that we might go ahead and move to Mexico City or Beijing for the peace we would have there."

"But Mom, you used to live there, and you said it was lovely." insisted Kristopher.

"Yes, and because of that, I agree with your father that there are much better choices than California,"

Mary said.

Not deterred, Kristopher asked, "Then how about the middle of Texas? And don't say tornadoes, because we know the dome can protect us from them."

"That might be more reasonable, but I can imagine that Stacy Buttons will think we have traded one color – white – for another – tan," Nick chuckled as he said this. "But at least that has possibilities, though I would prefer not to be so 'open' without anything to prevent us being spotted in moving trucks, planes and rail into the dome, camouflaged or not."

"I also think you should give consideration to Jackson's request that there is a steady flow of water to be harnessed," said Mary, "Especially as he plans to use that as a main source for power."

Nick rubbed his beard and said, "Yes, that's right. He did specifically ask for that, hmm."

"Then here's another idea," Kristopher was not giving up, "The South of France, you both told us is quite lovely."

"Indeed it is," Mary piped in. "The problem is we currently do not have the resources including rail to tap into moving our products into and out of there."

"True," replied Kristopher, "But you are at least close to the sea, and that might make up for that."

Nick nodded and added, "I think since the bulk of what we ship to, and receive from, is in the United States, we should concentrate on that country. Also, the elves speak English, even if they have a different native tongue, and that goes along way towards getting what needs to be done when we do have to go outside the village."

"Boy, you guys don't make it easy," said Kristopher, a little crestfallen. "So what are your ideas?"

"Who said we have any, yet?" chuckled Nick.

Mary asked, "Did you remember the place you went in error with your father that Aeon mentioned?"

"Wait a minute," Michael looked incredulously at his father, "You mean Aeon knew about this and you didn't plan for it?"

"No, Aeon only said, 'Return to the first place you visited with your father before the error, and follow your heart and direction from that place', or something close to that. He never mentioned having to move the village in the book, but did allude to it in a conversation once," explained Nick.

"So where is this place you went with Grandad?" asked Michael.

"No idea," said Nick, "I have been racking my mind and can't think what he means. Grandad and I never went anywhere by mistake that I remember."

"You two sure covered the earth together," commented Mary. "You took him with you several times after you became the official Santa Claus."

"And quite a few times he took me, before you and I met," reminisced Nick. He grinned and said, "He was so frustrated with me because I couldn't get the time continuum down until I ran across Aeon's book..." Nick trailed off and suddenly his eyes got big. "My God that must be it!"

Mary saw his excitement and became excited herself, "You remember?"

Nick rose from the table and was fully animated, "I think so, Dad was having a hard time teaching me how to move from place to place in the continuum, and he was frustrated when I accidentally took us to San Francisco, but what was that place he took me to first?"

Nick was beating the side of his head with his fist mumbling, "Think, think, it was a forest in the mountains; water was running and Dad said he wanted to take Mom there...I REMEMBER!"

Mary was out of her chair and Michael was standing, too. "Don't keep us in suspense!" Mary cried out.

Still talking more to himself than his family in the room he said, "Yes, it is perfect! Centrally located, natural resources, beautiful area, lots of people, but with plenty of privacy..."

"Nick!" Mary fairly yelled.

"Dad!" both sons called out.

"The Great Smoky Mountains in Tennessee and North Carolina! Dad took me there the first time he tried to teach me how to move from place to place. He said he wanted to take Mom there, and that if I ever learned what I needed, he would be able to do that." He looked at Mary and said, "I'll bet that was their first stop on their second honeymoon."

Mary laughed and said, "You mean first honeymoon, Annie told me they never got to take a honeymoon after they were married."

"Yes, Dad said the same thing to me," said an excited Nick Kringle. "But that must be the place! Tomorrow I will take us there and show you!"

Now the boys were highly excited, as they rarely got

to travel with the time continuum, though Kristopher kept at his father to teach him its secrets. This would be another chance to learn.

Nick described the area and talked about the plentiful water, seclusion in the woods, accessibility to roads, rail and air and many other things that would be a benefit to the villagers of the North Pole.

Mary agreed that at least on the surface it sounded ideal. She also thought it sounded a good deal like her native upstate New York, where she was raised as a child, until she moved to Southern California.

"Wait until you see it," said Nick. "I don't know why I left it off of our honeymoon itinerary."

Mary laughed and said, "I certainly have no complaints about that wonderful whirlwind tour of the world! But maybe in a way you wanted your parents to go first. Who knows?"

"You can see it tomorrow, and perhaps we will take a couple days to explore the area," Nick said and thought for a moment. "In fact, this would be a perfect time, as there would not be many visitors in February."

"How many visitors do they get? Any idea?" inquired Mary.

"If memory serves, I think it has the most visitors of any national park in the U.S.," responded Nick.

"How will the village remain hidden among those people?" asked Michael, "That must mean they get millions of people!"

"You'll see son," Nick smiled, "It will be like hiding in plain sight."

"I think if we are going away for a couple days, we

should advise the Council so they don't think we ran off or something," Mary said to her husband.

Nick laughed at the thought and said, "I'll call Ella right away." Nick moved to the phone and tapped the number 5. Ella picked up the other end and said "Hello Santa."

Nick told her of their plan to visit a particular place as a possible relocation point for the village and that the whole family will be indisposed for a couple days.

"Is it wise for all of you to go?" asked Ella. "What if something were to happen?"

"Nothing untoward will happen Ella," he chortled. "And it is most important we find the place we need to relocate without hesitation."

"Okay, Santa, I will relay your message to the rest of the Council. But before you go, I have other information to relay to you and a request..." Ella began to pass on her conversations, first with Whitey and then Cory.

Nick took the information concerning the gondola pretty well. He expected that after the problem with the mine and some of the shops, it would soon follow that some of the larger buildings and structures in the North Pole would begin to develop problems. They would have to use the ramps more and that wasn't too inconvenient. At least for now. He said as much to Ella and listened as she transmitted her conversation with Cory.

The other Kringles heard Nick practically bellow, "What? Now? Is he crazy?"

A few moments of silence and a more calm. "Okay if he deems it that important then schedule it for the first of next week when we get back." More silence and finally, "No, I agree Ella, and if Cory sounded that shaken, I am certain it is important. He has never 'Cried wolf' before, and I hope it is something we can deal with quickly and easily."

As Santa hung up the phone Mary came up to him and asked, "Another problem?"

"Can't say for sure." Nick was staring at the phone. "Cory said he needs to meet with me over an urgent matter and he told Ella it can't wait."

"I pray it is not a health issue with either of them," Mary said now also concerned.

"No," said Nick. "Something about a public relations problem."

"Lets not put any thing else on our plate than what we already have," counseled Mary. "Besides you promised us a vacation!"

"OH! Now its a vacation?" choked Nick. "I merely said I wanted to show you a possible area for relocation – strictly business."

"If the Kringles can't mix business with pleasure," Mary chided, "Who the heck can?" She punched her husband in the arm and walked off with a smile saying, "I'll be in the bedroom packing."

Chapter 9

Packing Up

The next morning found three of the four Kringles packing for the trip. Nick was on the phone since early morning making arrangements both in the village and at their destination. He was currently on with half the Council members, as instructions were being left for them of items to accomplish while the Kringles were away. The discussion centered mostly on whom to secure from previous visitors to return to the North Pole in their hour of need.

"We definitely need George Mendez, as Ion told me he has, or is, close to achieving sustainable cold fusion power," said Nick.

"That is truly exciting!" Jackson exclaimed. "And my son, Sparky Terawatt, has been making some serious advances on this end. If we put the two of them together, we may be able to achieve more than enough power without relying on hydroelectric or solar power, to say nothing of wind generated..."

"Okay, Jackson," Nick chuckled, "Save your enthusiasm and make sure Ion gets him up here. Also I think we should get Bill and Susan Fredrick, we will need his engineering and her architectural skills. We also need Jim Atherton, he is a geologist, among other fields of study, and may be able to give us more insight as to how much time we may have to accomplish this."

"Did you speak to Cory, and can any of his Santa Ambassadors lend a hand? Keeney asked Santa.

Ella answered for Nick, "He will be up here next week to discuss this and to put together a list of potential helpers, though I told him that they may be needed much more at the relocation sight than here."

"Good thinking, Ella" said Britney. "And by the way, can't you give us a clue of where you think this new sight will be, Santa?"

"I am only prepared to say that I am fairly certain that the place I am thinking will be both functional and esthetically pleasing," answered Nick. "I really do not wish to say much more today, though I am confident in my assumption."

"Spoken like a true mystery writer," Denny laughed as he spoke. "I suppose the sooner you get to it, the sooner we will know something."

"Agreed," said Keeney, "So quit burning daylight and be on your way."

"I will call from my destination and give you a progress report," Nick said. "I will return as soon as Mary and I decide on this place."

"Hear that Ella?" Jackson teased nick saying, "Make sure you put a trace on his call so we will know where they are."

Ella ignored Jackson's comment and merely said,"Travel safely, Santa."

"Goodbye my friends," Nick concluded and disconnected the call.

Kristopher walked up and asked, "How long do you

think we will be gone?"

Nick thought for a moment and said, "I can't imagine more than a couple days."

Kristopher nodded and said, "Okay thanks." He headed back toward his room.

"Pack light, not like you and your mother usually do," Nick admonished his son.

From the master bedroom Nick heard Mary yell out, "I heard that! And you are the first one to always say 'Thank goodness you remembered...' this or that. So I will do exactly as I always do," she finished with humor in her voice.

"Well, do it quickly," he said with a smile from her cajoling, "I wish for us to be on our way soon."

Michael came down the stairs with his bag in hand and joked, "Is this soon enough?"

Nick shook his head and said, "Why can't your mother and brother be more like you? You are the model of efficiency." He gave his son's arm a squeeze.

Soon after, Kristopher came down with a bigger bag and Nick teased him about how he packed for 'a couple days'.

Finally, Mary called down the steps asking, "Nick can you help me, please?"

"Here we go," he mumbled more to himself, and bounded up the stairs. He walked in and looked at the large suitcase that sat atop the bed. "Good heavens woman," he said with an exasperated tone, "I said a couple days!"

"Remember dear, that bag is for both of us, and it is February. I have no idea about this area and how cold or warm it is, and if we..."

Nick held up his hand interrupting her and shook his head, "Alright, I got it." He lifted the heavy suitcase with a grunt and said, "Good thing I did the Christmas journey not too long ago. I still have the strength for this."

They gathered everything together and huddled close when Nick asked, "Everyone ready?" They nodded and answered, "Ready."

Then with a blink of Nick's eyes, they, and their luggage disappeared from the foyer of the house.

Chapter 10

Meeting of the Minds

Ella and Keeney sat together in her office and were going over the list of potential invitees so that she could start contacting them and making travel plans. As was customary, the North Pole would cover any expenses, including food, when they came to the Pole and throughout their stay.

In addition to the tallfolk, Ella had received hundreds of messages from elves outside the Pole offering to return and help anyway they could. Keeney thought it wise not to turn away any help, and so long as there were enough elves left at the warehouses to handle anything that might be sent their way from the North Pole, they should accept any offer given.

"I am not sure where we will put everyone," commented Ella.

"That's a problem for Christel, Gunther and the rest of the Innkeepers," stated Keeney. "The important part now is to get them here."

Ella nodded and verbally went over the list, "Okay, Fredricks, Peters, Mendez, Atherton, anyone else?"

"What about that one Hispanic guy that was here several years ago?" asked Keeney. He was scratching his head trying to remember their previous visitors.

"You mean Jose Sanchez?" Ella prodded.

"That's him!" he shouted. "He was some kind of wizard when it came to acquiring materials and supplies at his former job. We could use him to help us reuse materials from here, and to get more for the new village."

"I'll add him," she said deep in thought, "Sanchez, what about Kelly Nightingale?"

"Is that an elf? puzzled Keeney.

"No silly, she is that lovely lady who called herself a 'Reimagineer', part engineer and part designer allowing her to re-imagine any engineering necessity to a more purposeful use. She had commented on how many times she had pictured the North Pole Village in her dreams, but never thought she would see it in real life," finished Ella.

"Oh, I remember now, that tall, black woman," said Keeney. "She was quite intelligent and she could be a big part of helping design the new village. Plus as you said she is an engineer, an added bonus, sure add her name to the list."

They had spent much of the morning going over other former tallfolk that had at one time or other visited the North Pole. Ella and Keeney had records of everyone and where they were today, but they mostly tried to use their memories of particularly special folks that had visited.

After a time Ella said, "This is ridiculous, if they have been here they are special. Maybe we should make up a list of everyone and ask if they would be willing to help out. As you said earlier, we shouldn't turn away any aid we can get."

"True," answered Keeney. "But let's concentrate on ones that may have certain skills that can harnessed for the village and everyone can come to our new relocation when we are done. Any ideas?"

"For what kind of skills you mean?" she looked at him puzzled.

"No!" he laughed. "Where we may be moving to."

Ella shrugged, "I am sure wherever it is will have its own unique set of challenges." Then she laughed. "As long as it has bedrock under it, and won't sink, I'll be happy."

Keeney laughed with her and said, "Okay, let's look at this list."

CHAPTER 11

VACATION?

They landed in the middle of downtown Gatlinburg, Tennessee. There were a few people walking around the street and into the shops that were open. Nick was relieved to know he was right about how few the number of visitors would be at this time of the year.

"Wow," said his son, Michael, "This is really pretty, especially for the end of February."

The temperature was in the high fifties or low sixties, and the trees were devoid of leaves. There was no wind to speak of and the sky only had a few clouds dotting it.

"We seemed to have been lucky about the weather." Mary commented.

"Actually when I was looking at the websites for this place, it said this was the average for this far down in elevation," commented Nick. "The higher mountains will be colder, but nothing like our North Pole."

"How high do the mountains go and what are we at now?" asked Michael.

"We are only at 1,300 feet," answered Nick, "and the highest mountains here go a little past 6,500 feet. They keep most of the roads closed until late March or early April, especially if they are snowed in, which works toward our advantage."

"When do they close them?" questioned Kristopher.

"According to the Internet, the first of November,"

Nick grinned with his answer.

"So during the whole time between our busiest time until we are done retooling there are no visitors hiking around where we might be?" asked Kristopher with wide eyes.

Nick was smiling broadly and nodded his head.

"Hello Santa!" a passerby said cheerily.

"Looky there, it's Santee!" another person from the other direction said, smiling and waving at Nick.

"They know you here?" said Michael in a shocked tone.

"They know him everywhere little brother," commented Kristopher.

"Actually, they know our Ambassadors and other impersonators," Nick said. "I look like them."

"You mean they look like you, my husband," Mary said taking his hand and squeezing it. "And the vast majority are not nearly as handsome as you. They only wish they were."

"You're biased," he said in a kidding tone.

"Hey, as they say," responded Michael, "You can't improve on the original."

Nick was beginning to blush when a car had pulled up beside them. A shorter but thin man jumped out and waved, almost yelling. "Hello Mr. Claus!"

Michael said, "Oh this is getting ridiculous."

Nick began laughing as he yelled back to the man, "Hello Richard," then turning to his son, "This one actually *does* know me."

Nick was chuckling as he approached the elf. He shook his hand and asked, "So how are things in

Charlotte?"

Richard answered saying, "After your news, we are busy as a new hive of bees. We are making room anywhere we can, should you need to send anything our way. We are sorry to hear about the village up there and are ready to pitch in where you need us." Richard was shorter than most tallfolk, but he still looked like a long drink of water with his thin frame, wire rimmed glasses and flat brown hair.

Nick nodded and said, "Thank you, I know each of you will be invaluable. Now may I introduce my wife, Mary, and my two sons, Kristopher and Michael."

Richard shook each one's hand and said, "This is quite an honor to meet you," He turned back to Nick and handed him the keys to the car he just left, "Here is your transportation, and here are the directions to your hotel. I got the furthest one up that I could, considering most of the side mountain roads above Gatlinburg remain closed."

"I'm sure it will be fine," commented Nick. "Thank you again for your assistance. Now how are you getting back?"

"Oh, not to worry," Richard answered quickly. "Victoria will be arriving momentarily. She got caught up in a little traffic down the mountain. Uh, Santa, may I ask a question?"

Santa grinned and said, "You may ask, however I may not answer."

"Is there a coincidence between you being here now and the needed resettlement of the North Pole?" asked Richard sheepishly.

"If there is any speculation toward that thinking in Charlotte, I would appreciate it be kept under wraps and no rumors of that be spread anywhere."

"That's not a 'no'," Richard said.

"I truly cannot comment on that question officially or unofficially," said Nick evenly. "But I will tell you that even the Council does not know where we are right now."

Richard's eyes got considerably larger as he said with too much emphasis, "Holy cow, so no kidding, you are thinking about here."

Kristopher laughed and said, "That worked well, Dad."

Nick shot him a look and said sternly to Richard, "Listen, and I mean this," he paused for emphasis, "not a word about this to anyone. I am considering several possibilities, and this is only one of them. Mary and I need to see the benefits and challenges of this area compared to others."

Richard looked down at the ground and said, "I'm sorry, Santa. As you might imagine, most elves here would love to be closer to 'where the action is', and it would mean that many of us can visit family and friends that we hardly ever have the opportunity to see now. That is unless we transfer to the North Pole. Many of us are truly excited at the prospect that would bring you and the village closer to us."

Nick said more softly, "I'm sorry for practically yelling at you. I am concerned about word of any possible considerations reaching anyone before we have a chance to see if it will fit our needs first. Plus, and you emphasize this with your own comments, I do not wish to get anyone too excited thinking that may happen before any decision is made."

Richard nodded his head and a second car pulled up behind his. Victoria hopped out and bounded to the group standing there. She said, "Hello Santa, everyone, and welcome to the most beautiful place on earth." Her voice was as bouncy as she was, and the others sniggered at her antics.

Michael walked over to her first and said, "How do you do, my name is Michael."

She grabbed his outstretched hand and said, "Hi Mike, I'm Vicky."

Kristopher smirked at her greeting to Michael and said, "I'm Santa's eldest son, Kristopher."

"I assume you go by Kris?" she said, but was already turning toward Nick.

"Not as of yet," he said tersely.

Vicky looked at Nick and said in rapid fire speech, "So you're him? The real Santa Claus? It is an honor to meet you...is that Mrs. Claus behind you? She's lovely. Is it true you may be moving to the mountains here? Is there any possibility of moving to Charlotte? Do you think we could combine the two together?"

Nick watched Richard wilt before him. Richard tried to stop Vicky from saying anymore, but it was too late, She had shot off her questions and comments as fast as bullets shot from a jet.

Nick looked at the exuberant elf who reminded him of a high school cheerleader on steroids. She was cute with blue eyes and curly blonde hair. She was shorter than Richard and was proportioned much the way a cheerleader would be, with a few freckles dotting her cheeks for emphasis.

Nick said, "I'm sorry Vicky, we would love to stay and answer your questions but we have an appointment and we need to run along." Nick realized he had told three white lies in about the same number of seconds. He was anxious to get out of there and quick.

He thanked Richard for the use of the car again and whispered in his ear, "Remember what I said."

Richard nodded and said, "Yessir."

With that the Kringles got into the car and headed away. As soon as they were out of earshot Michael laughed and said, "Sometimes I think we have to worry less about the people of the South and more about our own elves."

Mary said, "I couldn't have answered that gal if I wanted to, and I definitely did not want to. I thought Richard was going to fall at your feet and beg for mercy when she showed up."

Santa laughed at the thought. "He did look a little squeamish after her introductions. But we needed transportation and now we have it."

"Do elves provide whatever you need when you need it?" asked Michael.

"Part of the job, I think," said Nick. "Truth is, they often offer before I ask."

"It's good to be the King," Kristopher crowed.

"Hilarious," Nick snickered.

The four of them bantered the whole way to the hotel. Nick and Mary thought it best to check in and drop their luggage before they went exploring too far. It also was on their way up to the mountains they planned to see.

When they arrived at the hotel, because of the light season for tourists, their rooms were already prepared and they were able to check in immediately. Kristopher and Michael shared one room and their parents had the other. Both rooms had spectacular views of the mountains and a stream running right below their balconies. In the dead of winter it remained beautiful, and Michael commented as to what it might look like in summer.

They unpacked and settled in briefly, then Nick announced it was time to get moving. They loaded back into the car and Nick took one of the state routes toward the top. The roads to Balsam Mountain and Clingman's Dome, and others like it, were closed. As said, these would remain so until the end of March, but State Route 441, Little River Road and the Cades Cove Loop were open for sightseeing and driving. Nick planned on spending a day or so on the Tennessee side, and one day on the North Carolina side visiting Cherokee and Bryson City.

As they rode along Nick told them of what he had learned from his short time online looking at information. "They get approximately 10 million visitors a year to the Smoky Mountains," he sounded like a tour guide, "It is a free national park, one of the few in the U.S. The states of Tennessee and North Carolina, and local communities, paid to construct Newfound Gap Road, which is the road we are on now, or US-441. When the state of Tennessee transferred ownership of Newfound Gap Road to the federal government, it stipulated that 'no toll or license fee shall ever be imposed...' to travel the road.

"Also a large donation by the Vanderbilts insured that maintenance would be kept up on the area and roads. This area is home to various types of animals and birds. We will be trading white for black with the bears, as there are over 1,500 black bears throughout this area."

"Hey isn't that mansion close to this area?" asked Michael. "You know, Dad, the largest private home or something..."

"The Biltmore Estate, you mean?" Nick nodded. "It's over in Asheville, North Carolina. If we move to this area maybe we'll send Mom and some elves to get some ideas for our new home,"

"Ha, ha, that's funny," said Mary sarcastically. "Maybe they will provide you a room if you keep making comments like that."

Nick feigned being hurt. "I was only trying to help you with some decorating ideas, dear."

They drove up the mountain in silence for a period taking in the sights and occasionally commenting on the beauty of the area. It seemed like one vista after another was laid before their eyes. They passed several roads that were closed for the winter and nodded at each other smiling the whole time.

"In some ways," Nick finally said, "it is a shame we can't drive up there. I'll bet there are incredible views to be seen."

Mary nodded. "In good time husband mine.

Remember today we are tourists like any other. But I must say I believe this might be perfect, exactly as Aeon hinted to you. Open highways, plenty of forest, abundant water, and beauty to delight the eyes."

"Yeah," said Kristopher, "The only problem is it belongs to the federal government of the United States! How are you going to get around that?"

"Actually, we won't, and that's a good thing," replied Nick.

"How do you figure that?" asked Michael.

"By being owned by the federal government no one can decide they want to start harvesting trees and come into our area. Also by limiting visitors and their movements it will be easy to hide in plain sight among the millions that come to this park," answered Nick. "If we agree, I will send Topo Geosphere, Jackson and a few others down to scope out an area that would receive the least possible interference. Besides we only are asking for a couple square miles out of the 816 square miles that makes up the park. We may be in the Appalachian part of the forest, but not too close to the Appalachian Trail."

"So you are going to start building in the middle of the mountains?" questioned Michael further. "Don't you think we will be noticed?"

"Not if we raise the dome first," Nick said slyly, "Once we establish where and how much we need, Whitey, and just a couple others, will begin the process so we will be undercover before we break ground on the first structure. Plus we will establish in an area where not too many visitors frequent."

"Does the dome require much in the way of equipment to set up?" Mary asked.

"Not really," answered Kristopher. "Whitey said that most of the construction happens in the village and then they take the pieces south to assemble them."

Nick was surprised at his son's knowledge and asked him how he knew that.

"I do get around and talk to people and the dome is something that fascinates me. Since Whitey is in charge of it, I asked him," Kristopher responded.

Nick was impressed and realized his son was taking a deeper interest in the North Pole than he might have guessed.

"And I was pleased when Jackson said we could do with far less land than I had expected," Nick continued. "We need a much smaller footprint than I first thought."

So they continued on their excursion discussing both, the promises and the pitfalls, such a move would entail, never taking their eyes off the scenery they were exploring.

CHAPTER 12

SLIP SLIDING AWAY

As the Kringles were discussing their plans and possibilities, Whitey was having a tough day. The foundation had cracked under the crayon factory and half the building was listing dangerously. This put a strain on the remainder of the building and formed large cracks in the walls and ceiling. "Any suggestions?" Violet Colorwheel was asking Whitey. She was the director of the factory and was looking at the damage with him.

"I'm afraid you will need to evacuate this premise," he said. "If any more stress compresses that roof and ceiling, it may come down on your heads."

"Are you saying I can't pack up?" she begged Whitey.

"Not at the moment, I can't let anything happen to you or your fellow workers," Whitey explained, "Look, after I take care of a few other things, I will get some of the construction crew over here and see if we can make it safe as you pull your things together."

Violet began to tear up and said as one escaped her eye, "One hundred plus years we have been here," she said and then sniffed, "Billions of gifts for children went through these doors, and now we have to walk away from it."

Whitey said sympathetically, "Try not to look at it that way. When we get to the new village you will have a bigger workshop and will supply billions more children from there. Consider this a temporary forced vacation," he said and tried to smile.

"Some vacation," Violet returned. But she appreciated Whitey's efforts and told him so.

It was the third such news Whitey had to give during this morning, alone. One of the factories that he visited before was showing far more problems then the first time he was called there. Today the movement caused one of the water pipes to break and it was flooding the entire building. He and Britney managed to shut the water supply off, but the elves from the factory were continuing to mop the place out.

So far everything on the upper level was holding steady, and Whitey counted his lucky stars and hoped that would continue. He knew sooner or later their luck would run out, and he definitely wanted later.

His next call was to the Snow Cone shop, which was actually little more than a vending stand. The stand fell over from a crack in the ice that ran under the one side. Sy Snowpacker was already closed for the season, but he lost his snow making machine and several of his flavors when the store collapsed on itself.

Sy looked at Whitey and shrugged saying, "I guess I can lend a hand helping others pack up. No sense trying to do anything more here until we get to the North Pole – South."

Whitey was feeling badly for Sy, but he couldn't help but laugh at his comment saying, "North Pole – South?"

Sy smirked a little and said, "Sounds less confusing then the South-North Pole doesn't it?"

"I can see *that* going viral up here," Whitey chuckled.

but turned serious again. "I'm really sorry, Sy. If there is anything we can do..." his words trailed off.

Sy said, "Yeah, you can point me in the direction of who needs the most immediate help."

There was one thing that hadn't changed in the hundreds of years of the North Pole. If someone had a problem, everyone from the smallest to the tallest would pitch in and lend a hand anyway they could. It used to be that way in the South with the tallfolk, too. Back in the late 19th and early 20th centuries. Whitey remembered hearing about barn raisings and building homes for neighbors from Fredrick Salsbury, who used to deal with the tallfolk before he up and disappeared one day many years back.

But though the North Pole hadn't changed in that regard, where does one offer help when everyone needs it? He thought about this and concluded that this may be no different from other disasters like earthquakes, floods, fires and more that had occurred throughout history in the South. The elves would help the tallfolk in those instances as much as they could, and their efforts were always appreciated.

This was the first time the elves ever needed help from the tallfolk, and he wondered if they would be as generous in their assistance as the elves had been. *That's defeatist thinking and I am better than that,* Whitey admonished himself. He was worried how everything would get done, but right now he had to check on a couple other places.

Whitey went to two more shops that had called in regarding new cracks. The damage was minor in one and nonexistent in the other and that was a relief. However, the fact that this was happening throughout the lower level was disturbing.

After he answered the calls for assistance he sought Topo for some answers to his concerns. He found him in the lookout tower. It was an older, tall building that used to look out on the horizon for any potential trouble. It was eventually converted to a science station. However, everyone called it by its old name.

He walked in the front and immediately heard Bilge's voice coming from the next floor up. He guessed correctly that he and Topo were going over the latest figures. He walked in and apologized for the intrusion.

"Quite alright," said Topo. "In fact I was going to seek you out when we finished here. I am a lot easier to track down than you are my friend," and he chuckled at the last part.

"True, I am certainly getting my exercise lately," he sighed. "But I came to ask you, both, since you are together, is this problem accelerating faster than you may have first thought?"

"That is what we are looking at right now," answered Topo. "It seems that the Pole is not freezing nearly as solidly as we hoped it would."

"And for every degree higher than expected," continued Bilge, "it causes more stress on the ice that is frozen. I suspect you are seeing more problems than before?"

"At a rather alarming rate," he nodded as he spoke. "What started out as a problem or two a day is beginning to double and triple each day." Whitey then recounted the problems he witnessed that day alone.

The two men listened carefully and Topo said, "As we feared, it is happening faster than we originally thought. Do you think it is getting geometrically worse?" he asked his colleague.

"I don't think geometrically, but I do think our linear equations need to be readjusted determining a faster rate of decline. And I think it imperative we get Atherton up here as soon as possible," said Bilge.

"Ella was going to put a call into him, after I spoke with her. I will see if she was successful," said Topo and walked toward a phone in the next room.

"Jim Atherton?" Whitey asked and Bilge nodded. "I vaguely remember him, who was, or is, he again?"

"Jim was one of the tallfolk we invited up here a several years back," Bilge said. "He was quite brilliant for a tallfolk and he had an almost unquenchable thirst for knowledge, but he wasn't able to return to college because of financial reasons and his company wouldn't offer any assistance. Santa gave him a 'free ride' as they call it to go to any college of his choosing and apply for any degree he wished. He chose the sciences and now holds a Bachelors degree with two minors and two majors, two Masters degrees and is nearly finished with his doctorate."

"Wow, that's what I call applying yourself!" exclaimed Whitey.

"Ah, but what is really amazing is that during his stay here, he told Santa that he was most concerned about something. Can you guess what that was?" the old professor grinned.

"That the North Pole was melting and that eventually we would slip into the ocean," said Whitey.

"Bingo," said Bilge emphatically.

"So does he know more than we do about this?" Whitey asked.

"It would seem he doesn't know any less," Bilge answered. "The chances are good that he could pinpoint fairly closely how long we have to evacuate. Plus he had been developing some things in his own laboratory that are similar to what we accomplished here."

"Anything important?" Whitey asked.

"How about a dome?" Bilge answered with a smirk.

"What?" Whitey asked with surprise, "*Our* dome?"

"Similar, with some interesting properties that we did not include in ours," Bilge said.

"Such as?" pushed Whitey.

"A discussion for another time," Bilge waved his hand. "I simply used that example as a demonstration how truly amazing he is, and why we need him here sooner than later."

"If and when he gets here, I need some time with him, too," insisted Whitey, "I'd like to know if he has any improvements to add to the dome, that would be significant since we will be erecting one in our new village."

Bilge acknowledged his request and said, "Of course, as soon as we find out how critical our situation is here."

Topo returned and said brightly, "All set, Ella got a hold of him and they already have him booked on the next flight from Atlanta to Fairbanks. He should be here early tomorrow."

Bilge and Whitey both nodded and said, "Good."

"Now can either of you tell me with your own best guess how long we have to get everyone out safely?" insisted Whitey.

"I don't want to hazard a guess until we have had time to confer with Jim and a couple other folks," replied Topo.

"Hazard one anyway, Professor." Whitey was humorless, "I really need to know what kind of danger we are in here."

"If I had to say right now..." said Topo looking at Bilge again for support.

"You do," said Whitey.

They both answered, "Six months," and Topo added, "at the outside, maybe less."

Whitey stood there with his mouth working but no sound coming out. He finally said breathless, "Six months!"

"Maybe less," repeated Topo.

"Getting us out of here, maybe," Whitey said more to himself, "But having a new village built is nearly impossible."

"Nearly is the key word there," said Bilge. "Actually we might take a page from the tallfolk on this one."

Whitey looked at him and asked, "What do you mean?"

Topo jumped in to explain, "Tallfolk have been creating what they call 'manufactured housing' for decades. Depending on where Santa decides we need to move, we could place everyone in these manufactured homes for the short term until we build new workshops and factories, concentrating only on the most immediate needs necessary first."

"You plan to put the Kringles in a trailer?" Whitey asked with disbelief.

"Desperate times, desperate measures," said Bilge in a matter-of-fact tone.

"Besides it would only be temporary and we could bang these places out in no time, as soon as you have the dome in place," added Topo.

"And what would we do with these houses after you have rebuilt the permanent ones?" Whitey knew the answer before he finished asking the question.

"Donate them to others in need of decent housing, of course," said Topo wearily.

Whitey thought he should leave this discussion there, as he was only one of the Council members and couldn't speak for the rest. "This will have to be brought before the Council and you best do it as soon as you can meet with Jim and get us an accurate window for how long we have," he concluded.

He said goodbye to them and moved to his next problem of the day.

Chapter 13

Preparing For
The Onslaught

For many years the Council of the North Pole had
met infrequently. In the beginning there had been much
to oversee and to resolve. After Kris and Annie Kringle,
Nick's parents, were placed in charge of the Council and
the village, respectively, problems were fewer and elves
resolved their differences more often than before without
need of the Council's intervention.

Prior to this new situation, it had been months since
the Council reconvened. And when it did, there was
almost nothing to resolve and the Council was
considered more of a social gathering than a legislative
one. Denny brought a cake and beverages for the
occasion, strictly as a celebration.

Things were busy but peaceful in the village.
Everyone knew their duty and went about it happily.
The North Pole Village was a 'well-oiled machine' and its
residents took pride in what they accomplished with
nary a hiccup.

Now every part of this was asunder. The village they
loved and were so proud of was sinking below their feet.
More than a few elves stopped and went into melancholy
moods for a period of time. This was unusual as elves

are nearly always happy. This was the worst situation that every elf faced since before coming to the North Pole. And for those born in the village, it was the worst situation, period.

Some had kept up appearances and some were so busy they did not have time to reflect on their predicament. Such was the case with Christel Bunkinstyle. She stood approximately four feet tall, and had a long face with soft dark blue-gray eyes. Her nose was slightly longish and ended in a cue stick point. Her ears were long as well, but not pointed, as one would expect an elf's to be.

Christel had called a meeting of the various innkeepers to discuss how many helpers might be coming to the North Pole, and where they might put them. Denny Sweetooth from the Council asked her to pull everyone together and said that he would attend, too.

They met at the Reindeer Inn, which was the largest of the Pole's Inns. This was where they typically housed their southern visitors as the ceilings and accommodations were larger to fit the tallest of the tallfolk.

Ordinarily Christel would be preparing the inn for the next inflow of these visitors. But this was put on hold when different problems began showing up around the village. Mrs. Claus asked Ella to hold off from sending the next set of invitations. Now here was Christel planning for many more visitors, both tallfolk and elfkind, than she ever would receive normally.

Gunther Crispinclean walked into the inn with Fergie

Keepitneat, Christel welcomed them both and said
Pierre was preparing snacks and refreshments, and that
they would be meeting in the big dining area in the
corner. The two innkeepers walked toward the corner
and began saying hello to several of the staff from both
the Reindeer Inn and Santa's Boarding House, or the
SBH, as they more often referred to it.

The SBH was where Gunther was manager. His long
history with the Pole included being one of the first to
welcome the original Santa and Mrs. Claus when they
first came to the village. At the time the hostel was
called the Elves Inn, but the name was changed after
the Reindeer Inn was built, both to prevent confusion
between the 'inns' and as an honor to Santa Claus, past,
present and future.

After a few more people came in, including Denny
Sweetooth and and Pierre Whiskeneg, Christel came
around the corner and said, "Okay, we best get this
started. As I am sure everyone is aware, we are about to
get a mass of people here, more than we have ever had
to cater to before at one time. These people are coming
to help us in our time of need, and I plan to make each
one as comfortable as possible."

Gunther asked, "Are we using the SBH for elves or
talls?" He used the vernacular for tallfolk.

"Probably talls," she replied. "We will have to come
up with something functional, but practical for the
elves. Is there any room in either bunkhouse?"

"Perhaps a room or two," answered Ethel Coversheet,
who was in charge of the bunkhouse accommodations,
"but not much more than that."

"If there is any room that doesn't have at least two occupants in it," said Christel, "then we need to bunk people up."

"I can think of several elves that wouldn't mind crowding together," said Ethel. "I'll work on that right away."

Christel nodded her head and continued, "Now what about utilizing one of the manufacturing areas as housing? Mrs. Claus suggested that a couple of the manufacturing buildings were pretty much vacant now and could be utilized if needed."

Pierre asked in his thick French accent, "Excuse me Mademoiselle Christel, but 'ow many total people are we expecting?"

"We don't have any exact numbers yet, but I would guess about four to five hundred elves and about 75 talls by early next week."

"Mon Dieu!" exclaimed Pierre.

"Don't worry about that now," said Denny. "We'll sit down and figure out how to feed them later. Keep this in mind, we can use many of them to help you, too."

"But Monsieur Denny" he said in a worried manner. "We couldn't offer them anything they want for that size crowd, plus it would wipe out our stores of food."

Denny said exasperated, "They will eat whatever we can serve. If this goes as planned, we will want to wipe out any excess food we have here, and begin restocking in North Pole – South."

"Where?" questioned Christel.

"Whitey said that's what Sy Snowpacker coined it. It is already spreading through the village as the mystery place we are going to," he chuckled.

Much of the room brightened as they tried the phrase and chuckled along with Denny. Which was exactly what Denny intended with the comment. He continued saying, "I have already gone over the inventory with Mrs. C., and we have plenty of food to feed everyone for a couple months, and if we use everything, possibly more. She said the less we have to pack and ship South, the easier it will be. I, for one, agree with her."

Several elves nodded and Pierre shrugged and mumbled, "...so many mouths."

"Now getting back to the manufacturing centers..." Christel continued.

"The problem I see with those is the minimal necessities, especially bathrooms, for any long term use," Gunther stated. "If we put more than 50 persons in there we could have a potential problem."

"Why?" asked Christel. "We have many more than that on a usual day, what's the difference?"

"The difference," Denny jumped in. "Is that they are not trying to take showers and baths in there."

"Since the buildings are pretty close to the bunkhouses, they could also use the facilities there," explained Christel. "Everyone will have to make concessions. We could put a schedule together to help keep order in the groups. We will have to work something else out for the elves."

Denny said, "Yes, you're right. It will work out. Now let's discuss what else we will need and if we have enough. I have a bad feeling we won't be able to count on too many more loads of supplies from the outside to get what we need, so we better make a comprehensive list and get it ordered now."

They discussed everything they would need and how to acquire it from soap and towels to laundry detergent. Everything was debated, and anything not of critical need was taken off the list.

This continued for another hour when Christel closed the meeting and everyone went their way to prepare for the onslaught of visitors.

Chapter 14

A Local Scientist

Jim Atherton had hung up the phone with Ella Communicado for the second time in as many days. He had always expected he might return to the North Pole. There were many things in his various fields of study that he thought could be utilized by Santa Nick and his village.

Jim Atherton had little room in his head for fantasy, as he called it a several years back. When he received the cryptic letter and tickets, he did as many had done, threw them into the nearest wastebasket. At the time he was living in a studio apartment, and used a small dining table as his desk. The wastebasket was underneath it.

When the ski outfit replete with gloves arrived the next day, Jim called his friends and family to find out who had sent it. He was particularly impressed because he had a long frame and long arms and was difficult to fit. He weighed about 185 pounds and his six foot frame was lean. He wore glasses for reading and his dark hair was beginning to lighten around the temples. And when he looked at you, his hazel eyes shone with intelligence.

After having no luck figuring out who sent the clothing, he retrieved the packet, thanking his lucky stars that he didn't rip the contents as was his first inclination.

He took the airline tickets to the Atlanta airport and verified them at the counter. Jim was a poor man and had trouble paying his rent and utilities in Atlanta. He learned he would be able to get a refund for this expensive seat in cash. But Jim was also an honest man, and he decided that it would be unethical to take advantage of whoever purchased the ticket, especially as he did not know who that person was.

When he returned to his apartment, he did as most tend to do, and attempted to verify the train and 'resort' with no more success than anyone else had. He finally decided that if it were true and that no additional cost was involved, he would take the flight and see what developed afterward. The worse that could happen is that he would lose a couple days, and if they asked for anything further, he would explain they wasted their money on a pauper.

He later joked with Santa Claus, that trying to get his rational mind to think in a more fanciful way had been like trying to turn a Muslim into a Christian or vice versa. The simple indoctrination of the way Jim's mind now worked in a "scientific fantasy" was an oxymoron to the greatest extent of the term.

After Jim's visit, he applied, and was excepted to Georgia State University where he studied Geology and Earth Science, at the same time taking online courses on Applied Physiology and Chemistry at Georgia Tech University. Each was funded through scholarships from the North Pole.

During his visit he had mentioned that the elves had

built the village over the Arctic Ocean and that
someday, it was going to melt, though he did not give
Santa Nick any time line. This, apparently they were
now realizing, would be sooner than later. Jim began
doing calculations as soon as Ella called him and was
greatly disturbed by what they revealed. He did not
know if the village was working with the time frame he
mapped out, but if they were, there must be chaos
indeed.

Jim's flight was almost eight hours from Atlanta to
Fairbanks if everything was on time. He also knew the
train was an hour and a half to the Village's Train
Depot. That would be almost ten hours not to mention
his flight did not leave until nearly 3:00 tomorrow
afternoon and arrived at Fairbanks at 10:45 at night
after a layover in Seattle. He dearly wished Santa Nick
would have used his time continuum to merely "pop in"
get him and return to the North Pole in an instant, as to
lose almost two full days was critical.

But Ella had said something about Santa being away,
so maybe it wasn't possible to come get him. Like
everyone else, he wondered where they were going to
move the North Pole to? With their technology, much of
which he didn't understand, he imagined they could go
nearly anywhere and not be detected.

Jim had not tried to investigate what the North Pole
already had discovered and put to use, but instead was
working with the government and a few colleges on
projects that had hit a snag, or sometimes a brick wall,
and had requested his help. He was in an enviable
position, as he could literally pick and choose which

project he was working on and how long he wished to spend on it. Especially for one who had not received his first doctorate yet. Such was the influence of the North Pole.

He did however, 'tinker' as he referred to it on existing technology to better understand some of the properties and to use a few of the principles for other needs he was working on, with permission from the North Pole.

But he knew and agreed, with the elves and Santa about having too many of the secrets and technology that existed in the village being 'handed over' to governments or businesses in this hemisphere. He said as much in his discussions with the elves. Some things had to wait until these entities could be further trusted with such important secrets. The dome being the most important of these.

He could imagine what a nation, any nation, would do if it could suddenly seal itself from any possible harm, including nuclear missiles while still firing its own without interference. The power of such a prospect was too much to dare contemplate.

But Jim did discover some new properties that could serve the North Pole further, and had mentioned it to a couple of the more scientific elves in the Village.

Jim wished it was otherwise, as he thought about how much food they could produce by controlling the weather inside an agricultural dome. If the domes were limited to only farming and agricultural areas and not used for military purposes, imagine the effect it could have on worldwide hunger. But as the British

Parliamentarian, Sir John Dalberg-Acton, said back in the nineteenth century, "Power tends to corrupt, and absolute power corrupts absolutely." So he had been proven time and again.

Jim shook his head to clear the cobwebs, and the aimless thoughts he was thinking, and turned his mind back to the problem at hand. He was privy to many of the village's secrets, though as with anyone else, was sworn to secrecy about the majority of them. But he now used his knowledge to determine a plan of events that he thought might be successful in getting the village and its residents out in time.

He knew about the the principles of the time continuum, but how it could not be used to move much beyond a few beings or items at a time. He also knew about the miniaturization machine, and wondered about the maximum yield that could be miniaturized in one 'shot'. Further, he knew about the three cargo planes that could carry more than a Lockheed Martin C-130J Super Hercules, and the North Pole version could arrive at its destination more than twice as quickly. Its larger cargo compartment at 50 feet, versus the 41 feet of the Hercules, was combined with a longer flight radius than the U.S. Plane, and contained other interesting properties to boot.

Not only did the North Pole and the elves have resources, but they had something that no one would ever expect. In a word it was 'brilliance'. Jim has never seen such a collection of extreme intelligence in one place, including the institutes of higher learning that he had visited, or worked at. Think tanks could learn a great deal from just a half dozen elves.

Jim was always exceptionally honored that they treated him as one of their number. It was times like this that he would cross all the oceans of the world to try to help them. Their most endearing trait was their 'lighter than air' attitude to nearly any situation. No matter the concern, they knew two things; one, there was a problem to be solved, and two, there was an answer to the problem. It only needed to be uncovered. No drama, no politics, no "woe is me", instead it was always, "what do we need to resolve this issue?" And after a time the issue would be resolved. You had to admire that kind of 'pulling together'.

He went back to his notes and looked at them another time. *Think like an elf,* he willed himself. He looked at the problem once more with a fresh set of eyes.

CHAPTER 15

EXPLORATIONS

The Kringles had returned to Gatlinburg during the afternoon and found a quaint little diner along the main road and stopped there for a late lunch. They were talking to a young waitress named Naomi. She had been telling them about the local history and how she loved to hike around the mountains.

"Do you hike any great distance?" Nick asked her.

"Oh, I have walked up Mount Le Conte, the Chimney Tops and Clingman's Dome numerous times and did the Southern leg of the A.T.," she boasted. "I am laying out my plan to do the whole A.T."

"I'm sorry," Mary interrupted, "What is the A.T?"

"That's the Appalachian Trail. It's a hiking trail that runs from Central Maine to Georgia and includes 14 states and a total of 2,175 miles," she explained. "I plan to do the whole thing in one season!"

"Has anyone done that before?" asked Michael. "I mean the whole trail at once like that?"

"Oh sure, lots of people, but it takes about six months if you don't hit bad weather," Naomi said. "I plan to go up to Maine in the late spring and hike south so I have a better chance of completing the trek before the weather turns against me."

Nick asked, "So tell me are there a lot of hikers through this area? And do many of them hike across from Tennessee into North Carolina?"

"Not that many," Naomi said biting her lip as she thought. "Mostly what we have here are tourists that will stumble in for half a mile or so along the easy pathways to the common sights and run back to their car and call it a day."

"Wow," commented Kristopher. "You don't like them much, do you?"

"Oh quite the contrary!" exclaimed Naomi. "They tip nicely, and because of their lack of adventure, it allows me to go deeper into the mountains and not interfere with my hiking." She began to chuckle and said, "Where would any of us be without our beloved tourists! No offense meant..."

"None taken," chuckled Nick back to her, "And yes, I do tip generously."

She blushed at his comment and began to stammer, "Oh, I, uh, need to check on some other orders, um, if you would excuse me." She walked quickly toward the kitchen.

"At least according to Naomi we shouldn't have too many bumbling tourists around the Village if we move here," joked Nick.

The other Kringles sniggered at his comment. Nick paid the check and left a generous tip for Naomi on the table. Once back in the car they headed a little further up the mountains, and after about another hour, decided to head back to the hotel.

"It sure isn't crowded at this time of year," commented Kristopher. "Are you certain it is this park that gets 10 million people and not some other?"

"I checked it more than once, as I was a little taken back when I read it," answered Nick. "It is obviously slammed during the nicer months. I only hope the assessment given by Naomi is an accurate one."

They began talking more seriously on the trip back about how they might establish the area needed, how they might move supplies in and out, whether to build an airstrip for planes or fly everything into the nearby Knoxville Airport, and how to attach to any local railroad lines in the area.

Nick wished they had time to do a full blown impact study on the area, but knew there was not nearly enough time to do that much planning. A lot of this would have to be guessed, and hoped for, as they went. This was something that didn't sit comfortably with him, but he had little choice.

When they returned to their hotel, everyone seemed tired of the discussion and Michael was the first to suggest giving the problems a rest. Everyone agreed completely. Kristopher said he was going to watch some television and Michael opted for a video game. Mary planned on a nap and Nick said he thought a little time in the whirlpool sounded good after the long drive.

Luckily Mary had packed their swimsuits, as did Kristopher, but Michael didn't think about that and was sorely disappointed. Nick kissed and thanked his wife when she handed it to him and he said sheepishly, "I know, you're right, I never would have considered it like Michael." He took the suit into the bathroom and changed.

When he got to the whirlpool he was pleased to see

the whole area devoid of people. *Boy, at least we lucked out on the right time to come here,* he thought to himself, *I love people, but it is nice to have some quiet time to think to myself.*

He had only a few moments to enjoy his solitude when a couple of young ladies walked into the pool area with their skimpy bathing suits. They looked at Nick and started giggling like a couple middle school kids, though they looked more college aged. They went into the pool after testing the water. Nick had tried it himself and thought it felt more like bath water than a refreshing pool temperature.

They were looking at Nick and twittering like high pitched birds. At last one of the girls swam to the side closest to the whirlpool and said to Nick, "Do you mind me asking, do you play Santa Claus?"

Nick had been asked this question countless times when he went among the tallfolk. He had developed an answer that was both right and sincere speech that he would answer when the question came up. He smirked to himself and said, "No. I don't play Santa." Of course the completion of that statement would have been, *How can I play at something if I am the real thing.*

The young lady looked disappointed and said, "That's really too bad, I think you would make an excellent one. Your hair and beard are so brilliantly white."

"Thanks, I'll keep that in mind if I ever decide to *play* Santa." Nick retorted.

The girls went back to their swimming and giggling about another subject. Nick settled a little deeper in the water and closed his eyes.

He might have looked like he was resting, but his mind was not. He was going over an infinite list of problems, and trying to plug many of them into the Great Smoky Mountains to see if they would render solutions.

He was pleased that many of them did. Many more were unknowns, and for every problem he wrestled with, there seemed to be three more behind it. After a time he decided he was making himself crazy with worry and that it might be best if he followed his younger son's advise and left it alone for a spell.

In their room, Mary was asleep as quickly as she laid down. She was exhausted from the trip and the other recent events. She not only had to do the packing first thing that morning, but had left instructions late into the previous evening with several elves from numerous shops. Mary had always been a "power napper" as Nick called her. After about 15 minutes she was refreshed and recharged and could jump back into the fray of whatever needed handling.

But the last few days she was not as strong as she had been in the past. She was worried about her North Pole and the people in it. Ever since she inherited the CEO title from her mother-in-law, which was almost the moment after her marriage to Nick, she had passionately carried out her duties as Nick's mother, Annie, had done.

Annie had given her little instruction and even less interference. She always praised Mary for continuing the work she began. Occasionally they would talk together about what needed to be done and how to do it, but mostly Annie said, 'However you think it needs to be.' and left it at that.

After Kristopher and Michael were born, Annie almost forbade any business discussion, but only wanted to spend time with her grandsons. As the boys got older, Annie and Kris seemed to become more tired. When Aeon came to collect them, Mary was not surprised in the least, unlike Nick.

Nick was caught completely off guard. Mary felt Kris and Annie were relieved, and though they hated the idea of leaving their children and grandchildren, they were anxious to move on. Aeon had known it too. Aeon rarely let anyone he came for say goodbye, because it was so hard on everyone, but he allowed it this time.

Many times since then, Nick asked Mary if she thought he was doing as good a job as his father might have done. She answered the only way she knew how, and that was to say, "No, much better." She knew this to be true. Nick had faced as many challenges as his father did, but they were completely different in nature. Nick's decisions had always turned out to be the best, but she knew Nick would doubt everything he did concerning this move if she didn't support him.

That extra burden, along with her own, had made her more tired than she could remember. She would have to make a pact with her husband that no matter what either of them decided, that it would be the best solution they could come up for the time being, as they would not have the luxury of deliberating ad nauseum on every possible outcome.

When Mary woke from her nap, she spied her

husband sitting in the chair watching her. "What are you doing? And what time is it?"

"I am watching over the woman I adore and it's about 5:30," he answered. "I think the boys are going to want their evening feeding soon."

Mary smiled at his comments, wiped her eyes and put her glasses back on. As she sat up she said, "Can we just throw meat into their cage and leave them be?"

Nick guffawed at the comment and said, "If only! But I saw there is a local pizza place and they deliver to this hotel."

Mary nodded. "That sounds fine with me. I am not in the mood for going out anyway."

"Yeah, I think we are a little worn out," added Nick.

So they called their son's room and collaborated on their order. Nick called it in and sat on the bed next to Mary. "Did you get enough rest?"

"Yes, at least until I go to bed in about an hour," she teased him, "Actually I feel better, but I'd rather have a moratorium on any discussions tonight."

"Agreed, with one exception," he countered, "At least tell me what you think so far."

"Sincere speech?" she asked.

"Sincere speech," he said cautiously.

"I think it is perfect from what I have seen. I think it is exactly the place Aeon had in mind," she said with a finality in her voice.

"Good enough," Nick said with relief. He grabbed the remote and said, "Let's see what they have in the way of local news." They waited for the pizza and watched television in silence.

CHAPTER 16

WRAPPING UP

Nick called Ella after his shower the next morning. "I was wondering when we might hear from you," she said sarcastically.

"I figured there was no reason to call until I had something to report," he replied.

"Oh, so you have something to report?" she asked.

"Not until you change that tone my dear elfling." He bantered.

"Yes, master." She teased back.

"Now that's better," Nick said followed with his, "Ho, ho, ho!"

"It's been an age since I heard that laugh! So what's up, Santa?" she sounded pleased,

"This may be premature, but I believe I found the place I was supposed to find. Mary seems to agree with me, and I think we'll know today for sure if we are right." said Nick excitedly.

"Can you give us a hint?" she asked hopefully.

"Truly I would like to come back tomorrow and give a full report to the Council along with what I see are our opportunities and concerns." he said, "But I can tell you we are cautiously optimistic so far."

"Should I set a meeting for tomorrow morning?" she questioned.

"Yes, please do, Ella. And say no more other than I

may have a location to move to," Nick said seriously.

"I can't say more because I don't know more!" she admonished him.

"And that's as it should be for today my Communications Director!" he said with a laugh. "Goodbye Ella."

Nick hung up before he could get into a further discussion with her. The Kringles got together for breakfast, and they agreed that after going to the North Carolina side and seeing the other side of the mountain that they should head home. If there was nothing to ward them off of this area after that, Nick would make the recommendation to the Council as soon as possible, supported by Mary.

They were already packed and the car was loaded. Nick had called the Charlotte Distribution Center and asked Richard to meet them at the base of the mountains in Asheville, North Carolina. He hated to make him drive another six hours or more in a round trip to Bryson City. He knew Asheville would cut a good hour off the journey each way.

After checking out of the hotel, they climbed into the car and headed to the North Carolina side of the Smokies. Once more there was little traffic and it took them almost no time it seemed to see the welcome sign for North Carolina.

They did as they had on the Tennessee side, and ambled through many of the overlooks and took a few of the passable roads. Everything they had seen added to the excitement of moving to this area. At one of the viewing areas Michael asked, "How will we know if we are in North Carolina or Tennessee?"

"Do you think it will matter?" retorted Kristopher, "No one will be drawing a line where we will be."

Nick and Mary agreed, but than Mary said, "I think I would like to be closer to the Tennessee side."

"Any particular reason?" her husband asked.

Mary shrugged and answered, "None that I want to get into now."

Nick shook his head and said, "Whatever the CEO wants, she shall have. However, I heard the North Carolina side is less populated than the Tennessee side. But I have seen a good many areas that are suited to our needs on both sides. Have you noticed these places that seem to be devoid of any trees or tall shrubbery?"

The other three nodded and Mary asked, "Do you think it is because its winter?"

Michael said, "Even the harshest winter wouldn't erase entire trees from the landscape. It's like nothing can grow there. Maybe its a problem with the soil itself."

Kristopher added, "If its the soil, it can't be toxic or no one would be allowed to hike up here. I haven't read or seen any warning signs."

"Whatever it is," commented Nick, "it could make our job of setting our own roots a whole lot easier if we don't have to clear forests. Plus we saw a good many grassy fields that could work, too."

After about two hours they pulled into Cherokee and spent some time looking around the town. Like Gatlinburg, it seemed to have lots of amenities, but without the hundreds of curio type shops that littered the Tennessee town.

Being a pleasant 52° and mostly sunny, they decided
to walk around the town. Richard had left a message for
Nick that he would meet them for lunch about 1:00-1:30
at an Italian restaurant that he gave the address and
detailed directions. As it was only 10:20, they had little
time to kill before making the rendezvous in Asheville.

Kristopher began laughing almost uncontrollably and
said to his father, "It seems you are expected!"

When Nick asked what was so funny, and what did he
mean, Kristopher pointed to a large sign that advertised
Santa's Land.

Nick got in on the joke and said, "See, there was
nothing to worry about! They already have a place set
up for us! What we have to do is get everyone down here.
Unfortunately they're closed, so we can't find out where
they are housing my two clowns," he said with a smile.

Mary was a little more reserved and said, "You know
what I think? I think its a sign that we belong here."

"It's a sign alright," grumbled Michael, "of how to
commercialize Santa Claus."

"Really Michael," she said sternly. "Don't you see, I
think this is God's way of telling us that this is where we
belong."

"I agree with both of you," Nick interjected. "I also
get the impression that he has been telling us to lower
our burden, this is the new promised land. I also kinda
hate to see such blatant commercialism, Michael,
though in some ways it is flattering."

Nick looked at his son, and placing his hands on
Michael' shoulders said, "I will tell you this for certain,
there is a great deal of commercialism of both me and

Christmas. You will need to develop the hide of a rhinoceros once we move down here, as we will not be isolated as we were up north."

Now looking at both boys he continued, "It is something your grandfather and I have both had to deal with, as will the next Santa Claus, and God willing, the one after that. We need to accept this in stride, and realize that our worldwide purpose will always bring fame wanted or not, and things like this are not meant to harm or insult us."

Both boys nodded their heads and after they began walking again, Kristopher mumbled under his breath, "I think it is pretty cool."

Nick, who was standing next to him, whispered, "Yeah, I do too."

They returned to the car and drove around the town making notes of what was available on this side, as they had done in Gatlinburg, Tennessee.

Before they did this, they stopped at one of those stands that had placards from every attraction and hotel in the area, including Santa's Land. They were having fun looking and passing the various cards to each other, and Kristopher said, "I sure don't think we'll get bored if we venture out of the Village. Between here and the Tennessee side, there is so much to do that we could be entertained every day and night."

"Yes," sighed Nick, "It will be interesting to be in the middle of so much activity. I hope the other villagers will appreciate that as much as we do."

After cruising through much of the town they headed toward the city of Asheville about an hour away. They were wondering what it might be like to be so close to civilization and how much interaction they might have with much of the populace.

Nick said, "I would imagine that like now, many elves won't have a problem moving amongst the people of the South, and many of them will never leave the Village confines."

"Do you think having too many elves moving around these towns might cause rumors and speculation?" asked Michael.

"Naw, they'll think they work at Santa's Land!" laughed Kristopher.

"And the fun part is it will be sincere speech, except it will be the REAL one," Michael was laughing now, too.

They traveled into Asheville and were amazed by the size and scope of the town.

"One thing is for sure," Mary said. "I won't have to stock the pantry as if we were never going to receive another shipment." She was smiling and looking at the various stores.

It was a good thing that Richard gave them explicit instructions as the town was more spread out. When they rolled up to the restaurant, they saw Vicky's car parked in front and Nick groaned.

They went in and Richard was there, but no Vicky. Nick was visibly relieved and Richard said, "I told her that since I didn't need to go over the mountain this time, that I would go solo. She wasn't happy, but understood. Especially since I admonished her for her display when she met you in Gatlinburg, and I apologize for that."

"Quite alright, Richard, it's already forgotten," said Nick in a sincere tone, then he brightened and said, "Now let's have lunch, I could smell this place two blocks away and I am famished!"

The five took a table and immediately got looks from patrons seated around him. Nods of heads and looks and smiles came from every direction. Richard also saw this and said to Nick, "Guess you've been spotted."

Kristopher said aghast, "It's not unlike sitting in a fish bowl. How do you deal with it?"

"I always feel the eyes and catch many of the nods," Nick explained. "I have several people come up and tell me that seeing me had made their day, which brings me great joy."

"For some time your dad would go out in the most muted colors he could find and added hats and sunglasses, each to no avail," Mary reminisced. "He wasn't gone for more than a few moments when someone would acknowledge him out loud."

"So that worked well," Richard sniggered. "We see copycats of you everywhere, and each one claims to be the real deal. It is really funny to those of us who know the difference."

"Ah, the price of fame," added Kristopher.

A young girl with blonde hair about seven or eight walked over to their table and right to Nick. "My dad said I should come over and thank you for my Christmas gifts," she said.

"Well that is nice of you. Uh, I'm sorry what was your name?" Nick replied as he bent toward the girl.

"It's Christine, but I thought Santa always knew our

names?" she asked.

Richard turned to her and said, "That's what us elves are for, Christine. Santa has to remember billions of things, and after he does his Christmas trip, he gets to let his mind rest. Kind of like you do when you go on your winter break."

"Oh, of course," Christine said, "Sorry Santa. I really did enjoy my Barbie Playhouse and the wonderful things you brought me."

Nick opened his arms and Christine snuggled into them. He gave her a warm embrace and said, "Christine my dear, you are most welcome."

With that she moved back to her own table and Dad gave a thumbs up and a smile to Nick.

Nick turned to Richard and said, "Thanks for the save."

Richard blushed and said, "I didn't say anything that wasn't sincere speech. You use the elves to keep track of the billions of requests and details. And if you didn't have some sort of shut down after Christmas, it would be impossible."

Nick nodded. "Entirely true. Now what we would like to discuss with you is with the highest confidence, but there are some things we need to know. Since we may be moving to this area, what can you tell me about the people, both residents and visitors, and the culture as it compares to the rest of this country."

Richard was honored to be asked to download the information for the Clauses. He thought carefully for a few moments to organize his thoughts and began.

"By and large, this is a heavily Christian-based area

and people are generally nice. It is not as busy or pushed to achieve things as like a New York, Chicago or L.A., until you get close to Atlanta, but things get done.

"It has a pretty strong work ethic, and of course we have great diversity. From the most impoverished areas to some of the richest anywhere, we have it. Similarly, some parts of North Carolina are becoming the new highest tech locations in the world, North Pole naturally excluded. We have a great many tourist areas, and as you probably know, millions come to this part of the country to recreate and relax. This town gets hundreds of thousands of visitors every year, so the population swells and abates depending on the weather and time of year.

"The people for the most part are kind and generous." The next part he lowered his voice to keep from being overheard, "I had heard a good deal about talls before moving here, but what I heard and what I've witnessed are quite different. I miss the Pole and some of my friends, but the people here treat us kindly, and I have not heard of any incidents when we have had to travel away from the center. I like this region, and if I never got back to the North Pole, I could live with it."

"As you know now, there won't be anything to go 'back to' pretty soon," said Nick sourly. "It won't be there, any of it. This is why we need to take great care in choosing the new location for the Village. We will be closer to the populace than most elves will be comfortable with, as they heard the same stories you did. It will be tough enough to quell their fears, without adding a less than desirable location to the equation."

They spoke throughout the lunch grabbing bites between questions and answers. The five of them were more hungry for information than food, and many times two or more tried to ask something at the same time.

After the plates were cleared, they huddled closer to talk more about how much help the elves in this area might be to the relocation, and whether they might continue the distribution center, or combine it if the Village would be placed so near by. Richard wasn't in charge of the Distribution Center as that fell to Charlotte Boleyn. Her first name was actually Jennifer, but it was habit to take the name of the Distribution Center you were assigned to, as it made it easier to refer to either the center or elf in charge. But Richard was a close second in command, and since he already had a sense of the Kringles and their plans, he was the best to get intelligence on the area.

After a good two hours in the restaurant, Nick felt he had enough to base his decision and did not want to keep Richard any longer. Again, Nick asked how he would get back. Richard chuckled and said, "Like you do in reverse! I will hitch Victoria's car to mine and drive them both back." With that, he opened Vicky's trunk and pulled out the towing harness.

"Can we help?" offered Kristopher.

"Naw, I do this a lot," Richard said with a wave of his hand. "Sometimes I am sent to pick up a load of supplies and I take a trailer into town." He began attaching the harness to Vicky's car.

"I can't thank you enough for your assistance," Nick said genuinely. He had truly begun to like Richard a great deal and was glad he had the opportunity to spend more time with him than he normally got to do on Christmas Eve. They shook hands and Nick said, "I may ask Charlotte to do without you for a little while if you are game."

"I am at the service of Santa Claus," Richard responded and increased his grip to show his loyalty. "Whatever you ask I will do."

Nick smiled and said, "You are a good elf, Richard and I am proud to know you."

"Thank you sir!" Richard said, and shook the other Kringle's hands and said how he had enjoyed his time with them and looked forward to seeing them soon.

He went back to his harness, and the Kringles unloaded their luggage from his trunk. When the coast was clear, Nick waved a final goodbye to Richard and blinked, the four had disappeared from North Carolina and reappeared in Nick and Mary's bedroom.

"Was this on purpose?' asked his surprised wife.

"Yup, I didn't want to carry that anchor you call a suitcase one more foot than I had to," he answered playfully.

The boys laughed and grabbed their own bags, happy about not having to manhandle them up the stairs and said, "Thanks Dad!"

Mary hit her husband in the arm again and said, "Oh, you!"

Chapter 17

Planning The Next Step

Ella had contacted each of the Council members except two. Jackson and Britney were off somewhere going over energy supplies and couldn't be reached because of magnetism interference. Ella grumbled to herself, You think with all this high powered technology that we could invent a communications system that would work around this magnetic field. I will be glad at least for getting away from that!

But then she thought about what others were saying about suddenly aging. She was pushing 400 and what if these were her last days on earth? *Oh well, it isn't like I thought I'd live forever. But maybe I should try teaching what I know to a younger apprentice. Besides, what if Aeon comes for* me?

As Ella was wrestling with her thoughts she saw Santa's button light up. She grabbed the line instantly and said excitedly, "You're back!"

Santa laughed his ho, ho, ho and said,"Yes, and Mary and I are ready to meet with the Council as soon as they can be convened."

"I have set everything up for first thing tomorrow morning at 8:00," she said. "I need to get a hold of

Jackson and Britney."

"And where are they?" Nick asked.

"Off making plans for the power and water supplies I suspect," said Ella.

"Of course," Nick said. "But I meant where are they? At the pump-house, the power station, in another land?"

"If I knew that I probably could have gotten a message to them to contact me," she said sarcastically. "No one knows exactly where they are or what they are doing together."

"I see," Nick heard the strain in her voice and asked if everything was alright.

Ella told him of the thoughts she had been having and how she was thinking it might be time to step down as communications director.

"Ella, I wouldn't last a week without you and you know it. Secondly, who could possibly replace you? No one knows how to reach everyone at the drop of a hat like you do." Nick was practically begging at this point. "And thirdly, if anything happens to you when we move, it may happen to the entire village and if it does, whether you are around or not won't matter too much as neither will we."

Ella began giggling then laughing at the thought of being so foolish. "I guess you are absolutely right. I am being a silly old fool. I am sorry Santa."

"Don't concern yourself, my dear lady," he said. "Everyone of us will be having thoughts like that, Mary and I are having the same ones, and I am not ashamed to say I am a bit concerned about what will happen next

Christmas if I am wrong. But as I told you, I may not
be here to worry about it, but somehow I don't think
that will be the case."

"Thanks Santa. Whitey asked me if I got in touch
with you that I ask you to call him," Ella finished.

"Okay, I'll give him a call in a little stretch, I want to
make some notes for tomorrow first." He pulled out his
'mental pad' as he called it.

"Goodbye, Santa. See you tomorrow morning," Ella
hung up.

Nick began scribbling in his note pad and by the time
he was finished we wrote several pages. He thought he
addressed every problem the Council might ask, but of
course he knew that probably wasn't true.

After he read and reread his notes a few times he
called Whitey.

Whitey picked up after the second ring and said,
"Hello Santa, I hope you are having a better day than
we are."

"Actually, Whitey, I am back, but yes, I would have
to say it has been productive. What's going on?"

Whitey filled Nick in on the occurrences of yesterday
and began to tell him what happened today. "We've lost
the skating pond in the woodlands. I walked out there
with Frosty Evergreen and the whole thing is cracking
and water is beginning to seep through the top. So
Frosty closed it down and had signs put up around it."

Nick said that although he knew some elves will be
sorely disappointed it wasn't the end of the world. Then
he thought about Whitey's tone and realized he wasn't
done. "Okay, you might go ahead and let the other shoe

drop."

"If you will remember the skating pond is close to another structure. And it developed problems also."

"You don't mean..." Nick began.

"I'm afraid so, Santa," Whitey continued. "Let's say Mrs. Claus doesn't have to water her plants at the greenhouse any longer. They are self-watered now."

"Is the shop gone?" asked Nick cautiously.

"No that is okay for the moment," Whitey answered.

"But I don't get it, the gondola I can understand, that's a massive structure, but Mary's greenhouse scarcely weighs anything in comparison."

"It's more due to the location," explained Whitey. "The woodlands are the furthest southern point of the North Pole. As we already knew there were problems with the refreezing in the past few years and this has been a mild winter thus far. We haven't had a blizzard outside the dome in as long as I can remember, and that's quite some time. Obviously, we have a melting problem and it is going to show up first where the normal melting takes place,"

"Is the whole glass area sunk?" asked Santa.

"No, it has about two, maybe two and a half feet of water in it. But I can't let Mrs. Claus or anyone else go in there because the additional weight might cause the whole thing to go with whoever is in there. I am not going to lose our CEO over some pine saplings and poinsettias," Whitey said firmly.

"Of course not," said Nick. "But just the same, maybe we shouldn't tell her about it."

"Santa, I don't want to take the chance that she may

wander over there herself," said Whitey warily. "She might take it upon herself to try and salvage something."

"Okay," Nick relented, "I will tell her today. Is there anything else?"

"That's not enough?" said Whitey in amazement.

"Of course that's enough, it's just you sometimes can drag bad news over a great deal of time. I am never quite sure when you are finished."

"Your dad used to accuse me of the same thing," chuckled Whitey, "He always said I would go to the moon via Jupiter."

"Dad was a great one for euphemisms," said Nick. "I best be telling Mary that she might want to take up growing water lilies."

"I don't envy you, Santa, good luck," Willie knew he was in for a bad time with the news.

"Yeah thanks. I'll see you tomorrow at eight. And no more bad news for today," Nick said.

"If it doesn't happen, you won't hear about it," Whitey said and hung up.

He had no sooner hung up the line when Ella called to tell him she had tracked down Britney and Jackson and that everyone would be there tomorrow.

"Do you want this to be an open meeting," she asked hesitantly.

"Not this time, Ella," he replied quickly, "We need to get this approved through the Council. and only through the Council. If anyone has an objection they can find their own place to relocate."

"I see you are pretty firm on this place," said Ella.

"It comes down to time, and the fact we don't have much of it," Nick softened, "Look there may be other choices, possibly better choices, but we can't take more time. We need Whitey to get a dome set up and we have elves and possessions to move."

"So you spoke with Whitey then…" she trailed off.

"Yes, I spoke with Whitey," he said.

"Are you going to tell her?" she asked.

"What choice do I have? I can't have her accidentally walk in there and have the whole place go under," Nick felt sick at the thought.

"Not a good idea, no" Ella said quietly. "I hope she takes it okay. I recall when she came up with the idea and when she had those garden supplies and that dirt and mulch shipped up. I thought you were going to laugh yourself silly. But she showed you, and you had so many trees and plants to deliver to families that couldn't get any. It was the most since your ancestor in Germany did it. And that began the whole Christmas Tree thing in the first place."

Nick reminisced with her and was sad to be the one to break the news to her. But he was also thinking, *Imagine how many trees and plants she could grow in the Smoky Mountains. Maybe that is how I will bring this up before I tell her about the greenhouse.*

He realized Ella was still talking and said, "I'm sorry, what did you say? My mind was wandering."

"I was saying I don't envy you being the bearer of that news." Ella repeated.

"I think I have a way to soften the blow," Nick smiled. "But either way I need to go and talk to her.

Again, I'll see you tomorrow. Goodnight."

"Goodnight, Santa, and good luck." she said.

Later that evening at dinner they as they talked about the Smoky Mountains, Nick saw his chance to bring up the greenhouse. "You know so many things will fit in so well with this area. I don't see any power issues, and the roads and rails will be much easier to utilize. Why I imagine the greenhouse will double in size. Think of it, Mary, how much bigger your new greenhouse will be."

Mary smiled lovingly at her husband and said, "It's okay, dear, I know about it."

"About what?" he asked feigning ignorance.

"About the greenhouse sinking," she said staring at him. "April Zinnia called me and told me the whole story. She discovered the problem when she went in this morning and she was the one who called Whitey."

"I thought Whitey discovered it after going to the skating pond with Frosty," he said confused.

"What are you both talking about?" asked Michael.

"You have it backwards, April called Whitey and after he came to the greenhouse, he called Frosty and checked out the skating pond," Mary turned to Michael. "The greenhouse is sinking and there is two to three feet of water in the glass atrium. Your father, in a truly sweet way, was trying to figure out how to tell me this, but I already knew."

Nick coughed. "I was saying after hearing about this one, that, um, how much bigger and nicer the new one will be."

"Of course, dear," Mary winked at Michael. "And you

are right about the new greenhouse, it *will* be beautiful. I'm sorry I can't salvage anything from this one. But Whitey wouldn't let April set foot in there, and I am sure he won't let me anywhere near it."

"He is worried something might happen to you if you try," Nick said softly.

"So I heard, something about how he would not lose the CEO because of a flower pot." Mary shook her head sadly.

"He's doing what he thinks is right," said Nick. "And personally I agree with him. There's nothing in there worth endangering yourself for, and nothing that can't be replaced. Plus it is questionable how much of it we could move south with everything else that needs to go."

Trying to change the subject, Kristopher said, "I guess that means there won't be any more Saturday night skating parties, either."

"Not for a while," Nick said, also anxious to change the subject. "We may have to find another recreation for Saturday nights. I doubt, unless we want to keep the inside of the dome below freezing, that ice skating rinks will be easy to maintain."

"Actually one of the elves came up with freezing large areas of water regardless the surface temperature, so don't be too quick to kill off our parties," countered Kristopher.

"It sounds like we lose nothing, and gain much," Nick said happily. "How do you think we should approach this with the Council, Mary?"

"Just use the enthusiasm you are showing right now," she said, "They'll catch the fever."

"I mean, should I do more research and come up with more scientific facts?" He pushed.

"You are not a scientist, and no offense meant, but you are not qualified to speak as one," she said, and held up her hand to stop him interrupting. "Tell them what we experienced and mention what Aeon alluded to, and let them put together a survey team of their own and send them to scope out the region. We have done what we promised, and we can defend our decision with what we already know and saw. Let them get involved and own a piece of this decision, too."

Nick's sons both nodded their heads and Michael said, "Mom's right, the more the Council feels that they have a say in this, the easier it will be to convince the rest of the elves in the Village. Our own voices won't have enough merit to carry the whole North Pole."

Nick considered this. "Yes, I guess you're both right, but I am prepared to defend this place with my last breath if necessary."

"I highly doubt it will be necessary, since they already said they would abide by our decision." Mary grinned at her husband. "I don't think you will need to fall on your sword for this. Though I would talk about the amenities and the ease of transition we will have moving there."

Kristopher asked, "Should Michael and I be there to talk about what we saw, also, or if you forget a few things?"

Nick looked at Mary, who nodded her head, "It would be nice to have you both there regardless of the reason, but yes, having four memories would be better than only your mother and me trying to think of everything."

"What time are we meeting?" asked Michael.

"Four in the morning," Nick said.

"What?" yelled Michael.

"Are you kidding?' cried Kristopher.

"Alright, fine. You two can come at 8:00 instead."
Nick tried to keep a straight face. Mary would only look
down at her plate.

"Oh I get it," Kristopher said in a knowing manner.
"This is like you used to tell us we had to be somewhere
an hour earlier, so we would be there on time, right?"

With that, Mary broke into a laugh. "It worked when
you were younger."

They recounted the times their parents would play
practical jokes on them as they cleared the table.

Once they had cleaned up, they each went to their
own room, except Nick who went to his office and
prepared notes for tomorrow's meeting. After more than
an hour, he rubbed his eyes and decided to join his wife
and leave this for tomorrow. *Let the chips fall where they
may.* He felt good about their united front.

Chapter 18

Gathering the Troops

Because nearly everyone that traveled to Fairbanks, Alaska, had to connect through the Seattle-Tacoma airport, the 7:55 pm flight was full. Elves and tallfolk alike crowded into the airplane, which was small to begin with. The attendants could not figure out why the flight was so packed, as the cruise ship season wouldn't begin for another several months. They also heard from other airline employees that every flight that day and the next was jammed.

As they got everyone situated and stowed the overhead baggage they noticed there were many short people on the plane, and they almost missed a few when counting heads prior to take off. Another strange thing was that a lot of the passengers seemed to know one another, and this caused the attendants to wonder if there was some sort of a bizarre convention or family reunion taking place in Fairbanks.

When their flight arrived at Fairbanks, they unloaded and more greetings were exchanged, as if long lost family members were finally reuniting. Jim Atherton and Cory Peters came in on the same flight and they introduced each other and talked about their first trips to the North Pole and the existing problem they were attempting to help with.

Jim kept his hypothesis to himself, but discussed it in general terms about how the Pole was actually causing itself to melt.

"You mean every sunny day causes more problems?" Cory said with a low groan.

"Precisely." Jim answered and nodded his head, "Because dark water attracts heat and snow repels it by reflecting the light away, with so much more ocean exposed, it is almost like a heat lamp on the area."

Cory shook his head. "That can't be good. Where do you think they will move the village to?"

"With some of the changes I brought for the dome, I would think anywhere they might desire," he said grinning to himself.

"You have changes for the dome?" Cory said astonished.

"A few," Jim smirked. "But I'd rather not talk about it until I meet with the Council."

"Wow, you're going before the Council?" asked Cory. "Santa Nick told me about them, and I met a couple of the elders, but I never have entered the council chambers."

Jim shrugged. "It's a rather august body. The leadership there has watched over the Pole for centuries. I am sure they are as baffled as they have ever been. They set up the North Pole back in the 16th century and have never had to consider such a monumental problem."

"All I know is that moving is the most stressful thing a person can do in their life," Cory added. "It's up there even beyond a death in the family. I can't imagine what might be going through their heads."

"Judging from the elves on this plane, they are obviously pulling out the stops to get as much help as possible up there," Jim said looking around the full flight.

A couple of elves came up to Cory and one said, "You're Mr. Peters, aren't you?"

"Yes, that's right, but call me Cory," he responded. "Do I know you gentlemen?"

"We came down a couple times to Eagle River," said the taller of the two. "We switched out some reindeer for Forrest Hedemup."

"Oh, I remember," He addressed the smaller elf. "You're Bumper, right?"

The elf nodded and grinned.

Cory looked at the other elf and shook his head, "I'm sorry..."

"Zedekiah, or as most call me, Zed," the taller elf said. He was stocky, but taller than Bumper. Both elves had dark complexions and their hands were like sandpaper. Bumper's hair was shorter and he wore it in a wave from left to right. The long darker hair of Zed was combed straight back.

"We are based out of the Chicago Distribution Center and work with Chitown," stated Bumper. "She said we could help out, after we got everything ready and organized in the Center."

Jim introduced himself to the elves and asked, "Are they clearing every DC to take whatever can be shipped down from the Pole?"

Zed nodded and said, "Actually, the DC got our first

shipment today from the NPV via Thundersleigh,"

Cory looked confused. "I'm sorry shipment from who of what?"

Jim chuckled. "The Thundersleigh, along with the Supersleigh and the Firesleigh, are three massive cargo planes that the NPV, or North Pole Village, uses to transport large amounts of goods to their worldwide distribution centers, or DC's, for short."

Cory nodded his head and said, "Okay, thanks for the explanation, I thought you might have switched to a different language."

Jim laughed. "I have worked with many of the elves, more than most I imagine, and have picked up on their acronyms. In fact, Ella says she sometimes forgets she's talking with a 'tall' or tallfolk when talking to me."

Cory said, "At least I know some of it, like tallfolk, though I never heard the abbreviated version."

"I have a feeling that you are going to come away from this trip with a whole new vernacular for talking with the Village."

"I am not sure I will be up there that long," said Cory. "Unfortunately I am bringing Santa Nick another problem to deal with, and my stay may be short. It depends on what he wants me to do."

"Gosh, something else?" asked Zed with wide eyes. "Hopefully its nothing serious. He has enough to concern himself with."

"I am afraid it is serious," said Cory in a resigned voice. "And yes, I've already been told about how full his plate is. Believe me when I say I would much rather this not have happened, more than anyone."

Jim sensed that Cory didn't wish to divulge any more information now. He patted Cory on the back and said, "I wouldn't fret too much, Santa will handle it, or find a suitable way to take care of the issue, whatever it is."

The plane had begun its descent and the passengers were asked to return to their seats and fasten their seat belts. The little group broke up and followed the attendants instructions.

A little later they departed the plane into FAI, the Fairbanks Airport, and the walk to the terminal instantly reminded them of where they were, as it was only 3° outside. Cory now had a closet full of heavy parkas and came prepared. Jim only had his ski jacket that he received several years back from the "Warmth of Faith Company," which was another tongue-in-cheek company of the Village. Since he lived in Atlanta, it rarely was needed much during winter.

They climbed into the two buses and moved off quickly toward the same old barn they had seen before, although this time they could see the engine and coal tender of The Northern Express and a car behind them exposed to the outside. As they pulled into the barn they realized why. Instead of three cars, as they had seen during their first trip, there were now more than twice that many.

When they boarded the train, it was more crowded than the plane. Apparently passengers had arrived from Barrow and Anchorage and everyone had been waiting for the Seattle flight to get there. As they crowded together, the train valet elves herded the mass of people, also mingling around outside, into the cars and said they could get moving. They promised they would serve a late dinner snack shortly.

Elves and tallfolk entered the cars and through a flurry of discussions managed to get settled. The other tall folk were the first to respond to Ella's calls, and there were quite a few. Many more would arrive tomorrow with additional elves from the DC's.

The train pulled out of the station, and most hadn't noticed it moving, as they were getting themselves situated. Cory was sitting two-thirds of the way back in his car and he was watching someone. One man stood toward the front and was moving cases around. He looked to be in about his mid-twenties, handsome, with dark brown thick hair. He stood just shy of 6' with a slender build. But it was his dark brown eyes that Cory recognized. He still had that inquisitive "bad boy" look that was irresistible. Cory wondered if this was the best time to interrupt him, as he looked a little frazzled.

The man must of felt Cory's eyes on him, as he suddenly stood up straight and looked around the car. When his eyes locked with Cory a big smile bloomed on his face. He waved and held up his index finger as to say "one minute." He moved a few more cases around and began to make his way toward the back of the car.

"George Mendez." Cory fairly shouted. "As I live and breath!"

"Hi Cory," George responded. "How have you been?"

"I'm doing good," Cory grinned. "Still running the school and B&B. Katy and I had another baby and we named her Amethyst, so Todd has a younger sister to look out for."

"How is the Santa training business?" George asked.

"We get busier every year," said Cory. "Unfortunately there are still many more 'bad Santas' than good. We keep trying to stem the tide, but it is an uphill battle."

"You sure see them everywhere at the end of the year," commented George. "I see them in every store and event in the area."

"And now a few of them are causing us problems," said Cory. "I have to see the big guy about it. I wish I didn't have to do that now."

"What's happened?" asked George.

Cory explained the problem he was going to talk to Nick about. George listened carefully and shook his head as Cory spoke. George said when Cory finished, "Not an easy problem to solve, but I believe you will find your answers at the Pole. They have solved larger problems than this, although this is a big one."

George's response didn't make Cory feel much better about the task at hand. George sensed this and decided to change the subject.

"So how is Todd?" George asked, remembering the toddler he shared his first North Pole adventure with.

"A typical teenager. He likes to think he knows more than Katy and me," Cory laughed. "Much as I suspect *you* were when you were last here!"

"You're kidding, Todd is in high school?" said George astonished.

"Yup, turns fourteen next month," grinned Cory.

"I can't believe that much time has passed," George shook his head, "Of course I was in high school back then. I have two Masters degrees now.

Jim had been led to a different car by Bumper as he
wanted Jim to meet one of their science elves who was a
meteorologist from the Chicago DC. Pepper Windenrain
had also begun his calculations upon listening to the
broadcast from the North Pole. He was now spreading
his charts out before Jim and going over his calculations.
Jim had added a few new parameters to consider that
Pepper hadn't included and they were now readjusting
his numbers to fit the new data.

Pepper upon arriving at similar numbers to Jim's sat
back and wiped his brow. "This is terrible," he said
stunned.

"Unfortunately, yes." nodded Jim, "I have looked at
this from every angle and that is what I keep coming up
with."

"Now we know why there are so many people coming
up to the Village," Pepper said thoughtfully.

"Uh, I don't think they know how bad it is yet," said
Jim uncomfortably, "They gave me different figures
when we talked, and no one has contacted me with
anything different."

"How much were they off?" Pepper asked.

"Two to five," Jim whispered.

Pepper whistled and bowed his head.

The valets of the train were bustling getting food out
to anyone who wanted it. They had prepared a small
menu as there were too many to try and serve as they
normally did. Many had gotten something to eat earlier,
but some had traveled the entire day to get this far and
hadn't been able to stop for something more filling. Most
ate as they talked. All were in a hurry to get to their

destination and begin working.

The train approached the village and began slowing upon reaching the woodland area. Even in this extremely late hour you could see several folks out walking around. When they pulled into the station, many more elves were moving around and carrying large loads or bundles.

As everyone disembarked from the train, it look like an invasion force had landed at the North Pole. Many villagers were waiting for one person or another to arrive and greeted them with warm hugs and sometimes tears, but the sheer number of people wanting to help bolstered everyone's spirits.

Cory, Jim, and George, along with a few other tallfolk were the first to arrive at the village, and were ushered back to the Reindeer Inn. Christel came out and welcomed each one warmly. She explained that this time, attending to their needs would be less accommodating as the Inn would not only be full, but most of her staff was out helping other inns.

She also informed them that they would have to share rooms and apologized for the inconvenience, as there would be many more visitors than they had seen previously at one time.

Jim laughed and said, "My sweet Christel, I think you believe we are here on vacation. Nothing could be further from the truth. We are here to serve the residents of the North Pole, not the other way around!"

The usually stoic Christel suddenly released her pent up emotions, worries, sadness and exhaustion and fell apart right before their eyes. She fell against Jim and

George and began crying. Cory came over and rubbed her neck saying that everything would be all right. They and others would be there to help everyone make it through. Jim and George put their arms around her and held her tightly. She cried for a couple more moments, pulled herself together, wiping her eyes. "I...I'm so sorry, I don't know what came over me."

Jim said softly, "We do, this has to be so painful and worrisome for everyone in the Village. I, for one, will be surprised if this event isn't played out several times as we do this."

She showed them to their rooms and talked about how much work had been accomplished to take care of so many visitors coming to assist them in the time of need.

The innkeepers had indeed accomplished quite a lot and had been able to prepare one of the manufacturing centers for the elves to stay in. Fergie Keepitneat was in charge of this housing facility, and with the help of the construction elves, they built several comfortable rooms within the large structure. Each unit could house up to four people, although they needed to share bathroom facilities. As the finishing touches were being done, Fergie was working with yet another previous visitor to the North Pole, helping him install the last amenity.

Fred Wu, with the help of the North Pole, had invented the Hydroless shower, which used a mineral-like substance instead of water. The minerals were not only exhilarating but would clean hair, skin and massage the body while using it. It required no shampoo, conditioner or body wash, and the minerals came in four fragrances that left the hair and body with a fresh clean scent. These were mountain fresh, mango-pomegranate, coconut-passion flower, and green tea-avocado. After the 'shower' the minerals would run themselves through a filter and be ready for the next use. The filter would only need to be replaced once a year. The minerals to this point hadn't needed to be changed out. Wu was about ready to introduce this product, and thought that the current need at the North Pole would make an excellent test market case.

He and Fergie were installing the last of the stations around the building. Since no water was required, they were able to place them at each of the four corners of the building and two on each side for a total of eight, and the elves had built a small room surrounding each 'shower' for privacy.

As the first of the elves checked in by the front door, Wilhelm, one of the elves from the SBH, was checking them in and setting them up in their dormitory. There were only about 20 elves for this makeshift hotel, as most of the rest would arrive tomorrow. When this building was full it would hold almost 200.

It was decided that both 'talls' and elves would be placed in Santa's Boarding House. Many of the ceilings in the SBH were only six and a half feet high, but the thinking was that it could accommodate the talls without an issue. The SBH did not contain the cooking facilities that Reindeer Inn had, but it could handle breakfast for the occupants at least. After that, the strain would be on the other eateries around town.

Ella, as always, was receiving reports of who had

arrived and where they could be located. She was coordinating meetings of various individuals and was on the lookout for particular talls and elves. When she heard George, Cory, and Jim were in the Reindeer Inn she immediately called Bilge and Topo about Jim and George, and then contacted Santa about Cory.

"Let's set his appointment for right after lunch tomorrow," said Nick. "I'll probably need to rest up a little after tomorrow's Council meeting before I take on whatever problem he is bringing."

Ella felt bad for Santa and in an attempt to cheer him said, "Perhaps it is not as bad as he thinks."

"I haven't known Cory to ever bring a problem to me in the last ten years since he and Katy have run this school. And I am sure you appraised him of what we have going on here?" asked Nick.

"Naturally, Santa. I told him this wasn't the best time to trouble you with more." Ella quickly defended herself.

"Then that says it all," he said. "Clearly, Cory wouldn't run up here without a valid concern. I hope it is something we can juggle as everything else is happening. Who else came in today? Anyone we needed immediately, elf or tallfolk?"

"Pepper Windenrain arrived today, but mostly it was elves from the various DC's," she said.

"Hmm." Nick considered. "Why don't you have Jim, George, and Pepper along with Topo and Bilge join the Council meeting tomorrow?"

"Anyone else?" she asked hesitantly.

"We are bringing the boys, but no, no one else for

now," Nick knew what she wanted. "Cory and anyone else will have to wait. I think we need an update on our situation but we don't need any grandstanding going on."

"Got it, Santa," Ella said. "I'll call them next."

"I'm giving up for the night," he said tiredly. "I'll see you tomorrow morning, and I think you will like what we present. Have a good night, Ella."

"Can't wait, goodnight," she said and hung up.

PART TWO

ONE STEP
FORWARD...

Start where you are.

Use what you have.

Do what you can.

Arthur Ashe

CHAPTER 19

THE NEW LOCATION

Someone had chosen snow for the previous night, and there was a fresh powder around the village. But the clouds had cleared and the "sun" was up and bright. The Village looked magical under the new snow.

Everyone in the Kringle household was ready by 7:30. Michael and Mary were padding around before 6:00, and Nick got up around 6:30 and went immediately into the shower to clear his head. Kristopher roused a few minutes before 7:00, and they met at the breakfast table at 7:15.

Nick usually made breakfast, but today Mary and Michael let him take his time getting ready and made French toast for everyone. As they sat around the table they saw he was deep in thought and let him chew on the days events with his food saying little.

A few minutes before 8:00 they began walking with purpose toward the Council Chambers. As they walked in, Mary and Nick saw Jim and George and gave them both hugs. Santa did the same to Pepper and gave a hearty handshake to Topo and Bilge. He turned to Pepper and said, "A little different from giving me an updated weather report at the DC isn't it?"

Pepper said, "Indeed," and told Santa he was surprised to have gotten the call last night from Christel.

"Right now I want any elf or tallfolk to help study,

and keep an an eye on, what is happening here,"
explained Nick. "Meteorology figures prominently into
this problem. I need to know any changes to the weather
that could have a bearing on our situation."

Pepper nodded his head and said he would work with
the other meteorologists at the North Pole and keep him
informed as best as he could.

Nick said, "I thought since they were already
working on this, I'd invite you to this meeting to get
brought up to speed. Also, since you have spent the last
several years in Chicago, you might find what we have to
say particularly interesting."

Pepper smiled and said, "I'm sure I will."

With that, Nick and Mary made their way to their
seats on the dais. As they did, everyone began to find
their own seats and the conversation volume fell to a
whisper.

Once more Nick brought the Council to order and
began by introducing the guests that had come that
morning. Most knew about George and Jim, though few
of the Council had met them. Pepper had spent about
150 years in the Village before heading down to the
Chicago DC at that center's behest. So they had known
him and a few said how good it was to see him returned
to the Pole.

After the pleasantries were completed, Nick opened
saying that he and his family had spent a several
interesting days in the place he felt would be the next
Village location. He talked at first about the allusion
from Aeon to where he and his father had visited
together, then he said how the area contained any

resources they would need, and that although not secluded, the Village would be easily concealed and hardly disturbed.

As Nick did with his family he made it almost unbearable for the Council to know this special place. Mary finally gave him a look and gesture as if to say "Get on with it!"

Nick said, "The place we have found is in the Southeastern United States and it is called the Great Smoky Mountains, which borders the states of Tennessee and North Carolina." The Council and everyone else applauded the announcement. Whether that was because they were pleased with the decision or the fact that he finally spit it out could not be determined. After the clapping died out, a few Council members raised their hands.

Nick first recognized Freida Cutinglass and she asked, "Won't it be difficult to get supplies to the top of a mountain?"

"These are extremely old mountains, not like the Rocky Mountains or the Sierra Nevada Mountains in California which can get up to 14,000 feet. These are gently sloping mountains and are only 6,600 feet at their highest elevation," explained Nick.

"What about volcanoes or earthquakes?" asked Alfie.

Topo raised his hand and Nick recognized him at once, "Actually these mountains were formed primarily through the uplifting of one tectonic plate upon another, and though there was some initial volcanic activity hundred of millions of years ago, volcanic activity has ceased and the mountains, as Santa mentioned, had at once reached heights like the Alps and Rockies, but have eroded ever since the Ordovician Period approximately 480 million years ago. Hence their gentle sloping nature. They show no sign of movement and are one of the most stable places on the North American Continent."

Turning to Santa and Mary, Topo said, "I believe you have made an excellent choice." And then he sat down.

Nick had told them about the places with no trees or foliage located in several areas they saw driving through.

Topo again stood and explained that the areas Santa was talking about were called balds and that the Appalachians contained both grassy and heath balds. These were areas in which little vegetation grew except grasses or in the case of heath balds, low shrubbery. He said that the grassy balds were still a mystery as to why nothing grew there, but there would be no danger in establishing a village on one as there was no toxicity in the soil or any other geologic danger. "It's one of those strange unexplained curiosities," he finished.

Nick had both boys talk about the towns surrounding the area, and Mary discussed the overall culture of the area that they learned from Richard, Naomi and others they spoke with. They addressed the beauty of the area, particularly in winter and said they saw paintings and pictures of the other three seasons, and the beauty was breathtaking. Nick also told them that with the exception of a few ski areas and the towns further down the mountains, the region and the back roads were 'closed up' between November and April.

Britney asked how many people lived in the area, and

how big was the visiting population they referred to?

Nick told them and they gasped at the number, but he went on to explain that although the Great Smoky Mountains National Park received that vast number of visitors, only a scant few actually wandered into the mountains, and that the dome would be able to protect them from almost any visitors.

"Are we not concerned with people 'bumping into' the dome and trying to figure what they struck?" asked Whitey. "I realize we can easily throw off their GPS and satellite fixations, as we do with radar and the like now, but I am concerned about too many people stumbling into the dome."

Nick knew this would be his first genuine challenge and attempted to allay their fears on the infrequency of this when he noticed Jim Atherton stand up and signal for recognition. Nick said, "Do you have a suggestion on this Jim?" he asked hopefully.

"How about a solution more than a suggestion?" Jim grinned.

"Please, tell us," Nick said anxiously.

"As a few of you know, I had been working with the properties of the dome from time to time," he began. "I actually found a way to permeate the lower surface of the dome and form a type of bubble within the bubble, so to speak. In other words, we could construct a dome with its current protective qualities, while allowing someone to walk right through the Village in their own hologram, and never interfere with our residents within the dome."

"Wouldn't we run into them, ourselves?" asked

Whitey.

"Think of it like a one-way mirror," said Jim, "We can see them walking around but they would not be able to see or hear us. And before you ask, any structure inside would appear as a large rock without any easy hand grips in their hologram, so they would avoid walking into them."

"A couple elves told me you had done some work on the dome, apparently these are the changes they mentioned," said Whitey. "But tell me, would we have the cloaking capability outside and the protection from electronic eyes and ears?"

"Yes the dome I constructed carries the properties as the ones here and at the DC's. I actually successfully tested mine at the DC outside of Atlanta. It remains in place and no issues have taken place in the six months it had been up," said Jim.

"You replaced our dome with your own?" asked Jackson.

"That would be impertinent, no. I placed a dome next to yours in a higher traffic area to test the properties of the 'bubble in a bubble' as I call it. So far it has tested successfully and without fail," he said. "Needless to say, if it works in a greater populace, it would work efficiently in little to no traffic on a mountain. Especially as long as you didn't place the village on the A.T., or too close to any rest areas or campsites."

"What's an A.T.?" asked Ella.

Mary explained, courtesy of Naomi from the cafe.

As the Council whispered back and forth, Whitey and

Jim played question and answer with each other.

"Are there any additional requirements needed for the set up of this new technology?" asked Whitey.

"I need to reprogram the data already in your current circuitry and make a couple minor adjustments, which is how I knew I was not changing the parameters of your dome, but merely enhancing them," answered Jim.

"Have you tested the strength to see if it matched ours?"

"I have, and though I haven't crashed a meteorite into it, or fired a missile at it, it seems to hold up to the usual tests."

"Okay, gentlemen," Nick intervened. "Jim this is exceptional news and it couldn't come at a more opportune time. Whitey you know how to use the time continuum to move from place to place, why not take Jim to his test site and see this for yourself and if you agree with Jim's assessment. The two of you can join a survey team and go to the Smokies, as they are called for short, and begin scoping out a potential sight to establish the Village. That is if I have the Council's approval to begin?"

A couple more questions concerning the general area itself were asked. Nick did what Mary suggested and let his enthusiasm flow until he thought the Council was nearly as excited as he was. Nick asked the big question, "I would like to ask the Council to call for a vote on the proposal to move to the Great Smoky Mountains."

Mary called out, "I move for a vote on the Great Smoky Mountains as the new location for the Village of the North Pole."

Denny said loudly, "I second the motion for the vote."

Nick said, "Moved and seconded, will it appease the Council for a verbal vote?" They each answered "Aye." Nick continued with the the vote saying, "I will ask each Council member by name and take a tally."

A few moments later the great migration from the North Pole to the Great Smoky Mountains was officially underway.

Chapter 20

Heading North

Bill Fredrick had been standing in line at one of the fast food places in Seattle-Tacoma airport. Susan wanted something to eat before they had to board the plane for Fairbanks. Though it was only 10:00 in the morning, he thought it might not be a bad idea. Especially as he forgot to ask Ella if there would be food on the train this trip.

After getting his order he walked over to Susan and acting like a waiter, began unwrapping and serving the food with a flourish, "Your kosher-style all beef hot dog young lady. And here are some crispy fries freshly prepared for you, and one large ice tea with lemon, of course."

She giggled at his antics and told him to sit down. Bill Fredrick was an engineer who had graduated from the Viterbi School of Engineering at USC, complements of Santa Claus and the North Pole. He carried degrees in both computer engineering and industrial and systems engineering. He had done well since college and now had his own business as an independent consultant who, like Jim Atherton, had his pick of clients to work with, and as highly sought after.

Susan was also a North Pole funded graduate from USC, from the School of Architecture, and she worked for one of the top architects in the San Diego area. She had asked for, and had gotten, a leave of absence as soon as they hung up the phone from Ella. Luckily she was in between projects finishing a new high rise bank building downtown.

They both had met at the North Pole and began their romantic entanglement there and then. Susan was instantly drawn to Bill. He was over six feet tall and solidly built. He was very handsome, with blond hair and warm blue eyes. His neck was short and thick, his chest broad, and he looked like a pro football player from the waist up. He always wore his hair short and combed forward, as he had back then. Bill was equally attracted to Susan with her slender shapely figure, auburn hair and brown eyes. Although she now wore her auburn hair shorter.

Both were stunned beyond belief when Ella called. Susan had always known she would return to the North Pole, as Santa had told her as much when she went the first time, but this was not how she thought it would be.

When Bill proposed to her after her graduation, she told him about how Santa had seen them together at the North Pole. She had imagined it would be after they had a couple of children, and they would return as a family. But this? She felt sick at the thought that the North Pole wouldn't be there in the future.

They told Ella they would book the first flight out of San Diego, but she beat them to the punch and gave them the flight information she had already reserved. They said that would be fine and Ella said she was confirming the booking as they were talking. They left the return flight as 'open' since they were not sure what would happen when they got there or how long they would be needed.

They also called their parents to apprise them of the situation. Jared was the most surprised and said he hadn't heard a word from his company, which was tied to goings on in the North Pole at the highest level. He wondered if he and Julie might get a call, but heard nothing thus far. Like their kids, they would be on their way, if asked, at the drop of a hat. A similar sentiment came from Bill's parents, Clark and Jillian, as Clark had retired that year he said, "I certainly got the time available to help out." Both parents made Bill and Susan promise to let Santa know they would be happy to lend a hand doing whatever they could.

Now sitting at the airport eating their lunch, they spoke idly about the situation and what they might be needed for upon their arrival. Bill said, "Whatever it is they need, I am willing to do it." Susan nodded and agreed with her husband.

Susan asked if Bill thought there was anything in that engineering brain of his that could prevent them from having to move. Bill said that although he was pretty good at what he did, preventing a polar ice cap from dissolving was a little out of his league.

Shortly after their early lunch, they checked and saw their Fairbanks flight was boarding. They came to the gate and Bill began quietly laughing. There were passengers surrounding them and the vast majority of them were about four feet tall. Susan slapped her husband, as she held her own hand over her mouth, trying not to laugh as her husband was carrying on.

She couldn't help saying as she fished the tickets out of her purse, "Now I know how Dorothy felt when the house landed."

At that, Bill let out a full guffaw and dropped one of the overnight bags he was toting. The other passengers looked at the couple and smiled like they were in on the joke. As usual, they got looks any time they left the North Pole. This group had been living among talls for a time and were good natured about their short stature, especially when they traveled in groups. People were generally kind and many helpful when they met them. As elves were exceedingly patient in the first place, the comments and fun teasing about their height, or lack thereof, resulted in the comeback teasing about climatic changes around the tall's heads and the like .

After Bill got control himself he said, "It's been so long since we saw the elven community, and they didn't seem as short as they do now."

"You weren't 6'1" ten years ago and it was so new that everything seemed out of place, remember?" she commented.

Bill looked into her soft brown eyes. "I am amazed at how much I *do* remember about that whole week."

"I wish our return trip to the North Pole wasn't under these circumstances," she said sadly.

"I'm happy to go back anyway we can. We owe Santa and the North Pole so much. Anything we can do to help repay that debt would make me feel better about it," he confessed. "Besides, how do you know this will be our last trip to Santa's Village? Just because they are moving doesn't mean that we won't return again."

She shrugged and said, "Yeah, I guess that's true."

As they moved to the Jetway they could see a lot of people with concerned looks boarding the plane with them.

CHAPTER 21

SHORTER AND SHORTER

Back at the North Pole, immediately following the vote, discussions turned to what was needed and in what order. Teams were put together and duties were assigned. Everyone was ready to begin making this a reality starting that day. Discussions also centered around who had already arrived at the North Pole and who was expected today and later in the week.

The first thing to be decided had already been discussed, and that was for Whitey and Jim to go to Atlanta and assess the validity and implementation of the new dome. A second group consisting of Mary, Topo, and Bill Fredrick, who were scheduled to arrive around two that afternoon, Susan, who is Bill's wife, and a couple of the construction elves would go to the Smokies and determine a potential area to establish the new village. After their tests, Whitey and Jim would join them at a rendezvous sight to lay out the new place and determine the size of the new dome.

Michael and Kristopher were to head up the packing and shipping of the manufacturing warehouses including any machinery, squibbles or fixtures that would be needed after rebuilding the new manufacturing structures. Michael would have use of Firesleigh, and Kristopher would have the Supersleigh to ship everything south. The village would retain use of the

Thundersleigh for its residents and their shops and belongings.

The meeting was going fine and they begun to discuss contingency plans and schedules when Jim raised his hand. Nick asked, "You have something else to add, Jim?"

"More of a point of clarification, actually," said Jim, "I would like to ask the Council, since you are talking about schedules and the like, what time line you are working with."

Nick motioned toward Topo and Bilge and said, "They advised us we don't have as much time as we first thought. We have to vacate this area in about six months to remain safe."

"That's as I feared." Jim said sadly, "Actually you can shave a third of that time off. As near as I can tell, you have four months, and even then, there are portions to the north and east that may go before that."

The Council erupted into shouts and objections to the new information. Nick suddenly realized he was standing, as were others, but stood in stunned silence.

Nick slowly picked up the gavel and started to bring the room to order.

When the room was quiet again Jim continued, "Coming up here I showed some of my calculations and data to Pepper and he came to a similar conclusion. I haven't had time to verify my data with Topo or Bilge, but I am confidant that I am right, as I ran it by some of my colleagues in the south. In four months, the North Pole will be uninhabitable."

This new wrinkle was almost too much to bare. Nick

had been thinking to himself it was going to be next to impossible to have everything salvaged in six months. Now he had lost two more months, and then they could lose structures before they could get everyone out.

Nick said quietly, "Jim, if you and Pepper would please verify your findings with Topo and Bilge, we would appreciate it, though I have little doubt of what you say to be true. Whitey has already seen some disturbing signs that this is happening faster each day."

To this Whitey nodded.

"I think we need to work toward clearing the village and its residents in three months and do everything we can to achieve that goal," Nick finished.

"Be out of here by May?" Freida clucked.

"The last thing we will allow is to have anyone left behind," said Denny Sweetooth, "We will do what we must, but we will accomplish this goal. We must consider ourselves lucky that we are finding out now, and not four months from now when it would be too late."

Jim, who remained standing, said, "I'm sorry to bring such bad news, but as Denny says it is better that you know this today than a couple weeks from now, at least there is time to react."

"I think it would be wise to set up a central location where we can pull everyone together and assign details and prepare for problems as they come up," Mary said. "Perhaps somewhere that may be safe for the longest period, so we can concentrate on the biggest threats first and move things out the fastest. I would ask our scientists to determine our largest threat assessments, and begin assembling teams to handle those areas by their estimated priority."

"We can determine that, and we will have recommendations for the Council by tomorrow morning," Pepper told the Council.

"I don't believe we have time to take things 'to committee' any more," said Nick "When you figure out the safest spot, tell Ella. Together you can figure out which building would be best to commandeer for your purpose. But don't go in like stormtroopers. Help that person move out, or take only the space you need to set up, perhaps do both."

Whitey brought up a question that Nick had previously thought about, but decided to keep to himself until someone else mentioned it. "About security," Whitey asked. "We will have many tallfolk roaming around both here, and at the new Smokies location. How do we maintain our law of limiting what tallfolk can see regarding advances beyond their culture? Forgive me," he said nodding at George and Jim, who both waved it off. "Are we really going to open Pandora's Box and let the whatever happens, happen?"

Everyone thought for a minute until Kristopher stood and upon being recognized by his father, addressed the Council, "Why not have a badge allowing anyone who had been here before, and is trusted, to see what they see? Especially since most of the technology will either be boxed up or not functioning anyway, and most likely they will have left the new village before we uncrate and reassemble everything. Anyone else, such as Santa Ambassadors or the like that we bring in will be restricted to established areas, much as they would have been before. I assume we intend to split the village into areas again?"

Mary nodded and said, "Yes, at least that is my assumption, as I plan to continue the Visiting Center and its activities. It stands to reason that the manufacturing and loading area would be away from the other parts of the village as it always has been."

"That sounds reasonable to me, especially since there is one very tall, tallfolk here who already breached our security once," Nick said laughing at George's now reddening face, "Whitey, does that seem acceptable to you as you are in charge of security?"

Whitey nodded, "A 'security clearance' huh? Yes, that makes sense to me. I can live with that if no one else on the Council objects?"

The others on the dais shook their heads or mumbled "No." Nick sighed and thought that another bone of contention was diverted without a major debate. He ticked that one off to everyone being in a hurry to get the village to safety at any cost.

Nick asked the Council and gallery, if any other bombs needed to be dropped before they began implementation of the plans they had discussed. No one spoke up, so Nick said, "Than I call this meeting adjourned, and ask that we meet again in three days to check our progress." He brought the gavel down more gently than usual.

Chapter 22

Escape For a Moment

The meeting lasted until 10:45 and when they came out they found a crowd milling around the chambers. They immediately asked exiting members about what had been decided. Nick thought Alfie was going to dash to the Polar Times newspaper and run a special edition for the village, but saw he was bogged down by questions from the crowd before he could escape.

Their own boys also had people trying to get information as the crowd heard they had traveled with their parents. No one had approached Santa or Mary Claus because that wasn't done without invitation. It had been that way since Kris Kringle had become Santa Claus in the late 18th century.

"I guess it's no surprise," Mary said.

Nick shook his head and said, "I expected as much. I was more surprised when there wasn't a crowd here like the other day."

"They were probably thrown off by the earlier meeting time," said Mary.

"According to Whitey, the other day they gathered at six," he said thoughtfully. "Perhaps their curiosity was stirred later this morning."

"What time are you meeting Cory?" she asked.

"*WE* are meeting him at 1:00 this afternoon," he said

with conviction. "I am not going in there alone! If this is as serious as he claims, I will need you to help either pick me up off the floor, or hold me back from running out the door screaming my head off."

Mary laughed. "Okay, but I don't know how much more I can handle either."

Nick nodded. They at least had a couple of hours to try and clear their heads and grab some lunch before Cory came over.

The walk back to their home was uneventful and they both plopped down on the sofa once inside. They talked little. Mary eventually asked when she should leave for the Smokies again.

"Poor Bill and Susan will barely get here and you will have to bundle them up with everyone else and head out there," he said, "Whitey told me he and Jim would leave later this afternoon for Atlanta. I would imagine you should follow tomorrow or certainly the morning after."

Mary nodded, "I will play it by ear. I need to figure who else I want to accompany us."

They talked for a few more minutes and then Nick said he was going to root around the kitchen to see what he wanted to make them for lunch.

Chapter 23

Another Wrinkle

At 1:00 sharp there was a knock on the door. Mary opened the door and gave Cory a big hug saying how good it was to see him again. She had helped Katy set up the bed and breakfast in the beginning and had returned a few times with Nick. She told them she thought of the Eagle River school and resort as their own private retreat.

Cory smiled and said how good it was to see her again. He entered the home and felt worse for bringing such bad news to this bastion of happiness and hope.

Nick walked up and also gave Cory a hug and said he was also glad to see him, whatsoever the reason behind it.

Cory said, "Believe me Santa Nick, if this could have waited for another time, I certainly would have." Nick had asked Cory many times to only call him "Nick," but Cory said that wasn't respectful to his position. So Cory compromised, as some others did, and he and Katy referred to him as Santa Nick, to demonstrate both, the friendship and the respect.

"Come on in then and let us see if we can help ease your troubled mind," Nick said warmly.

The three of them settled into the living area where there was a nice fire going and the room smelled of burning Eucalyptus wood, Nick and Mary's favorite.

Mary asked if Cory would like a drink or something to eat.

"Perhaps later," he said anxious to get the discussion underway.

Nick looked at him and said, "Okay, what's up?"

Cory had been running this through his mind dozens of time and he began, "Let's start at the beginning, about a year ago, I had received numerous applications for the school, as I always do, and had Keeney run them through the scanner array as is our policy. We rejected several, as we always have to do based on their scores. But in that batch there was a man by the name of Phillip Weazle, a self professed historian on Santa Claus. His score came back a negative eleven."

"A minus eleven!" Nick and Mary both exclaimed. Nick asked, "Are you sure there wasn't some mistake? Did he pass more than one scanner?"

Cory nodded, "Actually numerous, each one red or double digit negative, he lives in the Midwest and travels around quite a bit."

"Okay," said Mary, "so you rejected his app, then what happened?"

"He went ballistic and swore revenge. He kept calling and emailing me telling me he would 'bury' our whole sham organization and the phoney head of our corrupt company," Cory said angrily.

Nick chuckled and shook his head, "Empty threats and obviously he doesn't know any better."

"I'm afraid his threats were not so empty," Cory said with a deep sigh. "Apparently this guy spends a major part of everyday looking for trouble and making life miserable to anyone he decides he doesn't like. He is into the social media and has several websites that he either runs or has a large influence over. He has been putting out all kinds of lies about how we take money from honest hard working Santas and blow it on ourselves in ridiculous and frivolous ways."

Santa looked at Cory, "And what can we do about this?"

"Unfortunately I haven't been able to figure anything out so far. When I try to dispel anything his sites say, he notches up the attacks. He says anything he wants, knowing there is no truth to it. He makes things up as he goes along, such as numbers of attendees, amounts of money, costs, anything. And he has got a large part of the other Santas believing his drivel and making similar accusations using his 'facts and figures', of course." Cory was getting hopelessly emotional by this point.

"Settle down, Cory," Mary said in a calming manner. "We will figure something out."

Cory looked at her impatiently and said, "You don't understand. We have had several Santas back out from the next course, and I get dozens of emails from past students and other Santas wanting to know what is going on. We have received threats against us, personally and to our facility, saying they would burn the place to the ground. They have tried posting pictures of you and said that they want you to come forth and explain the fraud you have been committing in the name of Santa Claus."

"This is absurd!" Nick was now beginning to get furious himself, especially at the harm aimed at Cory and Katy, who like Nick and Mary, did so much to help people every year. They didn't have a mean spirited bone in their bodies.

"Every time I go South, inevitably some guy will come up to me and tell me he wants to be a Santa because he heard that Santas make a fortune," said Nick disgusted. "This is where it comes from. I keep telling these people if that's why you want to do this, then you are doing it for the wrong reasons."

"There are thousands of impersonators out there now," complained Cory. "Anyone who can grow facial hair, or anyone that puts artificial hair on, is trying to get into what is now termed, "The Santa Business." There are groups that have formed or are forming in states or regions throughout the country and abroad. Conventions are being held that are basically everything from 'professional' Santas sharing resources and ideas, to drunken parties of amateurs running around from one city bar to another as a joke."

"Are these groups anything like our school?" asked Nick.

"There are a few schools around," answered Cory. "Mostly teaching the same ideas every year over and over, because there are so many 'new' Santas popping up each year. Most of them don't really know the truth of what goes on here, and far too many aren't taught how to speak to children, nor really care. And the groups are worse, they are primarily egocentric men and women claiming to be the original Santa or Mrs. Claus. It's always about their costumes, their bleached hair, their experience 'in the chair' as they call it..."

"Hold on," interrupted Mary. "You mean they are impersonating me now?"

"I haven't met one yet that knows what you do, or that you're the CEO of the Village, or really anything about you, other than your propensity for baking," Cory continued. "They seem to be more window dressing for their ego maniacal husbands or friends. And the Santas are worse. Not one can explain anything that really takes place up here, or how things work."

Mary shook her head.

"Aren't some of these guys who you chose our Ambassadors from?" asked Nick.

"A small number of them are, most certainly," Cory nodded. "but so many others are nasty to one another. putting each other down, and telling children that they are the "real thing" and that the others are fakes."

"Doesn't that mean this Weazle guy is pointing fingers at these guys?" asked Nick.

"Yes and no. He is convinced that you are not real, but that you are another fake taking money out of these other Santa's pockets for your own gain," Cory stated.

"How much of a following has this idiot got?" asked Nick. He was clearly at the boiling point with this nonsense.

"Now dear," soothed Mary. "Keep your temper."

Cory thought for a moment, "It is difficult to say. He has so many separate websites that he works behind the scenes, or uses different avatars, or is friends with others that own their own websites and he influences them what to write or say. Unfortunately his network is pretty big. Also he has numerous henchmen in various

organizations. For instance, he has a friend called Robby
Ellis who is this clown that runs the Sunshine Santa
group. He can spit venom better than any cobra I've
heard about."

"You shouldn't be ungracious calling him a 'clown'
regardless of his actions against us," Mary admonished.

"I'm not, during the year he works as a
clown...really!" said Cory in defense.

"Oh..." she said.

"And on top of everything else, the various groups
are more often than not warring inside the group with
each other, or with other groups," Cory said. "It is
gaining a lot of press and it makes the entire assemblage
as a whole look ridiculous. They are accusing each other
of a variety of wrongdoings and terrible
misrepresentations. Unfortunately it is bringing the
whole concept of what you do into a black and ugly
world, rather than providing the light you keep trying to
bring."

"What ideas have you got?" asked Nick.

"I really don't know," said Cory dejected. "I kept
hoping this thing would blow over and would heal itself,
but it is only getting worse with websites like 'Santa
Speaks', 'Public Defender', 'Santa's Internet', and a
variety of natural and artificial bearded Santa Claus
sites. It has become so crazy. They are fighting over
everything from website names, to how to organize and
whom to let in to their little factions."

"I think we should focus on the personal attacks,"
said Mary, "I cannot think how to approach the
problems of the clubs, and I'm not sure we should. But

this Weazle person needs to be stopped. Does he have a wife we might appeal to, since his scanner score is so deep in the hole. Obviously he wouldn't listen to any reason."

Cory scoffed, "No help there. His wife Cynthia Louis-Weazle is almost a worse piece of work in this than Phillip. She is a member of many of the websites I mentioned and to say she 'fans the flames' is an understatement. She is pure poison on the web."

"What's her score?" asked Nick curiously.

"Minus eight," he answered.

"Hmm, yeah no help there," Nick rubbed his beard. "I think we need to bring Ion Crosswire and Indy Webbinhouse into this. They both know as much about this as anyone up here. Perhaps we might bring Mac Gelfeeney up from Northern California, too. I only know enough about the Internet to get me in trouble."

Mary agreed saying, "I know a good deal more than Santa, but he's right. We need someone who can really take hold of this problem and get people rallied around the truth, if that's possible."

Nick started going off about how once again society had taken something that should be something wonderful like the world wide web and twisted it into something corrupt and evil.

"Now you are sounding like your father used to," Mary chided.

"I don't know, Miss Mary, I think Santa Nick has a point. This guy took the web and turned the WWW into Weazle's Wicked Word, and HTTP into Harassing Tirades Toward People. Whether he is only being cruel, or the devil himself, he causes some real nastiness out there." Cory spat. "All I know is the hate mail we get is worse than when we were working with abused families, and for absolutely no reason other than this guy got a stick up his..."

"Okay, Cory, I get the picture," she broke in. "And I agree something needs to be done. I am so sorry this person has gotten under your skin as he has, and I am extremely concerned for both you and Katy. Perhaps she should come up here also and you both should stay until we can turn this around."

Cory shook his head, "Katy loves the B&B and doesn't want to leave it, and we have a class coming up in a few weeks. I will head back as soon as we have any kind of a strategy planned. I need to get ready, and I will work to implement any plan we can come up with. We absolutely need to get rid of this powder keg before someone really lights a fuse."

"How about we get together at 8:30 tomorrow morning with the other guys and see what we can come up with. For now, let's get off this subject and talk about something else for a minute or two." Nick sighed. "I find that often the best way to solve a problem is to leave it alone for a time. Tell me about the upcoming class, and by the way, I apologize, but I don't think I will make it down this time."

"Really?" Cory feigned astonishment.

"Alright so you figured that out," Nick grinned. "But I was truly looking forward to it after Christmas, I thought about asking Mary to join me."

"Thanks for the invitation," she said teasingly. "But

I'm afraid I also have to pass."

Cory said, "Before we talk about who is coming next month, how about telling me where the Village is moving to. I heard something about the Southeastern United States?"

Nick whooped. "Man, who needs an Internet around this place? News travels faster than electronically without so much as whisper, ho, ho, ho."

They paused for some refreshments and the Kringles talked about their trip to the Smokies.

Chapter 24

A New Noah

Christel Bunkinstyle had called Santa to advise him that the Reindeer Inn was filling fast. He asked about several people and heard that indeed they had arrived. He inquired about the idea he mentioned to her last night before going to bed.

She said that they could pull it off, and Nick asked them to call the guests at both the Inn and SBH and let them know. They planned it for 7:00 at the Inn.

Cory had left about an hour before. Ella had put a call forth to Mac in California, but had not heard back yet, but she did arrange the meeting with Ion and Indy for tomorrow morning.

Nick let Cory explain the problem over the phone to them, so they might begin mulling it over. They both said they would come with ideas and thoughts on how to best defend the attacks from "The Weasel", as Indy now called him.

Whitey had also called. Apparently a couple other houses had developed some structural cracks and if not in immediate danger, they also had some damage. One was the Woodworks building and the other was Willie's skating shop, which naturally was on the edge of the already condemned skating rink.

He told Nick that there was actually some good news

in this, in that Topo, Bilge and Jim were actually able to now predict the movement and destabilization of the ice that was melting underneath. They were working on a map with estimated slippage and time tables for the village. As suspected, the woodlands were in the greatest danger of going first, and would need to be evacuated before any other section. There was a part of the manufacturing area that border the northeastern end of the woodlands, that was also in trouble. This is where the Light Shoppe and Ornament Shop were based, and why they had already sustained damage.

"They don't have any pressing problems right now, but should be first after the Woodlands to get packed," said Whitey.

"What about the gondola?" asked Nick. "That's at the opposite end in the Visiting Center."

"We agree that was a case of excess weight," Whitey answered. "Since the thickness of the ice is thinner than normal, anything with that much mass will put a huge strain on the foundation. But Topo and Jim said there was sufficient base ice to hold everything until it melts this summer. As long as we are gone by mid-June we should be okay."

Nick explained the conversation to Mary and she began having Ella contact everyone in the Woodland Center and advise them to move faster and to get their goods and possessions to the miniaturization building for quick transport to a safer location. Ella had already received the news from Whitey and took it upon herself to start calling and giving them a heads up.

Nick was about to head to his office when there came

another knock on the door. Nick opened the door to an
able-bodied looking elf with blond hair and piercing blue
eyes wearing an Australian range hat.

"Hello Forrest," Nick said. "Can I help you with
something?"

"May I come in Santa?" he asked.

"Of course," Nick replied and ushered his range boss
in.

Forrest Hedemup was in charge of the reindeer. It
was Forrest and Nick's father, Kris, that came up with
using first horses, and then reindeer, to make the
Christmas Eve deliveries. Forrest looked like a range
boss with muscular arms and a broad chest. He sported
a small reddish brown beard that he kept closely
trimmed. He stood about 4'6" and was a taller elf than
most.

Mary came out of the kitchen and also greeted
Forrest. The elf tipped his hat and said, "Hello, Miss
Mary."

Miss Mary was a title used by only a few elves. It was
respectful without being as formal as Mrs. Claus, which
is what most of the residents called her. Forrest always
felt Mrs. Claus was reserved for Nick's mother, and used
Miss Mary to prevent confusion of the two women in
conversation.

"Why don't you come sit for a little bit and let's talk
about the movement of the animals," she said.

"You know why I came?" Forrest asked surprised.

"We know the Woodlands Area is in the most
immediate danger, and we have the reindeer stables, the
petting zoo and the other animal barns and stalls in the

Woodlands," she said with concern. "It didn't take a lot of deducing to figure it out."

"Yes, Ma'am," said Forrest. "No one has told me too much about what I am supposed to do."

"That would probably be because we haven't figured it out yet ourselves," responded Nick. "We are putting this together as we go along, and we are a long way from working out the many problems we are facing."

Forrest was not only in charge of the reindeer but anything on four legs in the Village. It was he and Mary that came up with the idea of the petting zoo for the visitors to the North Pole. But unlike any other petting zoo, this contained not only deer and reindeer but polar bears, wolves, arctic foxes, arctic hares, seals and sea lions, horses and penguins that Mary had Nick import from Antarctica.

"I have a few problems of my own and I am not sure about any of them, so if you folks have a moment, maybe we can discuss them," said Forrest.

"Absolutely," said Mary. Nick followed her lead and agreed.

"The first obstacle I have is how to move the animals down to the new settlement. I practically need Noah's Ark to get them migrated," he said.

Nick couldn't help but laugh at the illusion in his head, though Forrest was being stoic. But then he recovered and became more serious. "What if we used an ark of sorts?"

"Excuse me?" asked Forrest.

Mary nodded her head and said, "Good idea."

"What is?" asked a confused Forrest.

"We will use one of the transports and build shipping cages for the animals. We'll ship them down to one of the DC's until the new zoo and stables can be built," said Nick.

"Ah, I am not sure how the animals will feel about it," said Forrest. "Besides I don't know how the bears and some of the other animals will react to being flown away from here."

"They have always been docile. It shouldn't be a problem, and it won't be too long a trip," Nick countered.

"Which brings up my second dilemma," he said. "How do we know that once they are away from the North Pole they will remain tame?"

"Why wouldn't they?" asked Mary stunned.

"There has always been a magic to this place, which I have always accounted for as from the magnetism of the Pole. We don't know what may happen if we take them out of it," said Forrest.

"Is there a way we can test the theory?" asked Nick.

"I suppose I can try to take a fox or wolf down south and see how they react," Forrest considered. "But I wouldn't guarantee what may happen with the rest. Also, we can fly the reindeer down there, at least the ones that will fly. We know many won't leave the ground no matter how much of that weightless alfalfa we give them." He shrugged when he was done.

"These are fine ideas," said Nick. "Can you head down with the fox and maybe a penguin or something smaller and less fierce than a wolf can be. You don't want an angry wolf on your hands if it doesn't work out."

"Can I ask another thing?" he queried.

"Shoot," said Santa.

"What is going to happen to the rest of the animals?" he asked with deep concern.

"That is something I have been wondering myself, but haven't dared ask," said Mary quietly.

"I don't know how to answer that, except that we may be seeing the extinction or nearly so, of some of the life in the wild up here," Nick's eyes grew sad.

"I was afraid of that," Forrest sighed. "Since we can build whatever we need to, can we make a larger enclosure and take a few more animals?"

"Wait a second, here." Nick stood. "A moment ago you were concerned about how the animals we know might change and become dangerous. Now you want to take wild ones from outside the Village?"

"Basically Santa, each one is wild, including the ones that come to visit us. To be accurate they act differently when they are among us in the village," he said.

"Do we know what causes the change in behavior?" asked Mary. "Perhaps we could recreate that environment at the new place."

"I have never figured out what causes the change in them," he said. "I never questioned it, as it was so complete. Plus as I said, they come and go as they please. We don't keep them caged here. They show up when and where they want. I don't have a clue as to why they act the way they do, but I know we have never had an 'accident' and I leave it at that."

"Great," Santa said. "Another mystery that we don't

have a clue how to solve, or if it can be solved. I think the best thing is to try what we have come up with and take it from there. In so far as other wild animals, let's see what happens with the ones that already have a predisposition to coming around before we start herding others."

Forrest got up and moved to the door saying, "I will take several animals with me to Charlotte. I can only manage a couple of small ones as I am not as good at using the continuum as you are. But it should be enough to give me a clue." He said goodbye and headed back to the stables.

Chapter 25

Tomorrow's Bubble

Whitey and Jim were getting ready to head to Atlanta. Whitey, Forrest and a few other elves were the only ones Nick had taught the secrets of the time continuum. He made them each swear they would not use it for time travel or ill gain. He went through the basics of stopping time, and how to manipulate people and things within the stoppage. After they mastered that, he taught them how, for lack of a better word, to teleport to one location from another within the same time.

Time takes on an entirely different meaning in the North Pole. This is for two reasons. First the sun only rises and sets once each year. The North Pole has six months of sun beginning with the spring equinox, followed by six months of dark at the autumn equinox.

Second, because all latitudes converge at the geographic north, meaning their Village, technically the North Pole doesn't have its own time zone. They could leave their home and walk into any time zone they wished by moving south along a particular longitudinal heading.

It was decided long before Nick, or his father, had come to the Village that the elves would base their time on the Eastern Standard Time Zone of what had recently become the United States. Mostly because Aeon Millennium had advised them to do so. He told them that this particular area of the world would become a dominant cultural, and highly populated section of the world, and that it would make sense to them later. As he was their resident time traveler, they followed his lead.

When Nick's father left with Aeon, he decided that for safety reasons he had better teach some others about the time continuum in the event he needed any emergency assistance, or God forbid, something fatal happened to him. His own sons were not quite old enough or ready to be taught, so he gathered elves that made the most sense, including his reindeer wrangler, his security chief, his closest friend in the North Pole, Denny Sweetooth, Keeney Eagleye and his wife, Mary.

He was particularly thankful he had done this today. It allowed those who needed to move quickly and if need be, to hold time in one place, to accomplish the things they needed without his help.

So Whitey could take himself and a few others and a limited amount of equipment and go where he needed to go. Whitey had the peculiar habit of tugging his ear when he used the continuum to travel, which of course further limited what he could carry. Luckily he had Jim with him to help with the load.

They disappeared from the North Pole and reappeared in the center of the Atlanta DC that Whitey had visited a few times.

Jim commented saying, "That is one neat trick that you people know. I wish I could learn to use time and visit places like that."

Whitey scoffed and said, "Goodness knows what you talls would do with that secret. We really sweated bullets when we thought Albert Einstein had figured it out. Luckily, he never got the final equation to put it into effect."

Jim shrugged. "Perhaps one day we can be trusted with it, but I guess not yet."

They began assembling the equipment and Whitey asked where the dome was located.

"Why don't you find it?" Jim badgered.

"We don't really have time for games," Whitey said irritated with the idea of fumbling about.

"Okay fine," conceded Jim. "I'll take you to it and then you walk in."

Jim lead Whitey from the immense warehouse to an area right next to a road. He pointed and said, "There it is."

Whitey looked at him and said, "Where? Over the road?"

Jim replied, "It encompasses the road, yes but also around it and for about a hundred yards beyond it."

"You mean any traffic goes right through it?" Whitey asked incredulously.

"Through it, in it, around it, yeah," grinned Jim. "and they never know it."

"Than it is not protecting anything," qualified Whitey.

Jim picked up a rock and stood back a few yards and threw it as high and far as he could. The rock hit something and bounced back toward Jim landing a few feet away. He looked at Whitey and said, "I have the

protection grid set to begin at 15 feet to clear any
trucks. Above that we are as safe as in the North Pole."

Jim said, "Impressive, and you can change the
height?"

"Height, length, width, distance, anywhere within
the dome activation modules," Jim said plainly. "Now
lets go into the 'bubble'."

Whitey walked with Jim through what must have
been inside the protective part of the dome. He asked,
"When will we know we are in it, or out of it?"

"You have been in it for about forty yards, but you
wouldn't know it unless I click this little button," When
Jim clicked the device, the outside landscape changed
little, but now Whitey could see there were boxes and
bins to one side that hadn't been there before and a
makeshift structure on the other.

Jim said, "If you had walked any closer to those
objects they would have appeared to you as a major rock
or wall of rock," he pointed at the structure.

"Amazing," said Whitey more to himself.

They started with impact tests outside the dome and
moved to the interior to run a series of climatology
tests. When they were finished Whitey smiled and said,
"I think this will work out extremely nicely.
Congratulations on your improvements. May I take it
that you will help us install the new dome in the Great
Smoky Mountains?"

Jim chuckled. "You know, I had always wanted to go
there and now is my chance."

Whitey laughed back and said, "By the time you are
done, you may never want to return again!" He slapped

the taller man on the back and said, "We should return to the Village first and advise them that we have concluded our findings here. I'm sure they will be ecstatic to hear the news."

They began to repack the equipment and prepare for their jump back to the Village.

Chapter 26

New Players

Mary and several elves met the train when it pulled into the station. She was anxious to meet some of the passengers herself. When a tall handsome black woman stepped from the train, she garnered looks of admiration from the other passengers as her slender figure moved through the crowd. Mary called out to her. The woman almost dropped her bag in excitement and started moving quickly toward Mrs. Claus.

Kelly Nightingale was nearly in tears when the two women embraced. "Oh Kelly," Mary exclaimed. "It is fabulous to see you!"

"Mary you haven't changed the tiniest bit!" Kelly said wiping her eyes. "But then again why would you, living in the Magic Empire?" Kelly had begun referring to the North Pole during her stay as the M.E., or Magic Empire, once she learned that the fingers of the North Pole and elves extended worldwide and through as many vertical levels of the largest corporations on the globe.

"That's about to change," Mary said with a tinge of sadness. "But that conversation is for later, let me walk you over to the Reindeer Inn. We can catch up a little. But first, I need to grab a few other people."

Kelly gave Mary a kiss on her forehead and said, "You are not to worry about such things. Your

Reimagineer is here with you now. Go say hello, as I am sure there are many that want to see you again like me. I can get to the Reindeer Inn on my own."

"Hold on for a moment or two, I want to walk with you and I want you to meet these folks," Mary pleaded. Kelly smiled and nodded her head.

Mary next sought out Bill and Susan and also hugged them firmly and thanked them for coming on such short notice.

The couple was beaming and saying that there was no where else they would rather be than at the North Pole again, especially when they were needed. Mary asked Bill and Susan to join Kelly and her. She saw, waved and said hello to a few other tallfolk along with many of the elves that disembarked from the train, but Mary Kringle had her principal entourage that she came to collect, and she felt her spirits lift tremendously upon seeing them.

They walked arm in arm to the hotel. Mary introduced Kelly to the Fredricks and explained who each person was, and what they had accomplished since their first visit to the North Pole. Kelly had come the year following Bill and Susan in April. Bill teased Mary that she kept bringing them up in the dark of night so he would never *really* get to see the North Pole.

Mary teased him back saying that since he was only a man, he would forever be in the dark anyway. Kelly howled and said she would remember that one when she returned south, as it fit so many men she worked with at her company.

Mary explained Kelly's title saying the woman was

an imaginative genius and could see exquisite forms and structures in everything she saw. She said that she had hoped for a chance to get Kelly and Susan together. She knew they would become fast friends, since they were both so creative.

"I'm glad I can anchor such a bond for the three of you, do let me know when my part comes in," said Bill in a ribbing manner.

Mary laughed throwing her head back. "Oh my dear Bill, be careful what you wish for, especially here, as you know what can happen!"

Bill wondered what he had volunteered for, but enjoyed hearing Mrs. Claus laugh and enjoy herself. He correctly thought that hadn't happened much as of late.

When they reached the Reindeer Inn, Christel reacted as Mrs. Claus had, and welcomed them warmly. She let the boarders know that they would be sharing rooms because of the vast number of people coming to help.

"Matters not to me," said Kelly brightly. "I can guess that the time spent in my room will measured in seconds rather than hours."

"You may be more right than you know," Mary said. "In fact, I would like to talk to the three of you once you get settled, but I wouldn't unpack too much."

Susan said, "Got it, we aren't staying are we?"

Mary shook her head and said,"We have some important work to do elsewhere. The four of us and a few more. But I will lay it out for you in a twinkling, I need to check on a couple things. I'll see you later."

And she was gone before anyone could say any more.

Christel had put the Fredricks in a room with one of

the single men that had come up and told them that
there would be a large dinner that evening at the
Reindeer Inn, so there would be no need to find other
food. She looked at Bill and said, "I will send up some
sandwich makings for you in a jiffy. You look hungry."

Bill grinned and said, "Christel, I am always
hungry!"

Christel asked Kelly or Susan if they wanted
anything and they said no as they ate on the train.

She told them what room they were in and sent them
on their way. Kelly said she would drop her things and
perhaps come by their room to get to know them better,
since it sounded like they might be spending
considerable time together.

When Bill and Susan got to the room they knocked
on the door and heard a man say, "C'mon in." They
opened the door and Bill said to the man's back,
"Excuse me but we're your new roommates."

The man spun around and said, "I know, I've been
expecting you."

"George!" they both exclaimed, and Susan said, "I
can't believe it!"

George smiled broadly and said, "I was supposed to
be somewhere else already, but when Christel told me
you were almost here and that we'd be sharing a suite, I
had to wait."

Bill came over first and gave him a hardy hand shake.
Susan followed with a hug and said "My goodness you
sure got tall! How are you? We lost track of you after
you went to MIT."

"Yeah, it kinda got crazy for me after that," George

said almost apologetically. "Ion was practically my roommate. I don't know who was more relieved when I graduated, him or me. Since then, I have been working on several things both for the North Pole and for the D.O.E."

"The Department of Energy?" Bill said with surprise.

George nodded. "Yeah, some pretty high level stuff. But I walk a thin line. I have to run tests and results through here before introducing them there. One top secret organization, then the other. It has kept life interesting."

"Wow, a real live double-agent!" Susan whooped. "I can scarcely believe it."

George laughed. "Believe it, there is more, but maybe we can discuss it over dinner. This is the only place I dare talk about some of my work. Since we are more or less sworn to secrecy here, I feel comfortable that whomever Santa trusts, so can I."

Bill and Susan gave a brief discussion on what they were doing and George was interested but said, "I am sorry, I really have to go meet Jackson and Sparky about some power considerations for the new location."

"Where is the new location?" Bill inquired.

"The Great Smoky Mountains in East Tennessee or Western North Carolina," said George. "I am sure you will hear about it from many of the elves." He grabbed his jacket and told them he would see them later and left.

After he was gone, Susan looked at the bags and said, "I wish Mary would have told us more about the plan. I don't know if I should unpack, repack for a shorter visit or leave the luggage closed."

Bill said, "I would do the last. Until we know we should be prepared to leave. We can always repack or unpack after we know."

There was a knock on the door and before they could reach it Kelly let herself in, "If you are not decent, I'm taking pictures with my phone!"

They laughed and said to come in. Kelly sat on the sofa and said, "Okay I want life stories. Christel told me you two met and fell in love here. I want details. Then I will give you my sordid past and by dinner we will know all the scandalous details about each other."

"Do you think we'll have that much time?" asked Susan.

"Mary told me we are leaving in the morning and to plan on several days," answered Kelly.

"When did you hear that?" Susan asked.

"I called and asked her. I told her she needed to give us a better clue of the timetable," she said.

"Thanks for the heads up," Susan said with relief. "We were trying to figure out what to do as far as luggage."

"You were trying to figure it out," Bill corrected. "I'm kind of a 'go with the flow' type of guy. I was ready for anything."

"Okay," smiled Kelly. "So Susan is the organizer and Bill is the 'Come as you are type', now let's hear the rest about you two."

Susan began with occasional corrections and clarifications from Bill.

Chapter 27

A New Communicator

Though Bill never had a chance to tell Mary about their parents offer to help, they were being called anyway. Ella had finished the first priority list and was now moving on to the next group. Over the years, so many had been invited to the North Pole it was quite a long manifest. She had secured the help of April Zinnia, since she couldn't return to the greenhouse and was looking for something to do.

April was excited to be part of the organizing of the returnees, and she had always wanted to meet many of the tallfolk that the village would speak about from time to time. She also had always liked and respected Ella and her ability to determine sincere speech in the most tongue tied of elves.

But mostly she liked dealing with people, elf and tall, alike. So far everyone she had spoken to had reinforced her feelings. She had been on the phone most of the day with various tallfolk that had visited in the past, and each one reacted with the same shock and surprise, and then sprang into action and offered to come as soon as it could be arranged.

Ella had another agenda in using April, and felt glad she was available. Ever since the first Council meeting, where they had learned that the North Pole would no longer be inhabitable, she had been concerned with finding a suitable replacement for herself, just in case.

She was not alone in this quest. Nearly any elf over 100, and some less, had the same thoughts. *What if?* Once they moved from the North Pole would they begin dropping like flies? They thought that might be an absolute worse case scenario and not likely, but they wondered how long they would have away from the Pole's magnetism. One year, five, or another century or two? It was their biggest concern with no answer forthcoming.

April was a young elf, only 59, and she hadn't settled on a journeyman trade yet. She therefore had no permanent last name. She called herself Zinnia because she enjoyed working with flowers and thought those were among the most lovely types. Mary Claus was quite pleased with her work and had commented to Ella many times about how good and sweet she was.

The same could be said about 80 percent or more of the elves, Ella agreed that April had a special something that set her apart. April seemed to be good at picking up sincere speech from teasing or "shadow speech" as it was called. Shadow speech was when there was more truth to what was being said, but you couldn't hear it because it was hidden in the shadows. The elves wouldn't call it lies per se, because elves didn't lie outright, but it might contain misrepresentations. Ella could always recognize the difference. She was also good at cutting through tongue-tied or nervous speech to the heart of the matter. Something many elves sought her out to help them.

Ella believed she could hone those skills in April, and assist the younger elf in taking over for her. If there was only enough time. She hoped that April would survive many more decades if everything went badly for the older elves.

April had already contacted the King, Chan, Cottonwood, and Orlov families. She had hung up with the Conner family. Brian and Heather said that it would take a few days to get everything arranged and they would bring John to help, but they needed to see if Patrick could stay with his grandparents.

There were many more to contact on her list, but she was grinning from ear to ear about how everyone wanted to lend a hand. She was satisfied that with the assistance they would receive, that moving the Village would most certainly get accomplished and everyone would be safe at the new settlement.

Chapter 28

Revving Up

Elsewhere in the village elves and people were settling in and the newly arrived elves were getting ear fulls about what was happening at the North Pole. It was enough to make them wonder if they would have time to get everything together that could be moved. In the short time that Whitey was gone, a couple of the buildings had shifted, and although there was minimal damage, it was still disconcerting that the ground below them would begin to move or rumble without warning.

When Whitey and Jim returned, he brought them to the door of the Kringles. Moments later they were explaining the improvements that Jim had done and saying that as long as they could put up the nacelles for the dome, they should be able to begin laying down frames for the housing.

Santa asked if it was true about walking right through the center of the village once everything was established.

"I witnessed it myself," said Whitey emphatically. "Not only did Jim have me walk through it without knowing it, I witnessed several cars drive right down the middle of it without them noticing a thing."

"Outstanding news," Santa said. "This is the first real breakthrough we have had go our way," He turned to Mary. "When do you think you can leave to find a suitable place to begin setting up?"

Mary smiled. "I have everything set for tomorrow morning. The people I wanted are here, and if Whitey and Jim are ready, we can go by then."

"Fine," they both nodded.

"I have a few buildings to check on that Ella called me about," said Whitey. "Plus we need to get some things together for tomorrow. If you don't mind, or have any other questions, I will get going."

Jim said, "I heard George Mendez is in and I was hoping to talk with him about his latest findings in cold fusion."

Santa said that he could find George over at the power station talking with Jackson and Sparky about that very subject. Santa excused them and as they left he breathed a heavy sigh.

"My that was deep," his wife said.

"If things keep going this way we might make it," said a weary Santa. "At least there seems to be some hope now."

"Oh, we'll make it," said Mary fiercely. "One, we don't have any choice, and two, we have the finest minds on this earth working toward it. And not the least reason is that God will see this done and will give us all strength to accomplish it."

Nick agreed, "You're right as always, I shouldn't despair about it. So Bill and Susan made it?"

Mary nodded her head. "And Kelly also, I have them getting to know each other right now."

Nick laughed. "That should be an interesting

conversation. Who else are you taking with you tomorrow?"

Mary said, "I spoke with Rory Whittlesee and Rudy Clawhammer, and they both are anxious to join our little band. Topo asked to remain here to analyze the geologic and meteorologic changes."

"I don't disagree, and you have two of our best carpenters," Santa said. "Have they ever been outside the North Pole before?"

"Actually Rudy has. He worked at some of the DC's a few times," Mary answered. "But Rory has not. He will have to stay close to us, but he is tall enough that he shouldn't stand out too much."

"How are you going to take so many at once?" he thought of the crowd she was forming.

"Whitey can take Jim, Rory and Rudy. I'll take Kelly, Bill and Susan." she replied.

"This ought to be interesting," Santa chuckled. "None of them have ever experienced the continuum before."

"Neither had I when you first tried to teach me," she returned. "That was quite an experience. I am sure they will be as astonished as I was."

"How will you get around?" he thought suddenly.

"I took the liberty to call Richard at Charlotte," she said. "He and two other elves are arranging a couple cars, it was all I could think of."

"I guess the word is out at Charlotte," said Nick resignedly.

"My dear," said Mary. "The word was out as soon as the we closed the Council chamber doors."

Nick shook his head. "Again I say, 'Who needs an Internet'? Which brings up my next question, are you leaving before or after the meeting with Cory, Ion and Indy?"

"How about I stay for the first hour?" she resolved. "But I want to get going so we have the most time possible to begin looking for a sight. Especially if we have to start in Charlotte."

Nick agreed, but said, "I am not sure we will get everything resolved in that time, but at least I won't have to bring you up to speed on it. Should we plan breakfast here? I could have Christel bring something over."

"I think poor Christel has enough to do without you throwing more at her," Mary rebuked. "Besides, don't forget Fergie isn't there to help out tomorrow."

Again Nick nodded. "Sorry, I wasn't thinking."

She smiled. "With all the pressure you are under, I am not surprised, but we both better be at the top of our game for now. There is so much needing to be done, and this wouldn't be the time for mistakes."

Nick agreed and said he would be clearer if he could rest for a few moments.

Mary said, "Go ahead and take it easy for a bit, I promised Bill, Susan and Kelly that I would hook up with them and let them in on the plan. I am heading over to the Inn and will be back later." She gave her husband a kiss on the forehead and grabbed her coat. Seconds later she was out the door.

Chapter 29

New Inventions

Jim had hiked up to the power station to see George Mendez. He had been working on something that Jim himself was dabbling with. Roughly defined, cold fusion, is the fusing together of elements at "normal" temperatures, such that they release more energy than is required to fuse them.

Many companies had been working at this process and a few of them had demonstrated in principle that it could work, but they were years away from a practical use, or certainly a working model. Far too many questions were unanswered.

Jim met up with George and the elves responsible for the power supply to the North Pole. As he worked his way in, he heard George explaining to Jackson and Sparky, "The contents of the reactor were removed and weighed to be 59 grams of mass, most of which was a ceramic encasement. Therefore, the reaction appears to produce more energy than a chemical reaction from a known amount with an equivalent mass," explained George, "meaning that the reactor was operating in excess of a COP of five."

"So it is producing five times more energy output than input?" asked Sparky.

"Roughly, I almost had it to six a couple times"

nodded George. "And of course this is not a nuclear reaction per se, it is also not a chemical one, either. It is more of a Low Energy Nuclear Reaction or LENR is we call it."

Jim could stay quiet no longer and interrupted before Jackson could ask his question, "George do you believe this is more feasible than hot fusion?"

"Imminently more," answered George. "You need a heat level that requires a heat source approximately equal to the stars, additionally the housing and laboratories needed for hot fusion are massive and many times the size needed for cold fusion. And I'm sorry, have we met?"

Jim apologized and introduced himself saying, "You might say I was a couple classes after yours here at the North Pole."

"Oh yeah, you're the one working on the dome aren't you?" queried George.

"Guilty as charged," said Jim, then he asked, "If I may, I heard that there are more than 100 largely unsubstantiated reports of observed excess heat effects by some unexplained interaction of hydrogen or deuterium with metals like nickel, platinum, or palladium. Which products are you using for your experiment?"

George began laughing and was followed by Jackson and Sparky. "What experiment?" George finally said. "We will build a working reactor at the new place, we are figuring out how large of an area we need based on the current and projected village consumption levels now in play."

"But there has not been anything published in peer-reviewed scientific journals approximating a working model, and the last I read the Department of Energy wouldn't put any funding toward the idea yet," insisted Jim. "How is it possible you have not only a working model, but a full size prototype ready for installations?"

"I can't say, how is it you have a dome that allows people to walk right down Main Street and not see anything of the village?" George smirked. "Did the DOE, or the DOD, fund that?"

"Touche," resigned Jim. "I would like to learn more about this when we have a chance to sit down and discuss it."

"Let's see if we can get this extremely cheap and unlimited fuel source up and working as well as your dome I've heard about," George said to Jim. "Then we can determine the proper time and place."

Jackson said, "We need to take these specs to the R&D manufacturing building and have them begin work on the containment system right away."

"Before you do that, how do you intend to move it?" asked George. "It will be far too large to put in the miniaturization machine to shrink it, and the full size version won't fit on the transport planes."

"Uh, yeah well," Sparky began haltingly, "you might say that we, uh, have been working on some new ideas ourselves. We only have to make a scale model of the containment system and get it to the new area and we can make it any size we want."

"I don't follow," said George.

"Ion wanted to tell you, but I guess we can now,"

skirted Jackson. "We took the principles of the miniaturization cycle and reversed them."

Sparky blurted out, "Yeah, so now we have an enlargement machine sitting in a new building waiting to be moved, we need to create a larger exit area for the container and we can make it as large as you need."

Jim laughed and said, "So many secrets and so many new inventions, but the same old North Pole."

"Let's get started on it," said George anxiously. "Obviously we will wait until we get the working model to the new location and after the enlargement machine is up and running we can make it the final size."

"We need to make sure we have enough material to increase the size without reducing the solidarity of the walls," said Jackson, as the four of them began walking off toward the manufacturing center.

Jim said, "You know, if you have a working enlargement machine, you could design scale models of housing and enlarge them to full size. That could help get the Village up and running in no time."

"That's what Ion is working on now," said Jackson. "He wanted to be here to see how this worked, but he was needed to work on the EM instead."

"EM for enlargement machine," George said sarcastically. "What are you calling the miniaturization machine, M&M?"

"No," Sparky snapped. "We call it the miniaturization machine."

George shrugged off Sparky's tone as he was kidding around. "Are you planning to disassemble the EM and ship it to GSM for the new NPV, ASAP?"

This even made Sparky smile and he realized George was having some fun at his expense and he said with a grin, "Wisenheimer."

When they got to the manufacturing Center, Ion Crosswire met them and shook Jim and George's hands and said he was happy to see them both again.

"You work with this task-master, too?" George asked Jim.

"Ion would grace me with his presence from time to time. Mostly to help channel me toward a particular problem or challenge that they needed me to look at," said Jim.

Ion said, "Jim is a lot easier to work with than you ever were."

"You were probably a lot nicer to him," George teased.

George let Jackson fill Ion in on the cold fusion reactor and where they were on it. Ion shook his head and said to George, "Congratulations, that's great work. That should really help us out in the Smokies."

Jim said, "Speaking of which you will have to excuse me for a few days. I am going to the new area to help locate a suitable place for our new settlement with Mrs. Claus and Whitey."

"Some people have all the fun," George snickered, "I guess we'll pick up your slack around here."

"Geez George, can't you be a little nicer?" complained Sparky.

George feigned hurt, "What? I am fooling around! You know me, I am slightly acerbic in my joking."

"Slightly?" Ion glared.

"Okay, I'll tone it down a few notches," George relented.

"Seriously, George, a lot of people are really on edge around here, and we don't need you setting them off trying to be funny," Ion scolded.

"Yeah, I suppose you are right, my apologies," he directed his comment to Jim, but it included everyone.

They discussed the variances in the variety of plans concerning the move and set up of the new village. Everyone wanted Jim to know what was needed for each project, old and new, in terms of space and time to set up. Armed with this information Jim set off to find Whitey and the rest stayed behind to discuss other new projects that could immediately help the Smoky Mountain Village once they got there.

Chapter 30

Old Friends, New Friends

Mary knocked on the door of Kelly's room first. Getting no answer she walked to Bill and Susan's room and knocked again. Kelly opened the door. Mary was not surprised, but teased her saying, "I'm sorry I obviously have the wrong room."

Kelly came right back saying, "My dear lady, I think you are in the wrong building!" Then laughing, she opened the door wide to let her in.

The Fredrick's had met Mrs. Claus briefly at their last visit and dined with her and Santa on Christmas Day, but never really had the opportunity to talk at any length with her. They were pleased that she sought them out and asked them to join the 'scouting' party as she was now calling it.

"You both are perfect for our needs right now," she was explaining. "Bill with your engineering degrees you can be a big help working with Jim Atherton and Whitey Slippenfall in establishing the basic needs of the village."

Bill said, "Whatever I can do, I am happy to do it. Susan and I owe you everything."

Mary smiled at him and turned to Susan and said, "And you my dear, your architectural skill will be of immense help. Most of the elves will want your assistance in laying out their new structures. By the way, how bad is your morning sickness?"

Kelly shrieked loudly and said, "You didn't tell me *that*!"

Susan looked thunderstruck at Mary and said, "How could you know? Bill and I haven't told our parents, or my company! We wanted to wait until the second trimester to make sure everything is alright. Was that a guess?"

"I could see it in both your eyes the moment you stepped off the train," she stated. "You know Santa is not the only one with abilities. I've picked up a few tricks in the 100 years I've been around."

"I am sure," Susan agreed. "But if it is okay, we would like to keep this a secret from everyone, except our parents. At least for a few more weeks."

"Too late for that," laughed Kelly. "But hey, they won't hear it from me if that's what you truly want."

Mary said, "Let me guess, I would say you are what, two, or two and a half months along? I think you are worrying needlessly, but if that is your wish. I would like permission to tell Nick, though."

"Of course," Susan agreed. "And to answer your earlier question, it is not too severe, but some mornings are worse than others."

Mary nodded and said to Kelly, "And now to my wonderful reimagineer. You, Susan and I are going to design the center of the village and develop the look and feel of the Visiting Center for starters. I want it bigger and better than we had here."

"That sounds like fun," Kelly said enthusiastically.

Mary continued, "We had developed the Visiting Center long after the village was established and though I was pleased with how it came out in general, I would have liked to develop it from scratch. Since God seems to be affording me the opportunity, I plan to take full advantage of it."

Susan nodded and said, "I have always wanted to work on a whimsical project like this. It has been in my mind since my last visit here, In fact, I think that was what got me into architecture in the first place, remembering the various styles, lines and colors of the North Pole."

"I think the best way to begin this project is for us girls to take a walk around the Visiting Center and you can tell us what you like and don't like about what is here," said Kelly.

"Can you manage without us, sweetheart?" Susan asked Bill.

"Actually if you wouldn't mind Bill, I would like you to find and meet Whitey and discuss some of the engineering issues he is facing," said Mary. "Christel can help you locate him."

Bill nodded and said, "Certainly."

The three women put their coats on and headed toward the door. Mary turned back to Bill and said, "Don't forget dinner when Christel told you. Please try not to be late."

"Me late for dinner?" he boomed. "Mrs. Claus, I thought you knew me better than that!"

Chapter 31

Dinner At Seven

Bill found Christel hurriedly setting a large banquet table. He told her what Mrs. Claus had said about her finding Whitey.

"I think he and Jim Atherton are together by the train station," she said, "If your lucky you can still catch them there."

Bill took off and let Christel continue her racing about. She was in overdrive preparing for the main event of the evening. The feeding of close to a dozen talls and the entire Elven Council. She was used to serving large dinner parties and had done so ever since the first Mrs. Claus, Miss Annie, and her son came up with the plan for the Reindeer Inn and inviting talls up to the North Pole.

Like many elves, back then Christel worried about bringing tallfolk to their beloved and hidden village. But she had met, and served, countless tallfolk over the last 60 or so years. Everyone she met she enjoyed immensely. And though she knew these people were the cream of their societies, she nevertheless felt there was hope for the tallfolk race as long as such wonderful souls walked amongst them.

She began laying out the seating cards as ordered by Mrs. C., tall next to elf, next to tall, with the exception of having married couples sit together.

Denny and Pierre were working on the meal in the kitchen and the smells were already permeating the entire Inn. Even the huge fireplace with its roaring fire couldn't subdue the smells emanating from the kitchen.

Christel thought about how everyone was in for a special treat this evening. Normally the guests were able to order whatever their hearts desired, but after some discussion, it was decided to use up whatever stores they had in the village, so as not to have to transport the food south with everything else.

After taking an exhaustive inventory of the pantries and cold storage, and adding the number of people that might return to the North Pole, it was decided that they could continue to feed everyone for several months, so long as they were careful about it. However, tonight was not a night for frugality. They were putting on a feast their friends and guests would not soon forget.

The response had been overwhelming when the call for help went out. People and elves would be arriving for days. There would be another feast when everyone arrived, but the people that were already here would prove invaluable to moving and setting up the new community.

The menu would consist of some of the great delights of the culinary wizardry of Pierre Whiskeneg and Denny Sweetooth. It included prime rib and beef tenderloin, turkey and duck, ham and pork loin and varieties of snapper and cod, several salads, vegetables and sauces. The desserts were too multiple to list, and Mrs. Claus found time to assist with these between the meeting with Forrest and the arrival of the train.

As the time drew near, a few people had returned to the Inn, and as they got a whiff of the aromas wafting about the massive lobby they ventured no further. Many tried to guess what they were smelling, but because of the cacophony of dishes they had difficulty telling one fragrance from another, but the sum total was enough to make their stomachs roar.

Christel put out a few snacks to help tide them over, and they were gone almost as soon as she placed the trays. She couldn't blame them as she wanted to steal some bites herself by now.

The council began arriving between six-thirty and six-forty-five, and nearly every tallfolk had returned by then. Bill, Jim and Whitey had walked in together. Kelly and Susan had arrived earlier, as Mary excused herself and said she would see them later after walking around the Visiting Center. Fred Wu came in with Britney Clearwater still explaining the waterless shower system that he had installed in the manufacturing building.

Freida Cutinglass, Ella Communicado and Alfie Newsworthy came in together and George Mendez and Jackson Killowatt followed closely behind them. Jose Sanchez, who had arrived about an hour earlier, and Cory Peters came down from their rooms at the same time Keeney Eagleye walked through the door of the Inn.

Christel had them begin taking their assigned seats. It would have been comical for the elves and talls to sit together as it would have looked like some perverse roller coaster, but special chairs were designed for the elves that were higher to bring them to the same height as their tallfolk counterparts.

Denny came out of the kitchen and looked as fresh as when he went in hours earlier. He was smiling as he always did and was anxious to see the looks on everyone's faces when the food came out from the kitchen. Comments were immediately made to him about the delicious smells wafting about.

As soon as everyone had taken their seats, in came Santa Nick and Mrs. Mary Claus and took their respective seats at the ends of the table. Many of the tallfolk had seen this scene played out before when they visited the North Pole. The final day always ended in a large banquet and was one of the highlights of their adventure. Everyone at the table began applauding the couple.

Nick remained standing as Mary took her seat. He looked at the folks at the table and smiled. He spoke loudly enough for everyone to hear, but in a gentle tone, "My dear friends, although the reason you are here today is not one I would have asked for or expected, Mary and I are extremely pleased to see each of you in person once more. Each of you have held a special place in our hearts, and we have enjoyed witnessing your growth and exploits.

"We thank you for being here during our time of great need. We thank God for you, and with His help, we will see this great task finished. The Council of Elves, Mary and I wanted to show our appreciation in some small way for your devotion to us. So please enjoy this

feast of the absolute best we have to offer. Now let us
say grace."

Everyone bowed their heads and Nick continued,
"Heavenly Father, you bless us with the abundance of
this earth and you bring us this fellowship that we may
share the limitless bounty with our brothers and sisters.
We give you thanks for every day of our lives and for the
fortunes yet to come. We use this food to your service
and in your name. Amen."

As he sat down Denny rose and said to the diners
before him. "I'd like to raise a toast to everyone at this
table. Speaking on behalf and as part of the Council, I
second the sentiments expressed by Santa and thank
each and everyone of you for being part of this mighty
escapade. I know in my heart that we will be successful
in our task and that our next town will be as splendid or
more so than this one. Thank you and God bless us
everyone!"

Everyone raised their glass and drank to Denny's
toast. He clinked his glass four times and an explosion
of servants burst through the back of the Inn, each
carrying a different platter and moving to each of the
four corners of the banquet table. The oohs and ahhs
came from everywhere as each platter looked as good or
better than the last. Kelly practically yelled out, "I need
a bigger plate! In fact when one of those platters
empties, I'll switch with it."

Bill said in response, "All those platters can be left
right here so I don't have to reach!"

And so the bantering began and for the first time in a
long the North Pole was the North Pole again in spirit.

Everyone was smiling, laughing and having a wonderful time. Nick also managed to lay down his burden for a time.

As the patrons finished their meals and complained about the amount of food they had eaten, the discussions returned to the logistics of the move and some of the new things that would be incorporated into the new community. It also revolved around who would be dealing with what elements and how to get everything to the next hamlet as quickly as possible.

Nick pulled Whitey and Jim aside and asked them "Assuming no hiccups, how quickly can we lay out the area needed and install the new dome?"

"Those are two different questions, Santa," said Jim, "We need to generalize how much area we can and will be able to utilize, then we can begin setting up the nacelles for the dome."

"Okay, taking those together, how fast?" Nick pressed again.

Whitey answered, "If we can set our sights on an area within a day or two, I would guess we could have the dome up and ready to begin receiving everything in three to four weeks."

"What if we don't have three weeks?" asked Nick, "You have seen yourself how much is already going on, I am afraid that in three weeks we will lose vital structures and may have injuries or worse."

Whitey looked at Nick and rubbed his beard, "Yes, I had also thought of that. We will do everything as quickly as possible and aim for two weeks. But perhaps with regard to the Woodlands Area, maybe we should begin shipping down what we can to the DC's and not wait."

"And the animals?" Nick asked.

"Animals?" Jim asked in shock. "Oh, I forgot about the reindeer!"

"Reindeer, polar bears, wolves, horses..." Nick began the list.

"Holy smoke," Jim exclaimed. "I had no idea we were moving an entire zoo!"

"That's exactly what it is," said Nick. "Our petting zoo and the animals that live in the Village here."

Whitey let out a long sigh. "I suggest Ella begins calling the DC's and finds where might be the best place to house them temporarily. Because although we could get the dome up quickly, it will take time to build housing and stables, let alone a zoo."

Ella walked up and said, "Did I hear my name being bantered about?"

Whitey smiled and relayed their conversation.

"I'll get right on it tomorrow morning. I'll start with the closest DC's to the Smokies like Charlotte and Atlanta, then move west."

"We might want to leave Charlotte out of this one," said Nick. "We might need them for other things being the closest to the new area."

"The distances are almost a draw between Char's and Lanty's DC, and Lanty has a bigger warehouse by far," said Ella.

"Which is why Atlanta might be a better choice. These animals will need more room to move around and perhaps we can put other necessities there beyond the animals," countered Nick.

"Okay, I'll talk to Lanty first thing," said Ella.

When Cory and Bill walked over the subject changed back to the food and questions about what the Ambassadors might best be used for.

After about another half hour Nick and Mary excused themselves saying they needed to get some rest for their big day tomorrow and suggested others might want to do the same.

Kelly said, "Okay, but it really isn't fair, you don't bring us up here for years and years, and you expect us to go to bed early? Just when I was having some fun."

Everyone chuckled, but began moving toward their respective destinations.

Chapter 32

Scourge of the Internet

Nick was always envious that Mary could go nearly anywhere and not be recognized for who she was. For Nick to do that he would have to completely shave his beard and mustache and dye his hair a darker color. He had tried to wear different colors and types of clothing, along with hats of various types and sunglasses, and always with the same results. A child would point him out within a few moments and call out 'Santa'. He had also tried shaving a good portion of his beard off one year and had it close cropped. It didn't matter, adults and children still stopped him and addressed him as Santa Claus.

Mary finished dressing and asked Nick how she looked. His reply was, "Beautiful as always, and exactly like a tallfolk."

She laughed knowing what he meant by his comment. "I can't help it that you look like you, even when you try not to."

They heard a knock at the door and Kristopher spoke saying, "C'mon in Cory. I'll let my folks know you are here."

As he bounded up the stairs, Mary closed the suitcase she was taking later and and Nick opened the door before his son could knock. He nodded at Kristopher, and his son changed direction and returned downstairs.

Nick sighed and mocking a game show host said, "It must be time for our next challenger, who do we have June?"

Mary chuckled and said, "Remember we are not alone in these situations and we will get through them."

They walked down the stairs together and heard the door knock again. This time Kristopher opened the door to Ion, Indy Webbinhouse, and Mac Gelfeeney.

"Mac!" Nick called out before Kristopher could say a word, "It's so good to see you again!"

He grabbed the smallish elf and gave him his usual Santa bear hug. Mac smiled and said, "Now that you are finally having some fun up here I decided it was time to come back."

Nick ho, ho, hoed and said how he missed Macintosh's snappy wit. Then he put his arm around Ion and Indy at the same time and thanked them for also coming over to help them solve this.

They walked into the study where Cory was waiting and Nick and Mary gave him a hug again. Cory's mood had been uplifted since he left yesterday. He felt that if anything could be done, that this would be the place to return things to the way they were.

Nick introduced the three elves to Cory. Cory said he and Ion had already met several years back when Ion came down to wire the school to the North Pole. There were specific connections that needed to be hardwired to prevent any possibility of hacking into the North Pole's records and database.

Mary asked if anyone wished for something to drink or eat. Nick, Cory and Mac asked for a cup of coffee.

Mary had anticipated as much and had prepared the 'big pot' as they called it.

Once they were served they got into the problem. Cory described many attacks that were taking place and had transcripts of online conversations, articles and accusations against the school and Santa in general.

Indy shook his head and said, "This is really some kind of weird oxymoron. I mean here these guys are attacking Santa Claus calling him a fake, a fraud, a liar, and yet, they are trying to pass themselves off as Santa Claus. It almost makes no sense."

"They are actually attacking the school and the 'real life person' behind the school saying we are some kind of money laundering enterprise lining the personal pockets of this mystery Santa Claus who refuses to show himself," explained Cory.

"But who are these other crazies jumping on this?" asked Mac. "Are any of them our Ambassadors?"

"Not that I have seen," Cory quickly defended them, "In fact, many of our guys have tried to oppose the comments and entrench themselves against the attacks. When these other guys began to turn on our Ambassadors, I told them to leave it alone as it only seemed to be fueling the fires."

"How is it these groups sprung up?" asked Ion. "I can't figure out how or why so many guys are playing Santa Claus."

"Not to get ugly about it, but it falls into several categories as to why they became a Santa impersonator..." Cory began.

"Imposter, more like it," spat Indy.

"Whichever, but it comes down to the fact that real or imagined – they heard they could make a ton of money, they are obese and use this obesity as an excuse for Santa, or they are fame-seekers and since they cannot garner any notice for themselves any other way, they become Santa Claus and once people begin paying attention it becomes an addictive drug for them," Cory finished.

"Pretty lousy excuses to become Santa. What happened to doing it for the children and to bring hope and happiness to people of every age?" asked Mac.

"Those are the few we seek out and try to train," answered Cory. "Truth is, as a percentage that group is becoming smaller and smaller. You can't begin to imagine how many television and print commercials are made each and every year featuring Santa Claus."

"And let me guess, for every commercial there are a hundred Santas waiting in line to film it," said Nick.

"At least," nodded Cory. "Then add each of the malls and personal appearances that Santa shows up at. This is why so many are convinced there has to be a ton of money made by these guys."

"Is there?" asked Indy.

"Is there what?" Cory asked confused.

"Is there a 'ton of money' made in this field?" clarified Indy.

"As I tell our students, if you hope to make a fortune as Santa Claus, you can do that only if you can hibernate for ten months out of the year. Otherwise don't count on it. There are a few, and I mean a *very* few that I've heard do exceedingly well, but they have a particular job or exclusive clientele that they cater to, mostly these guys fight over the same scraps," Cory explained.

"I think it is the fame seekers that cause us the biggest problems looking at these posts," said Nick. "You can see by their attitude and tone that they feel they should be exalted over any one else. It is almost laughable in the fact that they want to be top dog, but if it weren't for the people they were standing upon, they wouldn't be the top of anything."

Mary shook her head. "The cruelty and the horrible blood-thirstiness of the whole thing is disgusting. How could anyone think they are Santa Claus with so much rancor in their heart?"

"And the problem continues in that now there are entire groups acting brutishly toward one another," added Cory. "And a lot of these people, male and female, are so ego-maniacal that they can't get out of the way of their own facades. It is a ruthlessness that goes beyond measure. The fact that they don't murder one another at these meetings out of pure jealousy is amazing."

"I think we need to deal with the ferocity generated toward us, and let the others go on acting like hateful children," Nick pushed. "We will pray that the good people in these groups will eventually will out, or at least keep it from becoming less malicious than it already is."

"Besides 'The Weasel', who else do we really have to worry about?" asked Indy.

"The worst offenders and the fire starters seem to

always be the same," Cory said with disgust. "It seems
to begin and end with Phillip Weazel and his wife,
Cynthia Louis-Weazel, then more or less in order is
Robby Ellis, Nicolai Trolski, Jeffrey Krautmann, Alan
Cagey, and some guy named Scotty Konan. They all put
out information "according to their sources" and
continually tear down Santas in other organizations and
make personal condemnations against anyone who
disagrees with them."

"This Cynthia looks really nasty at that, she censures
anyone who begins to take a different tact from her,"
Ion observed looking at the posts.

"Yes, she has learned from the best," sighed Cory.
"Do you know her husband gets up hours before dawn
every single day looking for trouble across the Internet.
He told one of our Ambassadors that, himself."

"I'll bet he is not alone," said Nick. "Looking at some
of the severe criticisms on a good many of these public
defender sites, apparently this guy does too."

Ion said, "Actually Santa, we looked up the names
and locations of some of these websites and it turns out
that many have the same ISPN addresses."

"Meaning?" Nick asked.

"It's the same person with different avatars or
monickers, if you wish," said Indy.

"So the same person is putting these out under
different names?" asked Santa in disbelief.

"Many of them, although he may be part of the
whole and the most active," nodded Ion.

"Accomplices?" Nick inquired.

"Probably. And I would further guess, as Cory has,

that a good many of them are strongly influenced by him, if not directly told to do what he wants," said Indy.

"Okay so what's our game plan against this?" Mary asked clearly wanting to get to a solution.

"Unfortunately there is little we can do about what is already out there. The terrible thing about the Internet is once it is posted it is impossible to completely remove it from cyberspace," Ion explained, "So that leaves us with two possibilities, rebuke it or shut it down. Possibly both, but I see problems with the first."

"Rebuking what has been posted will only be like pouring gasoline on a fire. Every time someone tried to defend us it only led to an entire series of new posts from every place. That's why I told our Ambassadors to stop trying to come to our aid," argued Cory.

"Mary has always said you can't have an argument with only yourself," said Santa. "I agree, nothing would be gained by continuing to play into their hands by trying to advocate our position, so how do we shut it down."

Mac, Ion and Indy looked at each other, then at Nick and Mary. Mac said, "You won't be happy about this but it is the only way we could resolve this. You will have to take legal action."

"You're right, I don't like it," Santa said sourly.

"Now Santa." Mary scolded. "I know you hate anything that involves the legal system, but I think they have a point. We didn't bring this on ourselves. These accusations came from them and without any bases of fact. We need to protect the Peters and our good works from such evil beings."

"We aren't talking about lawsuits or anything that would bring us down to their level," said Mac, "only bringing cease and desist orders against the people Cory mentioned by name."

"What if others decide to take up their banner?" complained Nick.

Cory thought about it for a moment and said, "I think they're right Santa, and if we cut the head off the snake the rest might back down. It certainly beats doing nothing."

"We could call Paul Shelton," Mary suggested.

"Who?" Cory asked.

"Paul Shelton was another visitor to the North Pole before you," Mary explained.

"He's a trial lawyer," said Santa. "He got his law degree to assist others that were wrongly accused or convicted."

"Sounds perfect," said Cory. "And let's not forget I have some legal background from my prior life, so I could work with Mr. Shelton and help you get this done as you concentrate on the move."

"Won't this require us to be exposed in the American legal system?" worried Nick.

"Since the brunt of their attacks are at me and the school, we can use that to get him to stop," said Cory. "Truth is, Katy and I could get a little of our own back that way. We wouldn't need to involve you or the village."

The elves looked resigned and nodded their approval.

He looked at Mary and said, "Have Ella contact Paul and let's get this ball rolling. Cory I want you to be point man on this and you can talk to Paul directly and begin figuring what needs to be done."

Nick looked at the elves and said, "I need you three to give whatever assistance to Cory and Paul you can, but remember your first priorities are the move and settlement of the village."

Cory said, "As soon as I talk with Mr. Shelton, I will be heading back to get ready for the upcoming class and the fight ahead. By the way, where is Mr. Shelton's office?"

Nick said slyly, "Madison, Wisconsin."

And with that the strategy was underway.

CHAPTER 33

HEADING FOR THE HILLS

Mary was ready. She had called the Inn and told Christel to please have the Fredricks and Kelly meet her in front of the train station. She looked again at Nick and said, "I hope nothing untoward happens these next few days in the interim."

Nick shrugged. "I expect any quiet weeks we hoped we would have are a thing of the past. I'll settle for nothing major occurring."

Mary nodded. "And I further hope I don't end up transporting us to upper Siberia by mistake. I don't do this all that often."

Nick assured her that she would do fine as long as she concentrated on her target destination. "Just as I showed you," he said, "If you hit a snag, call me. I can be there in two shakes and get you to a safe location."

He lifted her bag and teased her about it being lighter since she had to lug it about.

"Nonsense," Mary replied. "I know better what I'll need when I get there this time."

They walked out of their home and into the waiting sleigh and reindeer. Throughout the years and despite offers for swifter transportation, Mary loved this part of living in the North Pole most. She had never been in a sleigh before she met Nick. She insisted that no matter what the hurry, if they couldn't take the sleigh, oft times it wasn't worth going.

She wondered if this, too, would change in the Smokies? She thought they certainly didn't have snow year round, including at the highest elevations, and it would seem silly to keep the dome at freezing if it was a delightful temperature outside.

*We'll put wheels on the sleighs instead of using the runners,*she thought to herself. For Mary Kringle there was always a way around a problem.

As they pulled up to the station, Kelly said, "Which one's Dasher and which one's Cupid?"

"Neither," chortled Nick. "You would give Forrest a heart attack calling them that. This one is Cardamon, and she is Nefertiti."

"I don't remember those names in the poem," commented Susan. "Do they fly?"

"Not these two," Nick shook his head. "We tried, but they didn't care for it. As we have enough that do, we don't push it. But they are great ground reindeer."

Whitey, Jim and two other elves, Rory Whittlesee and Rudy Clawhammer, walked up to the rest. "Are we about ready to go see the new area?" Whitey asked.

"The gangs all here," said Mary. She gave Nick a kiss and said, "See you in a few days, dear. Don't lose the village on us I'm gone."

"I'll try to keep it intact," he chuckled. "You guys be safe and accomplish much." Nick scarcely got the last words out as Whitey, Jim, Rudy and Rory disappeared from sight. A moment later Mary, Kelly and the Fredrick's were also gone.

They popped into the same space and Rory and Susan got tangled up together and fell down. Mary and Whitey apologized and said they obviously had concentrated very hard on the exact same spot. They had aimed to the same spot to land in the Charlotte DC. The manager saw them appear and quickly ran to their aid. "Is everyone alright?"

"Just feeling a little awkward I believe," said Rory. Susan mumbled she was okay, also.

"Welcome to our DC, Mrs. Claus and friends of the Pole," she said with a slight southern accent. "We are honored to have you here. Hi Whitey," she said taking his hand. "Haven't seen you in a coon's age."

"Hello Char," Whitey smiled.

Charlotte Boleyn was 4'5" and had gray hair which she wore in a bob. She was an older elf, but looked in her prime. She had been managing the Charlotte Center for about a decade.

She took Mary aside and talked barely above a whisper to her. "Mrs. Claus, I haven't allowed anyone here to talk about what might be going on. Richard told me about the exchange he had with you in Gatlinburg. We are hoping you would shed some light on the situation, and if you could address everyone here that would save a lot of rumor-mongering."

Mary nodded and said, "Thanks, Char. I can tell everyone what I know, which isn't much yet. I don't know what will happen to this DC as to whether we would roll it into the new village or let it alone. The rest is probably what everyone already knows, that we are moving to the Smokies and it will take everyone involved to get us there."

Char nodded and asked hopefully, "Are we the unofficial headquarters for the time being?"

Mary smiled and said, "Since you are the closest, and so far your center and people have been invaluable to us, yes, we could call you that."

Charlotte grinned broadly and again asked if Mary would make that announcement to the group, to which she agreed.

After telling the same thing to the elves in the DC, an exuberant applause broke out and everyelf there began congratulating each other.

After her remarks Mary told Charlotte that they were anxious to get going as there wasn't a moment to waste. Charlotte said, "I took the liberty of securing you a van when Ella and Richard told me how many would be coming."

"That's great," Mary said with pleasure. "I was worried about having to do a caravan and getting someone lost. Thank you so much, Char."

They bundled into the van and Bill offered to drive if Mary would navigate. She agreed and pulled out her maps from her last trip. Once they were in sight of a possible settlement, they would use the continuum to transfer to the area and back.

After a quick goodbye, they were off to the mountains. They had a roughly three hour drive. Bill wasn't exactly going the speed limit, though no one complained.

As they started their ascent into the mountains Jim was pointing out various balds and said, "No one knows why they exist. They are an enigma. There should be at least some shrubbery or scrub at these elevations if not trees, but nothing more than grass grows on many of them, so they are called grassy balds. There are some that more exactly fit the pattern here with scrub and bushes and those are the heath balds. Either kind would be easy to clear and build on."

Whitey asked, "Do you think the heath bald might make more sense as there would be less traffic?"

Jim rubbed his chin and replied, "Possibly, although we could pick an out of the way grassy bald and most likely get the same result. Of course I believe any of the balds we will have to hike to to reach them."

As they moved up higher into the mountains they saw a few places that they might investigate. Whitey mentioned that the farther away from any roads the better. Mary wanted to disagree thinking how much easier it might be to get goods and services in and out of the village for a change. As long as they could hide in the dome, it might be easier for everyone.

They took a side road off into the mountains. The road was not closed and looked promising. There was no traffic going in. They could clearly see one of the places they had been discussing in the distance ahead of them and pulled off the road to get a better look.

Whitey said he might take a look and asked Bill if he would join him. Bill replied, "Anything to walk around for a bit, I am getting pretty stiff from driving."

Whitey said he would signal if it looked alright. He fixated on the spot and the two men disappeared from where they stood and a while later reappeared on the bald. Whitey walked around to get a better feel of what this bald looked like. He was pleased at the prospect of not having to tear down trees or do much in the way of excavation. Although they still had the problem of not having a road to reach the area. They had done little excavation in the North Pole when they settled there and he wanted to leave this land as unspoiled as possible, even if they were here another three centuries or more.

"I can't believe how flat this is," commented Bill, "I would have thought mountains would have outcroppings and jagged edges."

"These are ancient mountains," Whitey recounted what Topo told him, "More than 450 million years old. Their teeth have been worn down to nothing."

"Amazing, at this time of year, it is so beautiful up here," Bill said wistfully.

"Imagine how it will look in summer," Whitey smiled and said. He was doing exactly that.

They walked a couple hundred yards surveying the area. The ground rose and fell softly and Whitey again thought it wouldn't be too hard to lay out the village here. He was concerned about how far they were to the road, He could only faintly see the others, but the point was he could still see them.

He saw that the bald went on for a few hundred yards more in two directions, but was not the four square miles they would need. He said as much to Bill who asked, "Do you think there is a large enough one around here?"

"Maybe not. I think we should keep looking,"

answered Whitey. "Ready?"

"Yeah, thanks for the exercise, I needed it," Bill said and put his hand on Whitey's shoulder again.

They returned to the others and Whitey told them what they saw. Mary smiled and said, "That's the best news we have heard for a bit. At least you didn't come back saying it wouldn't work."

Whitey returned the smile and said, "I think you already knew it would. But you're right, it's nice to be sure."

They returned to the van and loaded in. They would go farther in for a time before heading back to the hotel which was in Cherokee.

They came to a spot toward the top of the mountain road and saw a sign posting a closed road. They looked at each other and Bill shrugged saying, "How daring do we want to be?"

"Maybe we wouldn't have to go too far in," said Mary. "After all, there is little to no snow up here, so I don't think we'd get stuck. What do the rest of you think?"

"I'm game," said Kelly quickly. "I am tired of this highway and would like to see something else."

Most of the other occupants agreed or stayed quiet, willing to go along with the majority.

Bill put on his blinker though there were no other cars around right and turned right onto the road. They came up to a cross bar blocking the way. Rory got out and looked at it. There was a large padlock holding the bar in place. He pulled out what looked like a small screwdriver and a moment later he pushed the bar back and signaled for the van to come through.

When it had he pushed the bar back and relocked the
lock. As he got into the van Rudy patted him on the
back and Mary said, "We better not lose you or we will
be stuck here for a long time. This road is closed until
the first of April."

They proceeded cautiously ahead and the road went
on for a few miles going up further and circling back and
forth from the mountain. It was perfectly safe and the
view was stunning. Moments before they reached the
top they saw another road, less traveled going down
toward a bald straight out from them.

As high up as they were, the temperature was a crisp
but pleasant 49 degrees. They unloaded from the car
once more, zipped up their jackets and looked at the
bald before them. The road didn't go all the way to it,
but it was an easy walk nonetheless. Without a word the
whole group began walking the trail to get a better look.

As they climbed the slight rise they began to see it. A
large open area with a grassy bald that stretched over a
good distance. Jim took the GPS coordinates and
started measuring with his pocket laser. It was scarcely
under a mile long in one direction with a valley in the
center going the other direction.

"If you add in some of the forest, this might about
the right size," he commented to the group.

"I wonder how populated this gets in summer?"
Whitey asked mostly to himself.

"Does it really matter with the dome thingy?"
questioned Kelly.

"Although it would hide the village, and now with
Jim's improvements they can walk through it without

knowing, I would not want a traffic pattern going down our streets the whole day long," he answered. He looked at the remains of the oat grass long since dormant.

Mary said, "At least it is solid underneath, I'd take that for now."

Bill asked Jim how far they walked to this point. Jim pointed the laser back the way they came. He aimed to the area where the road ended and the trail began. He looked at the readout and said, "It's about three quarters of a mile to the road and four tenths of a mile from there to the car. Not that far, really."

"I have a feeling none of these places will be that far from the road," said Susan. "It's probably the old adage which came first the chicken or the egg, but in this case it's the bald or the road. I'll bet any bald that can be gotten to by road will put it fairly close in proximity."

"That's going to attract a good many hikers," said Rudy. "Far more than we ever had to deal with up north."

"You're not looking at this the right way," Kelly said. "Think of how many picnics we could get from these people. You can probably cut the grocery deliveries in half!" Everyone shook their heads at her attempt at humor.

"Seriously, do you really think that leaving the North Pole for any place other than say, the Sahara Dessert, that you won't have people coming through?" she continued, "If that's the case you might as well give up now."

Jim said, "We should take some preliminary measurements and look at the ground structure to get a feel for what's here."

Whitey and Bill nodded and Mary produced a tablet to enter the data as it was gained. Topo and Ion had already set up a spreadsheet and all she had to do is plug in the numbers and strata for the type of ground, which Jim would provide her.

It took them about an hour to gain the information about the area including walking the length and breath of the bald. After they had the necessary measurements they headed back to the van.

"One thing is for sure," said Rory, "When that road is closed it is a good bet we won't see anyone. And Mrs. Claus you said it was closed from November first until April first. That's like the six months our sun is set."

They thought about that as they returned to the car.

Chapter 34

Invasion Force

The first of three trains coming that day pulled into the station at 10:00 that morning. As the passengers got off they looked like they could scarcely move and were worn out from traveling through the night. Santa greeted them personally and thanked each one for sacrificing their time and efforts to come and assist the village.

Nick made sure that the attentive train porters had help to get these people settled into their rooms and get them food if they wished and much needed sleep. He readily recognized everyone who stepped from the cars though many he had not seen for a decade or more.

They came from the United States, Great Britain, France, Japan, Australia, Germany and many other countries. Each were former visitors and most extremely successful today, at least partly due to the North Pole, if not entirely.

Tired as they were, every person managed a smile as they disembarked, and nearly everyone gave Nick a hug as soon as they reached him.

Christel was behind the desk at the Reindeer Inn and there were several sleighs ready to take other guests to Santa's Boarding House and the care of Fergie. The travelers, having been through this once before in their lives, obediently followed their bell-elves to their room as fast as Christel called out their names. Additional elves came to help cart luggage to the guests room as it was unloaded.

Nick thought about how many people would be here by the time the 4:30 train arrived that afternoon. He was assured they would have room for everyone, but wondered how best to coordinate this invasion of tallfolk and elves, all trying to help the village pack up and move.

They had already been working the miniaturization machine almost nonstop. His sons and the elves were loading items and personal belongings for Charlotte and Atlanta as quickly as they could pack the crates and move them by squibbles to the planes.

Kristopher and Michael were doing an excellent job coordinating everything at their end and seemed to be enjoying their new responsibilities. The planes were running a regular schedule and already much of the remaining warehouse products and toys had been shipped to other American DC's. They were now dismantling various machinery that they didn't need from the manufacturing area for now and preparing to ship that out. Nick was as proud as any father could be of both their efforts.

Problems were again beginning to break out in the woodland area and new places began developing cracks. Water was seeping here and there through the ice. Normally in February the ice was solid as rocks and little water flowed anywhere in the Pole, except through the plumbing inside the homes and factories.

This unnerved Nick, who received reports that morning of the new areas of concern. His home and workshop were located closer to the manufacturing area, so he was cautiously optimistic that their home would not see problems for a little bit longer. He kept his fingers crossed anyway.

The biggest concern Nick had at this moment was what if things *did* get worse as these people helped out? If anything happened to a single soul, Nick did not know what he would do. He tried again to push it out of his mind and concentrate on the events that were genuine, instead of the 'what-ifs' that hadn't happened and might not.

As Nick turned he saw Cory walking toward the station with Mac next to him. Nick walked off and said to Cory, "Off already?"

Cory forced a grin and said, "I have a snake to dispatch, and the sooner I get to it, the sooner the job is finished."

Santa nodded and looked at Mac and said, "And where do you think you're going?"

Mac laughed, "Before the end of the day you will have so many people around here that you won't notice I'm not one of them."

Nick ho, ho, ho'ed and said, "I think you may be right. Perhaps I could disappear also."

"Fat chance," Mac sniggered and gave Santa a handshake. He wished him luck with the move. "I'll look forward to seeing the new village in the Smokies." He told Cory he'd see him on the train and walked off.

"I know this is a tough situation, Cory, but I thank

you for dealing with it and I hope you are able to put an end to this hideous persons attempts at self-aggrandizement and cruelty," Nick said bitterly.

"Not to worry, Santa," Cory forced a smile. "I'll push this animal back into his hole and seal it.

"Please keep us informed after you talk with Paul and let us know how it is going," Nick said.

"Of course." He gave Nick a hug and said. "Please give Katy's and my best to Mary."

He moved toward the train and Nick said a silent prayer for the success of Cory and his mission.

Nick had a couple hours before the next train so he decided to walk over to one of the restaurants and get something to eat and a cup of coffee. He walked into a restaurant that was more like the 50's diners he used to see when he first started making his rounds as Santa.

He sat down and was immediately greeted by a young elf named Rachel. "Good morning, Santa," she said with a bright smile. Santa couldn't help but smile back at those dimples and returned the greeting.

He ordered an early lunch as he had been up at 4:30 and was living off a bowl of cereal. As he sat there he looked over the Visiting Center and thought about many of the people coming today. With rare exception, he had met almost everyone of them when they came to visit before. He had also asked on numerous visits to the hall of records about how certain ones were doing.

It felt strange that they were coming back to assist Mary, him and the elves. They had always been the providers, and for so many years before he took over as Santa, the elves had not allowed tallfolk in their village.

Now they not only welcomed them but needed them.

Nick further thought about what would happen if this changed and they were no longer able to help people as they had in the past. So many possible changes might come from this, not the least of which would be if physical changes occurred with their inhabitants. Without many of the elves, they would not be able to accomplish the great things they had come to expect as commonplace.

Suddenly, Nick felt his appetite wane, but he ate a little anyway. He knew he had a long day before him.

After lunch, Nick headed to his Visiting Center home, as he wanted to stay close when the next two trains arrived to welcome everyone.

He wasn't through the door for five minutes when he heard a knock.

CHAPTER 35

THE DEEP FREEZE

Nick opened the door to Topo and Bilge. Both smiled and Topo said, "Hello Santa, we come bearing good news!"

Nick smiled back at the elves and said, "Then don't leave it outside, bring it in and share it."

The elves walked in and Bilge asked if Santa had heard from Mrs. Claus yet.

"Not as of yet," Nick responded. "But I expect she'll contact me tonight when they get to their hotel."

"Good, you can share this with her," said Bilge. Both elves seemed to be brimming over with their news.

Nick motioned them to sit in the den and as the three sat down Nick said, "Okay, don't keep me in suspense, what have you learned?"

Bilge nodded at Topo and then Topo sat on the edge of his chair and addressed Nick, "We have been studying a system beginning to set up to the the south of us."

Nick was about to comment that everything was south of them but held his tongue.

Topo continued, "It's begun spinning and is gaining strength. It could be a real whopper in a day or two."

Nick said, "I'm not sure I follow. The dome will keep us secure from it. What's the worry?"

Bilge said, "The point is we don't think we should avoid it. This looks as if it could possibly refreeze much of the village if we allow it to hit with full force."

Santa looked at the elf as if he was speaking a foreign language that Nick himself didn't understand, "I'm not sure I follow, we don't want to protect ourselves?"

Topo reasoned saying, "We can handle it. It would only be two or three days at the most, and once through here it could restore the Pole to a more frozen state for an additional two weeks or more."

"But what of our residents and guests?" Nick argued. "We will be packed full up here. We are receiving several train fulls today alone. Many of these people aren't prepared for the type of weather you are proposing."

"So we keep them in the inns and they will be fine," said Bilge. "It could gain us precious time if the ice refroze deep enough. Afterward we can keep the dome at 32 degrees like we always do this time of year. But we have a real chance for a few days and it could buy us a couple of weeks."

"How deep will the snow be from this?" asked Nick.

"Maybe a foot to a foot and a half," responded Topo.

Nick thought about it and knew they could easily handle two feet without any concern or effort, but wondered whether the time spent recovering from the storm would net them that much more time overall. He began figuring and said more to himself than the elves, "So we lose two days, possibly three from the storm, and spend two to three for clean up and snow removal, and for that we gain possibly 10-14 days."

"At this point a week more night make a difference, and work could continue on the inside, however it would be prudent to limit activity outside for several days," said Topo.

Santa looked at the elf and said, "It would be next to impossible to move around through the village for nearly a week. How would these people get food or supplies if they need them?"

Bilge said, "We have a day or two before the system hits. We could stock up the individual inns and houses. Most of us are always prepared 'just in case' of an emergency. Think what it could mean if it helped freeze the Woodland Area solid for another two weeks."

Topo jumped in, "Forrest alone might be able to use that extra time to get the animals we plan to move safely south. Plus the Woodworks shop is continuing to make enough wooden crates for moving. Two weeks could net us quite a bit."

"The net effect might only buy us a few days," Santa thought aloud. "And the other elves and our guests might freeze, or get frostbite, if exposed to those kind of temperatures."

"As soon as the front moves through we could rewarm the village to a more comfortable 32° and stop the wind as before," stated Topo.

"To the best of your knowledge, what would be the worst of it?" Santa asked in a concerned manner.

Bilge came closer and said, "The storm would hit in two days and come in during the evening giving us two full days to resupply and stock up. The first night the temperature would go down around -25° and wouldn't increase more than a few degrees the next day. The winds would be sustained at 25-30 miles per hour with gusts around 40. The snow would hit the following morning later before noon. It would last through the day and into that evening accumulating to about 6-9 inches. That night the temperatures will fall to -35° and the winds will lessen to about 15-20. The next morning we should be at about a foot of snow and the winds will increase again and be about the same minus 25-30 mark. By the end of the second day everything will begin to stabilize and the winds and snow will diminish, but the temps won't rise until the third day and will be around zero Fahrenheit."

"Would we warm the dome to 32 at that point or do you suggest to let it freeze some more?" asked Nick.

"The winds are the key factor here, Santa," answered Topo. "Strong sustained winds will cause faster freezing and a more solid freeze. After the winds and deep strong temperatures so far below zero end, we can maintain the the temp at freezing and it wouldn't have a measurable effect either way."

"Everyone goes through climatic changes and a little inconvenience from time to time," said Bilge. "Whether its tornadoes, deep winter storms like this, hurricanes or tremendous thunderstorms, its almost unavoidable on this planet. They will survive and probably could use a minimal workload for a couple days."

"Everyone we expect will have arrived by then," Nick said rubbing his beard. "And I suppose we could keep everyone safe for that amount of time..."

"Worse comes to worse, we can revive the dome to its full level and shut out the remaining storm." Topo reasoned .

"Whitey is south and he will have to return here to do

this," said Nick. "I don't want to take any chance of error collapsing or reinstating the dome. I will tell Mrs. Claus she needs to have everyone back before this monster hits."

"They will have to be back in the early afternoon the day after tomorrow to be safe," agreed Topo. "Earlier if Whitey needs to do a whole lot to reduce the dome."

"We only have it at 35% now because of everyone and everything moving in and out. If that storm were to hit today, we would feel it in here anyway," said Nick.

"But not to the levels we are talking about," finished Bilge, "We really need the full force of this storm to do any good."

Nick nodded and said, "Okay, got it. Now after, and including, the effect of this storm, where are we sitting for evacuation time."

"We are working with some new figures, and although there is shifting going on in several areas of the village, nothing is too serious except the Woodland Area," said Bilge. "The sun is beginning to rise, and though it hasn't broken the horizon yet, the temperatures are already beginning to rise, but not to where it is melting the sea ice, which will have the greatest effect..."

"Time, Bilge," Nick said impatiently. "How much time?"

"We think June first to be safe," he said flatly.

"Why is it every time I ask you two it gets shorter?" Nick said annoyed. "What happened to my two weeks?"

"We always try and tell you the worst possible scenario," said Bilge defensively. "If we need to err at all, we prefer to do it on the side of safety. You may have a month or more after that. But as we had this blizzard coming, we could as easily get a heat wave in May."

"In other words," Topo continued. "In some ways, your guess would be as good as ours. But we don't want to see anyone fall into a crack and be lost anymore than you."

Nick backed down and said in a softer voice, "Yeah, I see what you mean on that. I keep wishing we had more time to prepare, move and rebuild. Doing everything at once doesn't leave much margin of error."

The two elves nodded and sympathized with their boss.

"You will succeed in this task as you have in so many others," said Topo as he put a hand on Nick's shoulder. "There isn't an elf anywhere that doubts that. And if we have more time, I am sure we will find a way to utilize it. Remember, we are not alone in this undertaking. Because of what you have done for the tallfolk, we now have many allies to assist us."

Bilge agreed and said, "This will be accomplished and Alfie Newsworthy will be writing another story about us."

Nick chuckled at the thought. He knew Bilge was probably right. He smiled at the elves and said, "Alright, thank you for the news and advice. It will be done as you suggest and hopefully these few days will gain us much."

With that he led them to the door and putting his arm around each, said how pleased he was for their help and guidance. He bade them farewell and went back to his study to await the next train.

Chapter 36

Changes in Latitude, Changes in Attitude

Forrest had contacted Lanty Givens who was the director of the Atlanta DC earlier that morning. He told her that he would be coming by today to try an experiment and to discuss the possible placement of animals in her warehouse. He had gotten an Arctic fox and two snowshoe hares and placed the two types of animals in separate travel cages. He took a small bag with some extra clothes and concentrated on the DC the way Santa taught him to do and with his eyes shut, winced as if in pain and disappeared from the North Pole with his charges.

He arrived in the middle of the floor as a squibble was going by and almost had an accident. He barely dodged the self propelled hauler as it passed by. The fox barked a quick admonishment as Forrest spun to his right.

"That was close," Lanty said as she approached Forrest. "Nice reflexes you have there."

Forrest chuckled and said, "Comes from trying to stay outta the way of those reindeer antlers!"

Lanty laughed and Forrest liked her instantly. She was younger than he imagined as she couldn't be much older than 175. She was lovely, wearing her long hair the color of spun gold in a soft ponytail on top of her head. She had dimples on both cheeks when she smiled. Her eyes were hazel and Forrest thought they almost matched her hair. She was a little shorter than him at 4'4" but looked strong for her size.

She came over and said, "So you must be Forrest? Welcome to my DC." She finished walking to him and gave him a little hug, "It's nice to have a village elf here again."

Forrest smiled back at her and said, "Thank you for having me and my friends." He held up the two cages for her to look at.

"Oh they're beautiful," she said breathlessly. "I miss our northern animals so much, but we have quite the menagerie down here."

"I am trying to figure out how many might be coming with us," he said as a few more elves gathered around, "Besides the reindeer and horses we stable, we have a sizable group of animals that hang around the petting area and barn regularly."

"Do you think you can migrate them to the Smokies without affecting their behavior?" asked one of the other elves that had walked up.

"That's what I am here to find out," Forrest answered. "Depending on how these guys do, I will bring larger animals and test them. If everything goes as it should, we will begin figuring how many we will be able to handle at the new location."

"Has the location been decided yet?" asked Lanty.

"Mrs. Claus and a team of others are looking at

potential spots in the Smokies now," he said. "I expect they will have a spot picked out upon their return."

"Let me show you where we have you set up," Lanty took the carrier with the rabbits from Forrest and began walking toward a corner of the warehouse. "We weren't sure what or how many you were bringing, so we got hay, oats, alfalfa, and probably every kind of feed except for rabbits and foxes, of course."

Forrest laughed. "Not to worry, I expected as much. I brought along my own in my bag. I promise to give you plenty of warning before bringing down anything much larger. Then we will have one of the flying sleighs bring down what we need ahead, or with, the animals."

"A flying ark, eh?" Lanty laughed at her own joke. As they got to the area she was heading toward she said, "I hope this will suffice for now."

Forrest looked at the set-up and said, "Ideal, this is far more than I expected." Before him were several paddocks with metal corrals and hay and straw laid around them and more stacked up against one wall. There was also a small office built to the side complete with computer, chairs, water cooler, a cot and more.

Forrest looked around and said, "You've seen to my every need, I thank you kindly."

"Anything for the Range Boss of the North Pole," she handed him back the cage and curtsied saying, "After all, it is not everyday we have so important a guest from the Pole."

Forrest thought she might be flirting with him and the thought didn't displease him in the least. He tried to think of something witty to come back with, but in the end only said, "You're kind, thank you again."

She invited him to dinner at 6:00 in the dining area upstairs and he accepted. With that she said, "I'll leave you to your experiment and see you then." She was gone in a flash and he stood there holding the cages in his hands.

He set them down in the makeshift office. The fox seemed restless to come out. The rabbits were content and snuggled into half the size of the pet carrier. He carefully opened the door of the carrier that held the fox. The fox stepped out carefully onto the granite floor. He seemed as he always did up north in the village, and Forrest thought this was a good sign.

He paced around and sniffed at the rabbits, but he showed little interest to his usual prey. Forrest wasn't sure if this was because he wasn't hungry, or if it was the unfamiliar setting or the fact that he was sliding on the floor and didn't trust his footing.

Forrest let the animal wander around the office and he curled up into a corner and laid his head on his tail and yawned as if bored with the whole trip. The rabbits had spread out as and looked relaxed in their carrier.

Sometime later, he had brought a leash for the fox and decided to take him outside. He placed the strap around the docile animal's neck and the fox walked dutifully out with the elf. Forrest thought the fox would enjoy exploring outside these new surroundings and took him close to a forested area off from the compound.

After he walked for a ways the fox began to get agitated. He started pulling at the strap and growled at

Forrest, which he had never done before. The closer
Forrest pulled him to the trees the angrier and more
unhinged the fox became. The elf was concerned about
trying to pick up the animal as it looked ready to bite
him if he tried.

After a few minutes, Forrest decided he better return
the animal to his carrier and leave him there. *Thank
goodness I didn't bring down a wolf or bear,* he thought to
himself. He was sure it might have eaten him alive.

So much for the idea of bringing animals down here, he
thought again. As he moved closer to the DC the fox
began to relax and became tame again. Forrest stood
there scratching his head. Did the fox sense something
dangerous in the woods? Was there a snake or something
close by? Although he thought it was a little soon for
snakes to be out and about from their hibernation, he
couldn't be certain.

He tried to spy something as the fox must have done,
but couldn't see anything moving. Now the fox was
moving in and around his legs and acting pretty much as
he had before. Forrest looked at the animal and said out
loud, "Perhaps I should call you Jekyll." He moved back
inside with the fox trotting happily beside him. He
returned to the office and again the animal showed no
aggression to either Forrest or the rabbits.

The fox returned to his corner and once more curled
up into a small white ball of fur. Forrest sat there and
pondered the event. He looked at the rabbits that were
sitting in the carrier and wondered what there reaction
might be.

As the trees outside wrapped along the warehouse

and were on both sides, Forrest decided that it would be
best to avoid whatever the fox saw or smelled at the
closer exit. So he walked the length of the building and
went out the other side door.

He carried the animals for a little distance and like
the fox, as soon as he reached the treeline the rabbits
began jumping around the carrier making it extremely
difficult to hold the cage. He set the carrier on the
ground and watched as the hares began acting as if he
had put a vicious animal in the cage with them. They
seemed terrified and were scratching at the door and
sides of the crate and thumping their hind feet in alarm.

Again and with difficulty he picked up the pen as
they hopped around frantically, he carried it back to the
DC with both arms. As he approached the door, the
rabbits began to settle down and were now moving
around as before, instead of their frenzied jumping
about.

By the time they had reached the office their
breathing had slowed, and they were both sitting before
as if nothing had happened. Again, Forrest set the
carrier down and studied the animals. The fox seemed
curious and came over and sniffed at the rabbits, which
didn't concern them or interest the fox beyond a cursory
glance.

Forrest sat puzzled and thought that perhaps they
were more tame then he first assumed. *Perhaps they are
more used to people than I thought they were,* he concluded
in his mind. As if to prove a point, another elf named
Marty came by and carefully entered the office so as not
to let the fox escape. He bent down and stroked the fox

commenting what a beautiful animal it was.

Forrest thanked the elf and asked him what kind of animals lived around the forest outside their doors.

The squat elf with brown hair and glasses looked at Forrest and calmly said, "There are a few deer, some rabbits, skunks and raccoons. You know your 'run of the mill' animals you would see around a residential area, as we are not too far from several developments."

Forrest questioned further, "What about snakes, bears or other predators?"

"I've heard we have a few rattlesnakes, but those would be deeper in the woods I think, as I have never seen or heard one, and it's too early for them to be around, anyway. As far as anything else, no one has reported seeing anything bigger or fiercer than the occasional house cat."

Forrest rubbed his beard and sat quietly contemplating as Marty went from the fox to the hares. He knew the reindeer didn't have any problem leaving the North Pole, they did it every Christmas Eve and several times before for trials and exercise. Would they react in a similar fashion if they were brought here? Forrest couldn't imagine that would be the case.

He thought, *Perhaps I will try it again later and see if I get the same reaction.* He figured that was the best he could do for now and that only time and more trials would tell if he had a real problem.

CHAPTER 37

REPORTING IN

Mary Claus called her husband as they were heading back from another explored area. This one was like many of the balds they had seen, either too small or too exposed to walking trails, or both. The balds seemed ideal as a starting point, but any plans for the village would need to spill into the forest that lay next to it. Whitey thought that they probably would not need to change the landscape much, as where the forest picked up, it was not dense until they got deeper, and in some areas, that was pretty far in.

She told him about the one bald that looked most promising, and relayed the concern of foot-traffic in the area. Nick agreed with Kelly saying almost anywhere they moved to, that this might be a concern. He said that if the improvements Jim had built into the dome were half as good as he and Whitey had spoken of, that a minor inconvenience may be the only result of moving there.

Nick relayed his conversation with Topo and Bilge and explained the timetable they suggested. Mary had said that perhaps they should wait the storm out where they were. She explained that if they did light upon a location, that plenty of plans could be started, and that it would be a shame to wait until after the storm passed.

After they married, Nick had never been away from

Mary more than a day or two, and the thought of a
week or more twisted his insides. He loved her so much
he thought he might die if he went more than a couple
days without her company. However he relented and
said, "Perhaps you are right. I'll meet you down there
later today."

Mary laughed and said, "Nice try, big boy! You know
you have to stay up there and take care of everything
else. Seriously Nick, I hate being apart from you also,
but we have so much to accomplish and so little time to
do so."

"The first train came in a short time ago. I honestly
don't relish telling these poor people coming to help us
to take shelter and try to stay warm for the next several
days," commented Nick.

"These people know the problems we are facing,"
answered Mary. "They are not coming up for a vacation.
As soon as you tell them what is happening, they will
probably feel better knowing their footing may be more
solid, than worrying about getting a little chilled.
Besides, if I know Christel and Fergie, they will have
everyone walking around in short sleeves, because it will
be so toasty in the inns."

Nick laughed knowing Mary was right. He could
picture Christel going through a whole cord of wood
each day if necessary to keep everyone warm enough.
"We may have no woodlands after this," he said
chuckling at the thought.

Mary laughed with him and they talked about what
needed to be done and when. Mary said obviously the
first efforts would be dictated by the approaching storm.

After that she suggested asking Michael and Kristopher what needed to be done at the warehouses.

"What about the Woodland Area?" asked Nick.

"If its true what the elves said about this refreezing this area, than it can hold off a few more days. Besides when we begin the new village the first thing I see us laying out are the manufacturing areas as they take up the most room," Mary reasoned.

Nick nodded his head and said, "Yes, you're right. We should get that up and running before anything else." Then a thought popped into his head. "Mary, why don't you think of splitting up the village if one area isn't large enough? You could put the manufacturing area into one place, the Visiting Center into another and the resort in a third. Perhaps we won't have to worry quite so much about keeping visitors out of certain areas that way."

"Hmm that's not a bad thought. I could ask Whitey and the others about the that," she said. "I'll bet a separate resort for the elves to get away from the village center and rest would be more effective, instead of watching their peers working as they tried to 'kick back'."

"It seems to me if we could build one dome, why not three?" asked Nick. "It won't be like at the North Pole where it is extremely difficult and uncomfortable moving around if we leave the dome for short trips."

"And it might reduce running the traffic through one spot of the village and interfering with the whole works," said Mary excitedly. "I'll talk to the others here about that."

"I would hold the limit of villages to three separate areas at most," finished Nick.

"Oh gosh, and here I was thinking we could have ten or twenty throughout the Great Smoky Mountains," Mary snickered. "No, I think three is quite right. One for manufacturing and training, one for the Visiting Center and a third possible resort and a plantation style area."

"I knew you would get that greenhouse of yours back," Nick chuckled. "And now you want it by a resort!"

"A lot of elves have told me that they think gardening and working in the dirt are quite relaxing and have asked me to let them help out at the greenhouse before now. I figure this is my chance to grant their wishes," she said quite frankly.

"My love, you are the CEO, so whatever you think is best." Nick suddenly realized the time and said, "I need to shuffle off and meet the next train. Do try and keep the three areas relatively close if you are able. And good luck with your plans. I love you."

"I love you, too. Please tell everyone arriving that I also send my thanks and look forward to seeing them," said Mary. "Goodbye for now my Hubby."

"Goodbye my Wifey, be safe," Nick said and hung up the phone.

Mary began talking to the other van occupants as soon as she hung up from Nick about the idea of three separate areas.

Whitey shook his head and said, "Why didn't we think of that before? It's a great idea, we don't have to

place all our eggs into one basket, we have plenty of
room to spread out. I think it may be wise however to
put the bunkhouses and trade school with the
manufacturing area rather than away from it."

Kelly jumped in and said, "This could be a lot of fun,
we could come up with three completely separate
designs!"

Susan asked, "Tell me how high might you want to go
up? If we could build more than two stories, we could
do a really nice training ground and dormitory for the
elves."

Mary was enjoying the ideas flying around and saw
the enthusiasm of the occupants. She smiled at Bill who
smiled back and nodded his head toward her. Whitey
and Jim were estimating the possible sizes that would be
dedicated to each section. Susan and Kelly were laying
out architectural details and ideas about each area. And
Rudy and Rory jumped in and said that the first area
they explored might be best for the manufacturing area.
There were several conversations going on at once and
Mary couldn't be happier about it.

As they came to the next area they looked at it with
fresh eyes and ideas trying to figure out what if any
section might fit best and what services might be easiest
to be trucked in, and whether they thought the
landscape would be lovely enough for a Visiting Center
and so forth.

Mary was enjoying the bantering and excitement
that was flying around, and for once what was thought
to be a terrible inconvenience, was now a pleasure.

Chapter 38

The Next Load

Nick walked up as the engine pulled to a stop in the train station. As passengers began disembarking, he walked up and hugged or shook their hands as he did before. When Jared and Julie got off he did both, hugging Julie and vigorously shaking Jared's hand.

Nick said, "I am sorry that Bill and Susan aren't here, but they will be back in a few days."

Julie smiled and said, "They called us, we didn't tell them we were coming up yet, so please don't mention it, as we'd like to surprise them."

Nick smiled to himself knowing they had quite a surprise for them also. "Not a peep from me," he said and crossed his heart. He motioned them to their valet and said, "Let's get you comfortable and squared away, and we'll catch up later," Nick would tell everyone at dinner about the coming storm and acted as if business was as usual as the passengers disembarked the train.

"You'll have to tell me later if Mary is taking good care of them," he told the Grady's as he began to move off to another passenger. Just then the Gradys saw the Conners walking over and Julie and Heather embraced as if long lost sisters and hugged Brian with the same enthusiasm. Brian gave Jared a hug as did Heather and they began talking at once.

"When did you get here?" Jared's question was the first answered by Brian.

"We arrived earlier this morning after flying all night from Michigan. Heather was so excited she barely slept on the plane so she crashed once we pulled in. I got a good nights sleep, and if we didn't have to change planes and the train, I probably would have slept the whole way here." He was chuckling as he finished.

"It's from those road trips he used to take taught him how to travel unconsciously," said Heather shaking her head. "But never mind that, you both look so great!"

"We feel pretty good, too. But can you believe we are here again?" asked Julie.

"Wish it were for a different reason," answered Heather. "But any reason to return to this magical place is a good one. I began feeling younger and more energized the moment I stepped off the train."

"Funny," said Julie thoughtfully. "Now that you mention it, I do too, there must be something in this air."

The valet was standing by and didn't say a word or move. Jared remembered he was there and apologized for holding him up. Charles shrugged and smiled saying it was no problem. He would be hanging around for another hour before the train pulled out again.

The five of them walked toward the Reindeer Inn and Julie fairly shrieked when she saw Christel. Christel broke into a large smile and said, "Lovely to see you again Mrs. Grady."

Julie stopped instantly and broke into a mock-scowl saying, "Now don't you Mrs. Grady me, Christel

Bunkinstyle, You call us by our first names or don't think to call us at all." She broke out laughing when she finished.

Christel came over and gave them a brief hug and said, "Fair enough, Julie, Jared, I have your room made up and waiting. I hope you don't mind sharing, as we are pretty full and are having to split our multiple bedrooms with others."

"Not a problem," said Jared, turning to Brian. "Do you know who you got stuck with?"

"Some oddball California couple. I heard the last time he was here he was moody and depressed," Brian joked as he watched their eyes get bigger.

Christel said, "Thought it made the most sense since I remember you spent plenty of time together on your last excursion."

Two bell-elves appeared next to Christel and began picking up the Grady's luggage. Christel said "Pocatello" to the elves and said to the Gradys, "Now go get yourselves situated, there will be a dinner in the lobby at 7:30 this evening and you are expected." She turned to another family that had come in from the train with more friends tagging along.

After Nick had greeted everyone, he walked back and bumped into George heading toward the Reindeer Inn. "How is everything going, George?"

"Hello sir, everything is going quite nicely, I think we have the configurations we need to create the fusion reactor when we build the housing at the new location," George answered almost as if he were still in school.

Nick ho, ho, hoed and said to George, "Relax, my

friend, I am not one of your professors. It's me Santa."

"Excuse me sir, but making a statement like 'It's me Santa' is like the the President of the United States saying, 'It's me, the leader of the free world', possibly bigger, I think you do a lot more than she does."

Nick roared a good laugh and put his arm around George saying, "You have come a long way in your years, and Mary and I are quite proud of you. I am curious though, have you ever regretted the path you took?"

"You mean compared with music?" asked George. Santa nodded.

"I guess I would have to say they were never really mutually exclusive, and I'm sure if it were important enough, I would have found a way to fit it in along with everything else," George shrugged, "So I guess the answer is, no, I have no regrets, at least not yet."

Nick raised an eyebrow and said, "You really have matured, that is quite an answer!"

George scoffed and said, "I know a few who would argue that point."

Nick brushed off the comment, smiled and said, "I am particularly glad you were so insistent and I was smart enough to allow it. This cold fusion energy source may be something to truly help the whole world. I hope we can share it in the not-so-distant future with all mankind."

"Thank you sir, but I need to make sure it does what I advertise, first," George said hesitantly.

"I believe in you," said Nick and squeezed George's arm. "It will work, and *you* will make it work."

"Thank you Santa," George squeaked, embarrassed by Nick's certainty.

Nick patted the young man on the back and sent him on his way. He was proud of George and was extremely thankful he never lost his life in the tunnel when he tried to sneak through as a train came.

A few more people cornered Santa as he tried to make his way through the village asking about updates and various tallfolk they had heard returned to the North Pole after many years. Nick confirmed what he knew and told the rest to check with Christel and Fergie if he wasn't certain or didn't know.

He made it back to the Visiting Center home and closed the door. *Two down, two to go,* he thought, *then dinner tonight.* It would be a long day, indeed.

CHAPTER 39

THE ICE STORM COMETH

Once everyone arrived and became settled, there seemed to be a major bustle of activity from storing up supplies, food and wood for the coming front. Britney and Jackson were versed as backups for the dome. And they stood ready to "pull the plug" on the village's defense when Topo gave them the word. Whitey told Nick in a call from Mary that Sparky was equal to the task of controlling the dome in his absence and that he should have no concerns with letting him take care of it.

The visitors reacted to the news precisely as Mary predicted. They said they were there to do whatever was needed and that a little harsh weather would not keep them from their promise. Christel began tearing up as she heard them evoke their insistence that the North Pole and its residents was everyone's concern, especially those in attendance, so let the ice storm cometh, they would be fine with it.

That morning Topo gave the word to begin lowering the dome's defense and that the storm would arrive in the afternoon. As people scurried like chipmunks gathering their last acorns, the temperature began to fall to match the environment outside which was a cold 10° Fahrenheit. Soon there was far less movement on the streets of the village as everyone sought warmer shelter.

Some decided to stay put where they were working.

Such was the case with Ion, George and Sparky as they continued to test and work on the cold fusion project. They had taken over a good portion of the trade school building and George moved to one of the dorm rooms on the upper floor from the Reindeer Inn.

Kristopher and Michael did the same each staying close to their respective manufacturing centers. Luckily, the building in between the two centers was the converted bunkhouse so it was a very short and quick walk from the manufacturing warehouse to the makeshift dorm and back again. Both boys joked about how this was a sparser condition than when they lived in their college dorms.

Secretly they were enjoying the camaraderie amongst the elves bunked with them and listened as many stories were told about the migration and early days of the North Pole Village. They both knew some of the history. But they were amazed at some of the hardships that were endured in the beginning, especially before Aeon Millennium brought the discovery of the dome.

"Exactly how far into the future did he have to jump to get that discovery?" asked Michael. "Even now we are only starting to make improvements and if we make them now, why wouldn't they have been included in the original plans if it were further in the future?"

An elf who had a beard long enough to trip over looked at Michael and said, "Time travel is dangerous and tricky. He was tight-lipped about it. And he never discussed how far he went. Come to think, we never really learned much about his travels. Sometimes he would come back with a discovery and not reveal it until a great deal later."

Sparky said, "And my Dad told me he wouldn't teach anything about the time continuum except to a select few. He was amazed he taught your grandfather so much."

Another elf, who looked younger than Sparky asked, "So no one was left to travel into tomorrow to find out if we will survive this move and live long lives like now?"

That silenced the discussion entirely. The point kept creeping into everyone's thoughts, but no one spoke aloud the concern. Each one secretly hoped that, like the elves that lived outside the North Pole, they would be alright. Although most, if not all, returned from time to time to the North Pole.

The old elf looked at the young one and said, "Dewey, the Chinese have a word that they use for such mysteries, it is 'joss'. It was used to refer to a deity or religious figure but soon came to mean simply the fates will be decided by the events as they unfold. We do not know what to expect, but whatever will happen will happen. That is our joss, and I am hopeful it is a good one."

They reflected on this for a moment and Kristopher shrugged and said he was off to get some rest. The others soon followed suit.

At the other end of the village, there was a party going on in the Reindeer Inn. Christel had indeed stoked the fire high and everyone who had come to the North Pole previously were telling about how they almost didn't make it to this magical place that changed their lives forever. Others told what they did before and after their transition from Santa's visit.

Christel said, "There are many that never do make the journey. We have invited them twice and one family thrice as we wanted to help them so badly. We generally receive only about 60% of the total we invite here." She sighed at her last comment.

"Many times we talk about how we almost didn't take the journey with me being out of work and well...the fact that it was so oddly unusual in its presentation," said Jared Grady, "Truth is if Marshall and Susan hadn't insisted so, we probably would've tossed everything in the trash."

"Ah, the influence of children," commented Christel, "God bless them all."

Fred Wu said, "We didn't have children at the time but we were trying. I said to Kaileen, 'Perhaps we are trying too hard and we should take a chance and get away.' Later of course we found out she really was pregnant, but needless to say we were glad we came."

Another couple asked Christel if anyone had ever regretted the trip. She thought for a moment and shook her head saying, "None that I know of. We had a few question their sanity once here, and had so much trouble believing anything they were told. One man was quite certain we were only an amusement park and was convinced everything he received was completely fictional. We received a letter from him long after thanking us and berating himself for not enjoying himself more during the time he was here."

"I can relate to that," scoffed Jared. "I almost did the same thing, thankfully Julie and the Conners brought me out of myself, and I am grateful for it."

Julie gave him a squeeze and said, "Another day and I would have had the nutcracker guards take you out to the Woodlands Area and leave you there."

That triggered other memories and discussions of George being escorted by them to Santa, to the astonishment of other visitors that those statues actually moved and could guard the other areas.

Brian said, "Oh they can move alright! Christel are they going south with everything else?"

Christel shrugged and said, "I really don't know. We may retire them and not need them according to the last thing I heard, but I can't talk about that, so please don't ask." She held up her hand as they had seen her do in the past and several thought that some things do not change, Christel being one of them.

Other visitors were actually staying with some of the elves at their homes and stores or workshops. These folks had volunteered to assist with the packing and preparing of their shops. The elves that had extra rooms or space welcomed the tallfolk as family, and were extremely grateful for the help.

Many of these tallfolk also learned a tremendous amount about the North Pole and its history. There were many colorful stories told in each shop, and the elves were delighted to share their experiences and inner history that other 'talls' would have no idea about. It was often difficult to see who was enjoying whom more.

Hardly anyone minded the howling wind outside and the frigid temperatures. When the snow began blowing to white-out levels later that night, those who were still awake or awoke to the storm's fury made little more than passing comments, and went back to sleep or their other conversations.

That night, as predicted, the temperature plummeted to -25"F and the next morning, because of the clouds and snow. it looked more like a typical North Pole night rather than day. A couple of elves commented how they were used to having the dome control their weather and light rather than Mother Nature. Some elves had never experienced a day solely contrived without help from the dome.

The next day's high never got close to zero and the winds whipped continuously through the day. If anyone stepped outside, it was for the briefest of moments for safety's sake. A few that were working at the manufacturing centers moved quickly and were heavily fortified in their garments against the raging storm.

Work continued more or less unabated in every shop, warehouse and home throughout the North Pole Village. Though they couldn't load anything into the airplane "sleighs", they were able to stage great amounts of packed and ready loads to be moved by squibbles as soon as the weather broke.

Kristopher already had half a load on Supersleigh before the storm hit. He had been a little more successful than Michael and had been flying loads at one and half times the rate of his brother. He was running three flights to Michael' two each week since assigned their duties. In fact, he estimated another three to four loads and his center would be moved to its temporary location.

The planes themselves were also secure, hiding in a large hanger on the fringe of the dome. The snow had begun to pile up around the doors and sides of the massive structure, but not a flake had made it inside. Like other structures around the village, it was warm if not cozy in the large open area. Supersleigh, Firesleigh and Thundersleigh sat dark like giants sleeping in a cave. Like Supersleigh, Nick had placed a partial load of the elves personal belongings in Thundersleigh that when filled would be going to the Charlotte DC.

The second day of the storm was much like the first with nothing but high winds averaging between 30 and 50 miles an hour and occasional gusts much higher. The snow had begun to drift against the sides of the buildings and had reached many of the window ledges. Surprisingly, the walkways and main paths throughout the village were mostly clear of snow because the winds had blown it away and onto other barriers around the village.

Once more elf and tall alike watched the streaking snow and listened to the winds batter the houses and shops, but knew they were safe and warm within their structures. And the work continued, in fact at a greater rate than what would have been normal, as there was nothing else to do and little distraction to compete with their attentions.

By the third day everyone was anxious to see how the village fared and to move to other locations and see the others. The weather was a frigid -5°, but the wind had died down and the snow had quit. More had accumulated along the paths, but was still no more than

6 to 8 inches at its deepest. However some had difficulty getting out of their doors, and the windows were mostly covered from the blowing and drifting snow.

Nick himself was on the phone talking to the various departments and making sure that everyone was accounted for and alright after the fury of the storm. He learned everyone was fine and not so much as a sniffle had been acquired. He did hear from Dewey Antlerhorn, who was Forrest's assistant at the petting zoo, that many of the animals had run away shortly after the dome had been reduced. The reindeer and horses were okay, but almost anything else took off in different directions.

Nick thought this curious, but decided he had bigger concerns at that particular moment. He would have to wait until Forrest's return and let him deal with that problem. He was sure that the animals felt more secure with the approaching storm in their own burrows and dens, and probably headed off to those and would return soon.

Communication with Mary and others outside the Pole was difficult at best during the past couple days and he was anxious to find out how they were. It was time to establish contact with his love and see how they were fairing.

CHAPTER 40

A PATCH HERE, A PATCH THERE

The intrepid band in the Great Smoky Mountains of Tennessee and North Carolina hadn't wasted a moment of their time in exploring their new homeland. They had identified several sights possible for the new village or parts of it. They measured distances of each locale and what may or may not fit within the parameters of each potential area. They were in agreement that they didn't want too much distance between the developments and they also needed some separation if they truly wanted each section to stand by itself.

They had chosen one bald in Tennessee for the central manufacturing area and had measured it out, and with Susan's architectural knowledge, estimated it would be large enough for two main manufacturing centers that were similar in size to the ones currently in the North Pole, two warehouses, the Elven Training School and a large bunkhouse or dormitory with three floors and a few buildings scattered on the woodland fringe for eateries and such.

Whitey questioned if Santa would want a small workshop in this area. Susan said she could work something in.

The second area they picked was located in North

Carolina. It, too was a grassy bald, smaller than the first, but adequate enough for the Visiting Center. Mary, Kelly and Susan went over several possibilities of what would fit and where. They were on their fifth draft of possibilities already. The area would be able to support most of what they needed with some structures again placed on the forest fringe after moving a few trees. With Mary's love of fauna, and the North Pole's ingenuity, long ago they had learned how to remove and replant the largest tree without causing any damage to the living organism. They had done it many times in the Woodland Area, as some nursery sections had to be thinned out to optimize growing conditions.

These would be easier, as they were not nearly the size or complexity of those in the Woodland Area. By relocating a handful of trees and shrubs they could make room for many of the supporting shops and restaurants that currently serviced their visitors and elves.

Kelly thought it was imperative that they keep the overall flavor of the existing Visiting Center with the various architectural styles and colors. Both Mary and Susan agreed, with Susan stating, "The very first thing that struck me when we arrived was the riot of colors and variety of roof lines and looks of each structure. It was more surprising to me than the elves, themselves. I definitely want to keep that overall feel and look."

Whitey, Bill, Jim, Rudy and Rory were measuring and remeasuring each section and Whitey and Jim kept consulting their notes for what would be needed and where it made sense to put it. Part of the problem of splitting into three separate areas is that each section would need its own utilities and three of everything including waste disposal, storage – both cold and hot water, roads, building materials, etc. It became like building three villages instead of one, and presented more than three times the problems and needs.

They thought it would be better than trying to 'put all our eggs into one smaller basket' as Jim put it. Bill's engineering skills began to play a vital role now as he was laying out the optimal angles and flows to each respective sight. Making suggestions and observations based on the geology they were looking at.

Constructing three domes wouldn't be a problem said Jim, but trying to fit everything to a tee, and to place and keep the vital parts like water mains and pipes, might prove interesting.

"We will have to place any outside pipes deep enough so they are not discovered or tripped over," said Rory.

They had already placed a tremendous amount of data into their tablets, and commented that it would take a small army upon their return to pull everything out of their electronic notebooks. Rudy commented, "Thank goodness Mac and Ion came up with these a few decades ago, they are a whole lot better than paper and pens we were using."

Jim laughed and said his was far more recent, and he was trying to figure out half the applications and uses for it, but agreed it was far less bulky and more efficient than the old way of doing things.

Mary had planned to return to the North Pole by tomorrow at the latest. She was ready to get back and begin finalizing plans and implementing their ideas in a more solid form. Besides, she was missing her husband and wanted more information on what had taken place there.

Nick had told her that indeed the storm did seem to solidly freeze the village again. Preliminary inspections of the Woodland Area showed signs of stabilizing the ice and that core measurements showed deeper ice than previous samples. In fact, Bilge thought they might have gained more than the two extra weeks hoped for, depending on how warm the surrounding spring might be. Proving their plan was a good one.

Nick told her that she would be able to return to the greenhouse and salvage what she could. He said that since the help had been coordinated for now in the village that April had asked Ella for a couple days to help pack up what she could there.

Ella had mentioned to Nick how she was grooming April to take over the communications, in the event of problems later. She did this to also get Nick's approval, which he gave reluctantly, saying it was too soon to make those types of contingencies.

Mary advised the rest of the group that if anyone wished to stay they could, but that she planned to head back no later than tomorrow morning. Whitey said he wanted to return also and truly see how the village was doing in the aftermath of the storm. He suggested that Jim and the other elves might want to begin mapping out the nacelles for the dome after reviewing some more measurements.

"Actually, I would like to talk with a few people back

at the village before I do much more," said Jim. "I want
to get a better idea about the size of three cold fusion
plants, and talk with Britney about water needs and so
on."

Bill wanted to go back with Whitey and Mary, as did
Susan and Kelly, if only to look again at the structures
and parts of the village as it stood now. Bill said they
could return after a few days and begin designing the
new town center and various satellites of the village
with his wife and Kelly.

So it was decided that everyone would return albeit
briefly, and the rest of the day was spent frantically
getting last minute measurements and cramming ideas
down to compare to the North Pole establishment when
they got back.

Later that evening they returned to the Charlotte DC
and found Char. Mary thanked her for the use of the van
and they recounted what they had decided and gave a
description of the new boroughs they had decided upon.
Char was impressed with their ideas and thought it wise
since the village would be more exposed to split it into
multiple entities and locations.

Char asked if they could stay for dinner and would
like to take advantage of the guest quarters they had on
site. Mary gave a quick glance to those around her and
she thanked Char genuinely, but said they were in a
hurry to return to the North Pole and their duties up
there.

They regathered into the two groups they came in
and Mary and Whitey focused on the Train Station in
the village and instantly vanished.

Chapter 41

Homecoming

The village felt quite a bit cooler than when they had left and they each hurried to their destination the moment they appeared at the station. Only a few people were out and about and they scarcely noticed the groups return. Mary estimated that the village was at 32°F and said as much.

"Freezing is freezing no matter what, so see you in the morning," called out Kelly and she was moving as fast as she could across the snow to the inn.

Mary decided that there was little chance Nick was in the village house so again she closed her eyes and thought hard about the foyer of their woodland home. She popped away from the station and appeared inside their front door.

Bill commented again to Susan about how convenient it would be to learn that trick as they did their best to keep up with Kelly.

Within a few moments everyone was snug and safe where they needed to be. None of them would venture out again until morning.

When Mary walked into the kitchen, Nick jumped out of his chair saying, "I have a mirage before me!"

Mary laughed and said, "I am as real as they come. Hello my hubby."

They embraced and Nick kissed her. He said, "I sure hope we never have to make a habit of being apart like that. I almost went mad."

Michael came around the corner and said, "I thought I heard you, Mom. Are you hungry? I have some leftovers from dinner because Kristopher ate in the village before coming home."

"Famished," answered his mother. "And sick of restaurant food, it will be nice to taste your cooking again."

"We weren't expecting you before tomorrow," said Nick smiling. "I'm glad you came back early."

As Mary removed her coat she said, "I couldn't stand not knowing what was going on here, and there was so much I couldn't discuss down there. I needed to talk with you and hear what was happening with my three men."

Nick and Michael laughed and both commented that they had been hiding like ferrets with a fox outside their den because of the weather. "I never appreciated the dome nearly as much as I have in the last few days," said Michael.

Mary smiled and said, "I must say except for one morning, we had delightful weather down south. A little cool, but compared to here, not uncomfortable. Oh Nick, I think the elves are truly going to love it there. It is starting to bud with flowers and leaves with the brightest shade of green you have ever seen."

"After you are fed and changed into something more relaxed, we would love to hear about it, right Michael?" asked Nick.

"Indeed," her son replied. "Dad has told me a few things. I'll call Kristopher, as I am sure he'd like to hear this too." He was pulling out dishes from the refrigerator and in between he opened his phone to call.

Nick picked up Mary's suitcase and ushered her into the bedroom. As she entered the room she was surprised to see the bed neatly made and nothing laying around. Nick was always neat and his mother, Annie, made numerous comments about how he always picked up after himself, unlike his father. However, she couldn't help but ask, "You haven't been sleeping in that chair of yours, have you?"

"No, except for the second night of the storm," he confessed, "It was so bad I couldn't sleep well, but only that one night. It sure is good to have you back again."

He set the luggage on the bed and went to her and hugged her again, "I've missed you so much."

"Me, too," and she kissed him again. "We accomplished a great deal down there and everyone was pleased to head back, but it will only be temporary. I think everyone wants to get started on this as soon as possible."

The Fredrick's dashed into the hotel and went straight to the fireplace, suitcases in hand. Christel saw them walk in and waved. She picked up the phone briefly and spoke into it. When she hung up she walked over to the fireplace and asked Bill and Susan if she could get them something warm.

Kelly had already dashed up to her room and was planning to take a nice warm bath. Christel advised them of this, but said of course the kitchen was open if they'd like some dinner. Bill, never one to turn down a meal, said he would love whatever the inn had cooked up. Susan smiled at Bill and said to Christel that yes, she would like some dinner.

"If you don't mind there is another couple coming down for a bite to eat, also," said Christel. "If it is alright, I'd like to put you at the same table and serve you at the same time."

The couple shrugged and said it was fine by them. Christel called a bell elf to take their suitcase and showed them to a table in the corner of the dining room. They sat down and Christel asked what they would like to drink, and they both requested a hot cocoa to take the chill off.

Before Christel could return with their cocoa, Jared and Julie walked around the corner and Jared said, "Excuse me, are these seats taken?"

Bill and Susan jumped up and gave their parents huge hugs. Susan said, "How did you get here? I thought you said you hadn't been invited?"

"We got the call a couple days after we spoke with you," replied Julie, "Apparently they needed to get hold of those more vital to the new village first."

Jared said he wanted to hear about their trip to the new location and what they thought of Mrs. Claus. And Bill said that would be fine as long as they told them what happened with the storm after learning that the Gradys had arrived before it hit.

Christel came with the Fredrick's cocoa and took an order for Kona coffee from Jared and Julie asked, "Is it still true that we won't put on any weight if we are up here?"

Christel laughed and said, "It's still the truth."

"Then I'll have a large chocolate shake," Julie said smiling.

"We have a beautiful prime rib standing by for dinner. Jared and Bill, I assume medium rare, and Susan and Julie would like medium?" asked the elf.

They nodded and Bill said, "Extra horseradish with mine, please."

She was off again and Jared said, "Julie and I have never been to the Appalachians, what's it like?"

And with that Bill and Susan began their tale of what took place, about Kelly, Whitey and the others, and of course a lengthy discussion about Mary that would have made her blush several shades of red if she'd been in the room.

Two hours later still drinking coffee and cocoa on the sofas in the lobby, the Gradys and Fredricks were caught up with each others exploits. The Gradys had also found out how Bill's parents were doing and what would probably be next in the events of the village move. Julie asked how soon they might be going back.

"We didn't decide today, but I think after Kelly, Miss Mary and I have a chance to make some notes and plans about the Visiting Center and a couple other places here, we will be heading back to the mountains," answered Susan. "Maybe a couple days at most."

Bill added, "And Whitey mentioned he'd like my help from an engineering standpoint figuring out much of the laying out of the water and electrical systems to the various locations."

Jared sat back and shook his head saying, "I'll bet neither of you would have ever, in your wildest imaginations, thought you would both be playing a vital role to Santa, Mrs. Claus, and the elves of the North Pole."

"Yeah, too bad I'll never be able to put this on my resume," Bill chuckled. "They would have me committed in an instant!"

Susan chimed in, "But you're right, I never thought for a moment that something this magical would take place. And speaking of magical, we have one more piece of news we would like to share with you."

After learning they would soon be grandparents both Julie and Jared jumped up and gave their kids hearty hugs and Jared called Christel over and asked, "I know that the North Pole is alcohol free, but do you have something a little more festive than coffee and cocoa to celebrate our coming grandchild?"

Christel smiled, officially congratulated and hugged Bill and Susan and said, "I might have something that could work." And she went back to the kitchen. A few moments later she came out with Sparkling Cider and four glass flutes. She popped open and poured the cider, and again congratulated them on the news.

As they drank a toast and started laying out plans for when the baby was due to arrive and what would need to be done ahead of time, Susan thought that there couldn't be a more perfect place to release the news to her folks. She also felt a twinge of remorse that Bill's parents couldn't be there also. But this was the perfect place, in light of everything going on, to celebrate a new life coming to the world, and a new delivery for Santa.

Chapter 42

An Important Discovery

The next morning another North Pole resident returned and as soon as he had dropped off his charges and luggage, he popped himself over to the Kringle's home and knocked on the door. Nick opened and said, "Hello, Forrest, Mary and I were asking each other if we had heard from you. Come on in."

Forrest said, "Thank you, Santa. I just now returned and I wanted to make my report as soon as I could. But I have a favor to ask. Could you invite Whitey over and that tallfolk person that is working on the dome with him? The one I heard made the improvements to it? I need to ask them something."

Nick did as the elf requested and asked, "What's this about, do you want them to make a similar structure to keep the animals in – or out of the new village?"

Mary came in and offered Forrest some apple fritters that she had made for breakfast. Forrest humbly took a couple saying he hadn't had time for breakfast and was most appreciative. He began telling the Clauses about his trip to Atlanta with the fox and hares and how they reacted down there.

There came another knock on the door and moments later Michael walked in with Jim Atherton. Nick introduced the two and gave Forrest a little background info on Jim. Finally Kristopher entered with Whitey and joked to his father about whether he should secure the council chambers for their guests.

After the last of the fritters were gone and a little idle conversation had ensued, Forrest picked up his story again backing it up so that the rest of the room could follow where he was going. He said, "Every time I took them out toward the forest the animals became agitated and would begin acting up, and the minute I got them back inside they settled right back down."

He paused for a moment to drink some coffee and continued, "So I came back here to pick up a penguin and learned from Dewey that all the animals had run off during the storm, which made no sense to me, as I thought they would all feel safer here than out in the wilderness. Luckily Dewey said that the reindeer and horses seemed fine, but it got me to wondering."

"My penguins are gone?" asked a distressed Mary Claus.

"Some have already returned Miss Mary," said Forrest.

"Relax my dear, they will find their way home. Go on, Forrest," said Nick beginning to catch a glimpse of where he thought this might be leading.

We had a polar bear cub, whose mother had wandered off before the storm with her other cub. So I took the cub down to Atlanta to see what would happen. When I took the cub outside a distance, the exact same thing took place, it was everything I could do to keep the little fella calm when we went for a walk and he was mewing for his mother as if I had introduced him to a killer whale. But in the warehouse he was as calm and gentle as a newborn kitten."

Forrest turned to Whitey and Jim, "Is there something inherent in the dome that somehow works like the magnetism of the North Pole. Perhaps a calming influence of some sort?"

Jim answered first saying, "I believe the two are unrelated anomalies as the dome does not use or require any magnetic properties. At least the one I constructed didn't, isn't that true with yours Whitey?"

Whitey shook his head and said, "Yes, mine uses none at all."

Jim looked at Nick and questioned, "How long have some of the elves been living at the various DC's?"

Nick said that his father and the council began setting up the warehouses as long ago as he'd begun using reindeer. "Some have been there quite a long time like 60 or 70 years, before they express a desire to return. Could be we have some down there since the start, I really couldn't say."

"There's your answer, and you may now put a major concern to rest across the village." Jim slapped his leg and murmured, "I'll be..."

Whitey's eyes got big and he said breathlessly, "Are you saying...?"

Jim nodded and said, "It was never the magnetism of the North Pole, it has always been the properties of the dome that has determined the longevity of your lives. I would guess if you took a survey you would also learn that the lack of illness, weight issues, and the like are due to the dome properties."

"Then that means that nothing will change once we move to the Smokies!" exclaimed Mary. "Oh, how wonderful!"

"We must call a Council meeting at once and make sure everyone here in the North Pole Village and across the world at the DC's knows about this," said Whitey with a broad grin.

Nick stood and held up his hand saying, "Hold on a minute. I am as excited as the rest of you about this news, but I believe we must find a way to confirm this before announcing it to the world. Is there some sort of test we could run?"

Forrest said, "Actually, in many ways I think that's what I did with these animals. You wouldn't have believed how they reacted down there, and when I learned that the other animals ran away up here, I discovered it was shortly after they turned off the dome properties to await the coming storm. Animals have far keener senses than we do about these things. I think that is why we have never had a mishap including with the most dangerous animals here. It's because of the dome and its properties."

Jim agreed and said, "And your own elves prove it, living for decades down south without a change in their aging or getting sick. I think you have had your experiments, and never knew you were conducting them. I would be positive in the hypothesis put forth, that it is the dome, more so than the magnetism of the Pole, that affects things. Especially as Topo and Bilge advised you that the magnetic north moves hundreds of miles every year."

Santa thought again for a moment and Kristopher
said to his father, "Wouldn't it be better to announce
this now and allay the fear that is the underlying tone of
the village, even if it is unspoken most of the time?
Imagine what that could do for the overall morale."

Nick thought about Ella's concern and plans for
having April take over for that same reason and
wondered how many other elves were making similar
concessions. He looked at his wife and Mary nodded.
"Okay, I'll call Ella and tell her to organize an
emergency meeting tomorrow, but please nothing about
this until we have had time to formally announce it to
the Council members and draft a proper release."

They nodded and agreed.

Nick dared for the first time since this discussion
began to utter a long sigh. "Imagine," he said quietly.
"All this time the answer was already out there." A
thought hit him and he looked at Jim, "Are you sure
that your dome will have the same properties as ours?"

"I took the initial design and added to it, so whatever
was there before, is still there," Jim said confidently.

Again Nick sighed and said, "Thank you Forrest. You
alone have solved the greatest question we have had
about moving from the North Pole. You are to be
commended on your discovery. Please be at the Council
meeting tomorrow so I may give credit where it is due.
And of course I will need you there as also Jim, let's say
9:00, to address any dome questions along with Whitey."

Both nodded and said they would be pleased. With
that everyone adjourned, as each had many other things
needing to be done that day.

As soon as the room was cleared Mary came over and gave a big hug to Nick and said, "Can you believe it? It looks like our worst fear is over."

Nick nodded and said softly, "Our work will go on."

Chapter 43

The Head of the Snake

In Eagle River, Wisconsin, Cory had been amassing tons of electronic data per Paul Shelton's instructions. Almost immediately after kissing Katy and his kids hello, he was on the phone to Paul. He relayed the information in great waves and Paul had already begun drafting a cease and desist letter to Phillip Weazle in his head before the conversation was half way through.

As Cory relayed what had been happening, Paul worked on a list with Cory's help on which websites this despicable person had under his immediate control or influence. They had also prepared a list of 'the Weasel's' henchmen that Shelton was also preparing correspondence for, ordering them to cease any further attacks.

Paul had already added names like Robby Ellis and the Weasel's wife, Cynthia-Louise. Cory told him volumes about Jeffrey Krautmann, Nicolai Trolski, Alan Cagey, Scotty Konan and he discussed Jack Eastover, who Cory suspected to be a Weazle alias, and then Mickey O'Rourke, who ran a website that Weazle had administration capability, and used it often, censoring some members and deleting their comments, at the same time fueling other vicious comments. Here is where he allowed nasty comments directed to the schools former students and deleted any rebuttals they attempted to make.

At every turn, Shelton saw clearly how the two Weazles would manipulate opinions and place falsehoods using their minions. Phillip was the best at it doing this without actually personally signing his own name to it. "The Weasel" was actually a good name for him, as he was as crafty and cautious as he was mean spirited.

Cynthia-Louise was less sly about her posts and often signed her name, not caring who agreed with her or not, but making sure if you didn't, you would be burned in effigy for it. You could see that sometimes Phillip would attempt to undo the damage she would start, but other times he let her spout, seemingly not to care about the consequences.

Initially, the draft for the cease and desist was actually geared more toward Cynthia-Louise, rather than Phillip, as his poison was harder to place to his own hand. Paul was still looking for a way to include Phillip. He remembered Cory saying that Ion Crosswire and Mac Gelfeeney had talked about the computers ISPN address, and that it might tie Weazle to some of the other posts. Santa Nick had given Cory both their cell phones, and Cory passed them to Paul.

Paul called Mac Gelfeeney in Northern California. He told him about his concern and discussed the ISPN theory with him. Mac walked Paul through how he could determine if the addresses were one and the same.

"Bingo!" Paul fairly yelled. "They're a match!"

Mac explained how he could also find out who owned the various websites. Though Weazle had tried to hide his ownership, Gelfeeney was able to ascertain that yes,

Weazle was actually Jack Eastover, and that the website "Public Defender" was actually owned and operated by Weazle.

Under the Eastover moniker, Weazle had brought numerous accusations and falsehoods against Cory, Katy and the school, along with their "so-called Santa Claus". He had made brash statements accusing the school of fraud and improperly using every dollar they had collected from their "duped pupils". Of course, no shred of evidence was offered in any of these accusations, except for hearsay and innuendo, of which there was much. Further, the Public Defender had made multiple accusations against the bogus Santa Claus that the school had brought in each year. It made comments saying that the Santa was in cahoots with the school and the school wanted a large percentage of the earnings that the Santa students would make after attending.

When the students tried to debunk this saying that they were invited rather than charged, Weazle's compatriots would attack them, or on some sights their postings would suddenly 'disappear'. In the beginning, Paul Shelton scratched his head wondering what Cory could have done to cause such wrath from this individual. Searching through Weazle's records he finally found the answer to this mystery. Weazle, it turned out had a major stake in an enterprise called "The Mystery Of Santa Claus School" in Indiana that charged great sums of money to teach potential persons how to be Santa Claus. *So that's whats behind this. He deems this as competition, and this is his way of destroying it,* thought

Paul, *How petty can you get?*

Paul Shelton now had plenty, including motive, to establish legal action against both Weazles, but was under strict orders to do so only as a last resort. So Paul sent a six page letter to them outlining exactly what he had on their nefarious activities and their wrongful defaming of the school and its proprietors. He stated in no uncertain terms exactly what he planned to do with it if they did not remove any and all of these postings and cease making any further comments, immediately.

He called Nick and received his permission, after a lengthy discussion, explaining that the only way to show how serious they were would be to legally cease any further malicious action toward the school. It would send a very powerful message to Phillip Weazle and his spouse. He had sufficient evidence to bring an injunction against the Public Defender and cease its comments and malicious conduct against the Eagle River school. He showed the judge exactly the damage the comments of that website had upon the school, including the personal threats that followed, each directly quoting the Public Defender as the reason these people were threatening them. The injunction was issued that same afternoon.

Paul had secured the names and addresses of those sending the threats and also sent them a letter informing them that the authorities had been notified of their actions and messages and would be paying them a personal visit, especially if anything happened to either the Peters, or the school, or any of its former attendees.

Within a mere matter of days of Cory's return, a

flood of correspondence had ensued from the Law Office of Paul J. Shelton, and the State of Wisconsin with a promise of prosecution if activities of the Public Defender did not immediately cease, and a public apology for its defamation appear on its website within 30 days.

He had sent copies of everything to Cory and Katy and assured them that no matter what it took, or how long, he would have every activity against them stopped. He said he would fall like a ton of bricks onto the Weazles, or anyone else who had anything bad to say about the school, them, or Santa and Mrs. Claus.

Paul said the the snake's head was exposed and the machete would fall, if a reverse of all action wasn't enjoined in rapid order. And Paul assured them his aim was true.

Paul finally felt that, at long last, he was able to do at least a little payback for the years of law school, and assistance in starting his own law practice, he received from Nick and Mary Kringle. They wouldn't let him do any personal legal favors, and had said everything was already taken care of for them. And Paul had come along many years too late to assist in any of the business dealings he heard about between Nick and the many companies he later learned had been involved with the North Pole.

Of course that last part was fine with Paul, as he never cared for corporate law, and generally refrained from its practice, recommending other more proficient lawyers for those services. One thing he knew, he would never allow either the North Pole, or its residents to have any harm come to them if he had anything to say about it. And he blessed the day God made sure he didn't pitch that invitation into the trash.

To watch a special video with author Joe Moore scan the QR code!

PART THREE

THE GREAT ESCAPE

Obstacles are those

frightful things you see

when you take

your eyes off the goal.

Henry Ford

Chapter 44

Pulling Together

After meeting with the Council and announcing the news brought forth from Forrest, Jim and Whitey there was great celebration around the North Pole and beyond. In normal times they would have had a banquet to celebrate such a monumental discovery, but these were not normal times.

Shortly after the cleanup from the storm was finished, the North Pole Village looked like a bee hive in full swing. People were coming and going in every direction carrying boxes, crates and running squibbles throughout the town.

Tallfolk were in nearly every shop and home in the Visiting Center. Jared and Julie were helping out at "Santa's Friend Theodore," which was the shop and center that made each of the Teddy Bears that Santa would deliver. They packed box after box and Julie made sure to give each bear a special squeeze before packing it away.

They knew that Susan's bear that Marshall gave her from here was still one of her most treasured gifts ever received. It sat on her bed everyday and often times with her if she was lounging around. They both reflected on those days in the North Pole and how so much had taken place, and now they were going to be grandparents.

Fred Wu was helping George with the set up and materials of the reactors, since there were now three units being made. George halfheartedly complained when the request came, but in some ways was relieved that he had three opportunities to make the reactors. This way the entire load would not be dependent on only one unit.

Bill had met with Britney Clearwater and Jackson Killowatt about how best to lay out needs for each center as it was being constructed. Susan and Kelly went about taking notes and pictures of the current Visiting and Manufacturing Centers and discussing design ideas. Since there were forests encompassing the three potential locations, it was decided, after talking with Nick and Mary, to absorb the Woodlands Area into the other three areas.

Whitey had done an inspection of the Pole the morning following his return. He was truly pleased at how much the storm had helped and stabilized the foundation of the hamlet. He reported to Nick that the entire area seemed more like its old self again, albeit if only temporarily.

However it was now a realization to everyone that time was against them. The Spring Equinox had occurred and the sun was now a fixed ball in the sky gaining altitude with each passing 24 hour period. They would not see it set again until they had left the Pole for good. Temperatures would soon begin warming, and regardless if they kept the area under the dome at freezing, the vast ice sheets would begin melting around them.

Bilge and Topo were working feverishly trying to predict the future weather and the impact it would have and how long. The greatest variable was not knowing how much weight could be supported as the ice thinned beneath them and how fast that might happen. They looked at the ocean currents and their flow and tried to guesstimate when the warmer currents would swing through the area and how large an impact it would have on the floating village. They believed they had until June to safely escape a disaster, but were not convinced that some areas wouldn't begin slipping into the sea before then.

Since Topo Geosphere was the Village's chief geologist, he had also been requested to accompany Whitey, Bill and others in the initial designing of the new centers in the GSM. He said he would have to pop back and forth as there was too much at stake in both locations and needed to keep checking figures and plans at both.

Back at the Manufacturing Center, Thundersleigh had already been sent down to the Atlanta DC by Kristopher with another load. There were more than 100 elves working at each of the two manufacturing structures. The flurry of activity would have made any other normal person dizzy, but this was actually not anything out of the ordinary to the North Pole Village and it felt, at least in terms of activity, no different than a few days before Christmas.

Michael kidded to his group one day saying, "At least the good news is we don't have to gift wrap it all!" This

led to a huge wave of laughter across the large building
as his statement was passed along from elf to elf.

The morale was noticeably improved since the
announcement of the discovery of the protection of the
dome and the aging issue. Gone were the murmured
whispers of "What if?" and the contingency plans of
heirs and concerns of the children not living past their
parents.

Throughout the village songs were being sung, tunes
whistled and a general feeling of euphoria was spread
around the North Pole, each knowing that their legacy
and good works would continue. Of course there was
apprehension amongst those who had never been outside
the North Pole Village, or at least since coming here,
about what would lie before them and how they would
assimilate once outside.

There was a far greater chance of meeting up with
tallfolk that were different than the ones invited to the
village by Santa. They had heard the stories from those
who had lived beyond the Arctic Circle, and from others
who knew others, and so on. Many discussions centered
around the new concept of three different Village areas
and having to commute from one to the next. This
caused some concern about running into other tallfolk
and having to interact with them regularly.

Many said they would stay close to their home and
shop and not move about too much. Besides, they had
done the same thing already up in the Pole. Why change
now? They would be safe under the dome and, as before,
have no reason to venture out of their comfort zone.

Shop after shop and the personal belongings of the

elves were packed onto Thundersleigh. This cargo carrier was making as many trips as Supersleigh to the various DC's for unloading and staging.

So the work progressed at a quicker pace than Nick would have thought possible. Many of the visitors came in exhausted from their toils, and Christel, Fergie and the others took care of them in every way they could from providing food, to preparing their rooms for their nightly rest.

Each was glad to have their help and support. Every elf knew this would be a far more daunting task without their assistance. None of the visitors uttered a word of dissatisfaction. Though the work was continuous and difficult, they were happy to be a part of this monumental effort and each thought how they could tell their grandchildren how they helped Santa and Mrs. Claus relocate the North Pole.

After a couple days, as Mary predicted, those from the trip before, along with several other elves offering assistance to erect the dome, met at the hangar area. This time they took Firesleigh down to the Charlotte DC. Bill had kidded Mary that he was getting used to going by way of the time continuum. Mary said it wasn't a good thing to get to used to and thought a more conventional transportation mode was in order, especially considering the number of people and equipment that was needed for this trip. Julie asked if the North Pole had to file flight plans and such to the FAA for their forays to the south.

An elf was moving toward the cockpit with short cropped brown hair and a thin mustache. He had a bright intelligent look to his eyes and as he looked at someone they were drawn to those deep brown eyes. His name was Willie Movinmuch and although he looked quite old, he also looked powerful. Willie addressed Julie's question saying, "Actually Miss, we had developed a greater stealth technology than your country has today. It was built into every aircraft we have at the North Pole, so we can come and go as we please, and except for occasionally being spotted briefly by a commercial airplane, we fly unnoticed from the FAA and your military, or any other government on this earth."

"Don't the other planes radio in when they spot you?" Julie pressed Willie wanting to know more.

"More often than not we are reported as UFO's, especially as we travel quite a bit faster than any commercial plane could or would be allowed. We used to pass the Concorde Supersonic jets when we were in a hurry. It is rumored that some of America's biggest aerospace companies are already on the drawing board with some ideas we incorporated several decades ago."

Now this piqued Bill's interest and he said, "Really, like what?"

Willie gave him a smile and said, "Perhaps another time, but right now I have to get all of you down to Charlotte, so I need to go to my office." He gave them a salute and headed to the front of the plane.

What Willie said was proven shortly after take off when an hour later he said they would be landing in Charlotte, North Carolina and asked everyone please buckle up. Bill exclaimed, "That's amazing! It took us

three hours just to get from Seattle to Fairbanks! I
scarcely knew we were flying."

Mary said, "One more reason we can do the things we
do. If people knew the secrets of the North Pole and our
elves, they wouldn't be so skeptical of how we do what
we can. Look how many refuse to believe how reindeer
fly or how fast. Nick and his team can go faster than this
and have to have an envelope to protect them crossing
vast distances."

Bill shook his head and Kelly asked, "How do stand
dealing with the rest of the world when you are such an
advanced civilization yourself?"

Mary laughed. "Kelly you make us sound like aliens,
but to answer your question, we do what we do because
we love to do it. Pleasing children and helping others is
something that is in our nature. We truly do love people
especially the younger versions of them."

As the wheels touched the ground, the plane came to
an immediate halt. Mary said, "Time to load up, we're
here."

Char had secured a couple more vans from the local
car rental office nearby and the groups became a
caravan to the mountains. As the group moved up the
mountains several made comments about how much
change had happened in a few short days. The trees
were becoming a brilliant spring green and flowers
appeared everywhere they looked.

Those seeing it for the first time each expressed how
beautiful the area was and Mary smiled to herself
thinking, *They are truly going to love this place!*

When they reached the first area, although there was

no one in sight, they felt that time was definitely against them and the tourists would be coming soon. They wasted no time setting up the parameter of the first settlement and laying out the dimensions of the manufacturing center as they had planned.

Bill began taking survey measurements with the laser theodolite he got from one of the elves and mapped out the angles for the pumping system that Britney gave him the measurements on and had demonstrated to him up north. Like most things in the elven village, it was more sophisticated and needed far less mass than anything he had learned about down south.

The new electric station with its cold fusion plant would be slightly smaller than what they had currently, and was much smaller than anything that could produce nearly as much wattage in the 'tall' world as he now referred to it, copying the elves.

By mid-afternoon, the first of the nacelles was being drilled into the ground. Once placed only a small cap would be visible and to any passerby, it would resemble a smooth faced beige stone, like so many other rocks laying around the surface of the bald. Of course, if for any reason they tried to pick it up, it would not budge a centimeter.

Jim had worked with Whitey adding the improvements he demonstrated in Atlanta to the pods at the North Pole. They had a total of 28 nacelles including four extra, in case anything was amiss. Jim was showing Whitey how to adjust the height and depth of the dome 'walkway' for tourists after they placed the second nacelle.

By 4:30 that afternoon, they had laid four of the
needed eight nacelles for the dome and Whitey said that
would be good until tomorrow. They packed up the
equipment and loaded up the van. Since it was only late
March, the hotels had plenty of room for the band of
travelers and no one commented about the stature of
the elves. *A good sign*, Mary thought.

The next day, exactly three weeks to the day Whitey
was asked by Santa how long it would take to get the
new village dome up, they launched the controls and the
first of the three domes was operational. Bill, Susan,
and Kelly stood stunned for a moment and then began
acting as if they were children testing out a new
playground dashing in and out, touching the hard
surfaces that were to repel uninvited visitors, and
basically playing hide and seek.

After a little time, Mary said, "Okay kids, lets get a
move on to Site B and begin work on the Visiting Center
Area."

Bill gave his best "Aw shucks, Mom" and acted
totally deflated. This brought laughter from everyone
and Mary threw up her arms in mock despair and said,
"Kids!" They had a good laugh over it and started
assembling the equipment again.

An hour later they were at it again, pulling out the
laser distance meters and other survey equipment and
measuring out the distance of the new area. Like the
first area this would also take eight nacelles. On the way
over Bill asked why they were called that, "When I first
heard that term I immediately thought of the fuselage
of an airplane, but I'd never heard the term used outside

of that."

Whitey said, "Exactly like an engine housing on a plane, spacecraft or ship, this 'nacelle' houses all the proponents of the engine used to hide and protect the village. Originally the word is French for 'small boat' and we like to think of the dome as our own private ark. It may not be little, but it sure has kept us afloat for centuries." He smiled at the end of his comment.

As Bill and Susan were working with Mrs. Claus down south, Santa had put their parents to work overseeing the delicate but needed items elsewhere. Because of his leadership skills and compassion for all things North Pole, Jared Grady was asked to help lead the packing and moving of the Woodland Area as quickly as possible. Since the storm had refrozen the area, everyone concerned wanted to take a shot at moving any belongings they could before the ice began to melt again.

Rather than get involved personally, Mary Claus placed April in charge of removing anything she thought salvageable from the greenhouse after the last sinking. Several plants and a couple tables were lost in that event, but April saw that there were plenty of pots, seeds and tools that could be saved and moved south. With the help of a couple visiting elves from the Southern California DC, the band worked quickly to get everything out. Not only because they were worried about the framework giving away again, but the fact that they were not used to such cold temperatures coming from a warm climate and wanted to return to the makeshift inn, which was much warmer.

Several places like the hot cocoa shop, the Skating

Party shop that kept a large supply of ice skates, sleds, toboggans, skis and the like were crated up and moved to the hanger area. This shop owned by Edward Elfman would be moving to the new resort area along with the cocoa shop in the new settlement.

The Kringles had decided to move their home to the new Visiting Center as they did as much there as the Manufacturing or Woodland Area and there was more room to rebuild a home similar to their grand edifice of the North Pole. Surprisingly, Kristopher had asked if it would be possible to have a small home of his own in the Manufacturing Area. They agreed and told Susan to please add that into her architectural plans for that section.

Michael was comfortable at his parents home wherever it was, and thought moving to the Visiting Area was a great idea.

Everything was moving at a strong clip and every other day one or two aircraft took off to the closer DC's of Charlotte, Atlanta and now Birmingham, Alabama, as the others were filling up and Atlanta needed to leave room for the coming of the "Polar Ark" as they were calling it.

To that end Forrest was making a short list. He knew he couldn't bring all the reindeer he wanted, as there were hundreds. He also knew that because the area wouldn't be filled with ice and snow that much fewer would be needed. He was worried about what would happen to the reindeer as they lost their habitat to the sea. He knew many would head south if only because that was their only choice. But he also knew that many might perish if they did not migrate quickly enough.

His same concern extended to the Polar bears, seals and other Arctic forms of life. A few groups from the United States and Canada were trying to come up with solutions, but nothing was being resolved quickly enough.

He had decided he truly would have to be like Noah of long ago and resolved himself to bring a mating pair of each species beyond the reindeer, sled dogs and horses. This was everything he could allow himself to bring to the new village. Further, unlike the North Pole, they would have to remain in the new zoo area as he couldn't allow Arctic wolves and polar bears to wander around the Smoky Mountains unabated.

With his limitations set, he popped in and out of Atlanta getting the temporary housing for each species set. He and Dewey Antlerhorn drew up plans with Kelly for the new Petting Zoo at the Visiting Center after discussing size and needs with Miss Mary, Whitey and a few others.

Things were progressing well thought Nick Kringle and he was pleased that everyone was ahead of schedule and would be moved before the crisis date, or so he thought. It was now time to talk with Ion Crosswire about Phase Two of the operation.

Chapter 45

The Cloaking Devise

"Hello Santa," said Ion as he entered the Clauses home once more. He had spent many visits and hours in the home of the Kringles, and wished as they did, that somehow they could move the entire structure down to the Smokies.

Nick asked if he could get him something to eat or drink, but Ion said he had breakfast at the bunkhouse and was fine.

"I know you already can guess what I wish to ask, so I will," said Nick. "How goes Phase Two? Have you come up with a plan?"

Ion smiled and said, "I would say I have most of the problem figured out, and some parts already constructed."

Santa said, "Let's not keep it a secret, what have you figured out?"

Ion settled back into the chair and said, "To recap the problem and make sure I have everything you are concerned about addressed, here is what you asked: 'How do we keep a huge caravan of trucks bringing everything from possessions to building supplies, food, sundries and people secret, or at least not drawing a huge amount of attention?' Am I right?"

Nick had worked with Ion long before he was Santa

Claus, and knew that Ion could drag out any issue into a long diatribe, but eventually he would get to the point, one only required patience. So Nick sighed and said, "That's it exactly."

Ion folded his hands and said, "I think we need to do deal with this as a military operation. And the best way is to use the cover of darkness for a good portion of the way and cloak the vehicles when they make their final approach."

Nick looked at the elf and asked, "Cloak the vehicles? How?"

"Let's start with the first part. We schedule the trucks to leave their various departure areas so that they will arrive at night in the mountains. We have vehicles that will work as leads to bring them toward their debarkation destinations. The drivers of the follow vehicles will drive without lights and use these." He held up sunglasses and handed them to Nick.

"You want them to wear sunglasses at night?" he asked in disbelief.

"Actually, sir, they are night vision goggles that have been made lighter and far more effective than anything we created thus far. Those are your personal pair with bifocals, so you can read in the dark if you need to. Everything will appear as if it were daylight with a cloudy sky through these. Each driver and assistant will wear a pair and they will have no trouble seeing everything." Ion was gaining excitement.

"What about oncoming traffic? If they can't see the vehicles without their lights, we could end up with a nasty accident," said Nick with concern.

"Hence the lead vehicles," Ion explained. "Any oncoming vehicles will see the lead with its lights and make corrections before coming to the other trucks. Once they pass the first truck, they will be aware of the others following, lights on or off."

Nick nodded and said, "Okay, you said the first part. What's next?"

"Would you be up to a short walk, so I can more effectively show you something?" asked Ion.

Nick could see Ion would be crushed if he refused, so he said, "Sure, why not?" and got up to get his coat. Once they were both prepared for the colder temps outside Ion began walking toward the footbridge that crossed the stream in front of the Kringles grand home and workshop.

As they reached the footbridge Ion asked, "Santa could you wait here for a moment?"

Nick did as the elf requested and watched as Ion went to the bridge and promptly...disappeared. Nick laughed his Ho, Ho, Ho and yelled to Ion, "Is this more dome magic?"

Ion reappeared on the other side of the bridge and answered, "Similar and from part of that design. It won't deflect objects the way the dome does, and its area of effectiveness is limited to about a 100 yards, but it will effectively hide any vehicles coming or going from the road."

Nick was pleased but asked, "Now what about any other traffic using the road, how will we keep them from becoming suspicious?"

He watched Ion begin to cross the bridge again and

this time he could see the elf clearly as he walked across. He held up a little hand-held remote and clicked the button and disappeared from sight again. As he came out the other side he said, "As you can see I have created remotes to turn the cloaking devise on and off."

"Cloaking devise? Ho, ho, HO! This is marvelous," Nick said with glee. "This should easily keep any suspicions to a minimum. Congratulations, Ion, you've done it again!"

Ion blushed and said, "The technology was already there. I adapted the pulse and changed the wavelength to match..."

"Whoa there my brilliant elf, I could never keep up with your explanations, nor do I wish to. But I always know who to call when I have a thorny issue that needs resolution," crowed Nick. "And once more you have proved me right."

Ion blushed again and Nick said he wanted to show Mary the new cloaking devise. On their way back to the home Nick suggested that perhaps there was a way to adapt this to his Christmas Eve visits.

"Already done," Ion said with a grin.

Chapter 46

Santa to the Rescue

With the problem of secrecy and moving about addressed, Nick now turned to the army of people he was going to need to rebuild the North Pole into three areas. He needed everything from ditch diggers to truck drivers. Though the elves could do much of the carpentry, plumbing, electrical, etc., Nick knew he needed far more hands than he had available to do this monumental job quickly.

No matter how grave the situation, they could not skip a year of delivering presents on Christmas Eve, and that took many months to prepare for under the best of circumstances. To miss a delivery would cause his ancestors to roll in their graves, or wherever they were.

Nick called Cory in part to hear the progress that had been made, but also to discuss this with him again. After a brief exchange of pleasantries Cory opened up the discussion saying, "It seems that we forced 'The Weasel' to stop his activities and pull much of the offending discussions off the Internet. We even managed a weak, but nonetheless sincere apology from him on several sites including Public Defender. The worst may be over. Something did pop up for several days from his clueless wife, but disappeared after that. I can only guess she put it up without Weazle knowing about it and when he

discovered it he yanked it from the internet or had her
pull it off."

"Have the threats stopped?" Nick asked.

"Entirely," Cory answered with a sigh. "And we had
several Santas 're-up' for the next set of classes, and a
few extra filled up the last class we finished. We had
several emails and phone calls immediately following the
apology, congratulating us on being able to stem the
flow of poison. We have been consulted to help some of
the groups on stemming the jealousy and nasty
attitudes going on in their ranks."

"I hope you are not going to get involved in that kind
of political turmoil," Nick stated hesitantly.

"Oh, perish the thought, Santa," Cory insisted.
"That's a quagmire of problems unto itself. I have no
interest in joining or getting involved in anything that
supports that much ego and envy. Besides I think Katy
would have my head if I merely suggested it after what
we went through. I merely bring it up as a point of
interest. So how goes the move?"

"That's the other thing I wanted to discuss with
you," Nick began. "I think it's time we try rallying some
additional help for the new settlement. Are there any
Santa Ambassadors you can think of that might help
out for the next couple months? Especially any that
could drive a truck, swing a hammer, or work with pipes
and electric, which is what we need most?"

For the next half hour, they spoke of general needs
and a few individuals and Cory finally said, "Katy and I
will get on the phone and begin calling. No promises
here, but you know over the past decade we have had a

lot of men and women come through our doors. I am sure that I can get several of them to help out, especially when I tell them they would be helping the real Santa and Mrs. Claus erect a new North Pole."

"Of course, make certain they know we would cover the board and lodging for as long as they would be willing to help out," said Nick. "We would probably put them up in Gatlinburg or Cherokee."

"That, I am sure, will sweeten the pot," Cory said enthusiastically. "Is there a limit of how many you would be willing to take?"

"Ho, ho, ho, Cory," Nick bellowed. "You just bring me everyone you can, and I will worry about the limit we can take!"

"I will be back to you in two days time and give you a preliminary count of volunteers." With that the two men said their goodbyes.

Two days later as he said, Cory called and said, "I have your preliminary count."

Nick said, "I sure hope you were successful as I have been doing some heavy calculations over the last couple days."

Cory said, "We are waiting for a handful of people to get back to us, but so far you are up to 564 total volunteers with another 30 or so that will get back to us."

"564!" Nick yelled. "That's unbelievable! How did you do this? I had no idea we had that many Ambassadors," Nick said dumbfounded.

"Think about it Santa Nick. We have been doing this for going on eleven years and more or less have had 100

or more students each year. Frankly, I am disappointed
we couldn't get more, but a lot of them have other jobs,
and some said they were too old to help out. Others said
they had no skills and would probably do more harm
than good, but to send you their best wishes and
prayers," Cory explained.

"What skills do some of them have, do we know?"
asked Nick.

"I have everything broken out as follows" said Cory
and he read from his list.

Truck Drivers - 27
Plumbers - 7
Electriticians - 6
Carpenters - 18
Painters - 21
Cabinetry - 3
General Workers - 238
General Maintenance - 130
Woodturners - 9
Craftmen/women - 11
Cooks - 42
Engineers - 19
Undeclared - 37

Total Volunteers - 564

"I sent you an email now of everything I read you,"
he concluded.

Nick said how that was so much more than he could
have hoped and began laughing. When Cory asked him
what the joke was he said, "I was thinking, I assume
that most of the men look somewhat like me with white
beards and long hair. Imagine the confusion this could

cause working in the village."

"Never mind that," laughed Cory. "Imagine each of these Santa and Mrs. Clauses walking around in Cherokee or Gatlinburg!"

"It will probably be both, due to the number you recruited," chuckled Nick. "Send me the list of names and I'll have Ella and April start working on the hotels and transportation. Looks like we will have to secure buses also!"

Cory said, "I would plan for about 30 more when making the reservations. Also, most said they were available for two months, but some could only do two weeks. I used the timetable of May 15th until July 31st when talking with them."

"Send me everything you have and we will work it out. Also if we can stagger some of them to come later...oh nevermind, we will work it out," Nick said , his mind reeling from the sheer number of volunteers.

Cory was pleased that he was able to make such a difference in Santa Nick's plans and said, "I guess you can say, Santa to the rescue! This could be the start of something exciting."

Nick shook his head, smiling and said, "Indeed."

CHAPTER 47

GREAT SMOKY MOUNTAINS
OR BUST

Kristopher had finished shipping his building contents, so he went to help Michael with his. Michael had managed to get more than three fourths of the center packed and shipped and they were still disassembling some of the bigger machines. Michael asked his brother, "What do you think we will be doing once we get this finished?"

Kristopher answered, "I, for one, would like to go to the new manufacturing site and help with the planning and building of the new manufacturing buildings."

"If we have a choice, I would rather stay up here and help some of the other elves get organized and packed," responded Michael. "I heard from Pepper Windenrain we are in for a warmer than usual spring. We may be cutting this close."

Following the big blizzard, temperatures had warmed into the 40's and actually hit the 50° mark a few times. Though they kept the village under the dome a brisk 32°, the perimeter of the sea ice was beginning to make a further retreat under the warm days.

"I heard dad is sending Thundersleigh down every couple days now to Charlotte and Birmingham," Michael informed Kristopher.

"Now that I finished, Forrest is packing the Supersleigh for the trip to Atlanta," Kristopher added, "He also built enclosures for some of the bigger animals in the dome that Jim Atherton built down there for his tests."

"Speaking of domes, have you heard how goes the efforts on that?" Michael wondered.

"Dad said they have the three domes placed and have been doing a little tweaking to adjust the amount of height and depth for any wandering travelers," said Kristopher, "In fact, I heard that one hiker actually walked right through the dome as they were making the adjustments, so they used him as a guinea pig on the acclimatization as he marched through."

"If the domes are ready, do you know if they have begun construction?" asked Michael.

"From what I picked up, a bunch of people including Whitey and several of the tallfolk have begun grading the place and laying pipes for the Manufacturing Area," answered Kristopher, "It won't take them too long to begin building the structures once that's done."

One of the elves walked up to Kristopher laughing and said, "You should see what a couple of the talls and elves did to the cargo jets. You really need to visit the hanger." He moved on to tell the other elves in earshot.

Michael shrugged and said, "I could use a break."

Kristopher agreed and they walked toward the hanger on the other side of the now empty building Kristopher had recently finished.

Because of the design of the cargo jets, there was no actual runway, just a patch of concrete large enough to support the planes. As massive as these planes were, they had a unique propulsion system that when fully loaded, lifted them vertically without a rolling start. This also allowed them to land at any DC with a minimum of area. Being able to takeoff and land from anywhere further kept the various DC's concealed, since no long tarmacs had to accompany each center and most had a domed hangar little more than the size of a large helipad.

There were several elves and a couple of people walking out of the hangar smiling and joking at the sight they witnessed.

As the two brothers walked into the hangar they began smiling also. Each plane had been completely repainted on the outside from nose to tail. Thundersleigh sported a beautiful panoramic view of the Smoky Mountains as Michael and Kristopher had seen it, only this scene was greener. Under the cockpit's window large letters were stenciled "Great Smoky Mountains or Bust!".

Supersleigh had been repainted with a rendition of Noah's Ark over a landscape of the North Pole. It carried an assortment of Arctic animals and reindeer. Under the window of this plane it declared itself to be "Forrest's Ark" in large bold letters.

Firesleigh had a rendition of the Visiting Center across its whole body complete with elves running back and forth with boxes, crates and luggage. It had been renamed "Movin' On Down" and had this in flowing script under its window.

The brothers couldn't help admire the works of art.

It had caused many to stare at each for long periods to see the immense detail of each diorama. After a time, Kristopher said it was time to get back to the building and finish dismantling the machine they had been working on.

On the way back, Michael commented on how much time it must have taken to repaint the huge jets. Kristopher responded that apparently some of the villagers had extra time on their hands and maybe this move was further along than they suspected.

Indeed, such was the case as many shops had already packed and moved their belongings south and were now helping others. Many of the elves that traveled north from their respective DC's had been released to return, and some of the tallfolk had gone back to their normal lives.

The trains were returning with mostly full loads of passengers to Fairbanks for departures to the various points south. Now it was time to begin the migration for the rest of the North Pole Village.

Chapter 48

Heading Out

If anyone needed extra motivation to leave the village, a few days later they received it. It began with a loud crack that sounded like lightning far too close for comfort. The rolling thunder that followed was the sound of Santa's Woodworks and several surrounding buildings crashing down and disappearing rapidly under the ice.

It had begun. Several cracks formed around the other buildings and Whitey Slippenfall had Ella issue a warning that declared the Woodland Area off limits to everyone. He called Santa from the new Manufacturing Area straight away with his report once he got the details.

"Thankfully everyone was out of the area and to my knowledge we lost no one with the buildings." Whitey was saying to Nick.

"How far do the cracks extend?" asked a concerned Santa Claus.

"About two-thirds of the way to the end of the Woodland Area. We will probably lose the greenhouse, cocoa shop and after that the reindeer stable. I can't say how soon," Whitey explained.

"Thank goodness Forrest had the sense to move the animals toward the Manufacturing Area before this happened," commented Nick mostly to himself.

"Now that this has begun, I must insist that you, Miss Mary and the boys move to the Visiting Center House until we leave permanently for the Smokies," insisted Whitey, "We can't be losing the most important part of this village."

Nick smiled at Whitey's urgency and said, "Not to worry, we had most things already packed up and either shipped or on the plane. Mary wants to go to the new area anyway. I'd prefer to have her and the boys head down before they have to watch our home disappear under the ice. I will go ahead and relocate to the other house this very day."

Whitey sighed and said, "Thanks, that will be a big load off my mind. But obviously we don't have until June like we thought. I asked Topo and Pepper for a status update and of course, once I got them to cut to the chase, I was told that they did not expect it to get so warm, so soon. They said if those temperatures continued to maintain or climb any higher, any bets were off about making it into June."

Nick had heard the same thing from Bilge and Topo. They were dumbfounded at the steady rise of temperatures and kept looking at the jet stream and how it kept dipping deeply south, bringing the warmer air from the tropics. Bilge had said that almost never happened this early in the year, and he was quite upset that they could no longer guess how much longer things could last beyond a couple weeks.

Nick was scared about losing someone to an accident if one of the dwellings suddenly disappeared into the

Arctic Ocean. The move was going faster than planned, but apparently so was the melting of the Pole.

Nick checked with Britney and Jackson concerning the water and electric to make sure there were no problems and got a thumbs up from both. Ion and George had already left for the Smoky Mountains to begin planning and construction of the new cold-fusion plants. Nick thought about the rest of the village.

He did not want to see a panic take over the village. Although elves were always methodical in their dealings and not subject to panic or rash judgment, Nick knew the same couldn't be said about tallfolk. As he thought about this along with the safety issues, he came to two conclusions. The first was that it was time to move the tallfolk out of this sinking landscape, and the second was the last train leaving the North Pole forever would take place in two days.

Everything else would either have to go by plane or vehicle to the Smokies. He was no longer willing to risk the weight of several tons of locomotive and cars returning to the North Pole. He was assured by Jackson that both utility plants were safe from harm for the time being, and would probably be the last thing threatened, as they were high on the hills behind the village. So losing power or water was not the biggest concern today, but Nick decided that whatever wasn't shipped in the next ten days, wouldn't be.

He had Ella call one last Council meeting for the North Pole telling her to excuse Whitey and Mrs. Claus, as they were otherwise occupied. He would make his decision known, and work out plans and details for what remained. He asked Mary to join him in the study.

When she entered they sat down and he said simply to her, "It's time for you and the boys to go south."

"Is this because of the incident at the Woodland Area?" she asked.

"Not entirely," he said. "But it is obvious that we don't have as much time as we anticipated. Besides you, Kristopher and Michael can do more good in the Smokies now than here."

"Especially since we have three locations to work on at the same time," she nodded as she spoke.

"Like you said, Mary, I am proud of the way they took charge of their respective duties," Nick said. "Perhaps you could charge them with a section of their own and let them oversee one part? This would allow you and Whitey more flexibility to work on the three areas."

"I agree," she said. "And though this is much bigger than supervising the packing of the manufacturing centers, it would be good experience. Especially for Kristopher, you know he is already dropping hints about taking over?"

Nick chuckled, "Yeah, he has said a couple things to me, but he has a few more years and white hairs to wait. I have only done this for the last 70 or so years, and my dad got to do it for over 250. I am not ready to hand over the reins yet, I'm still having too much fun."

"There are other things he can do in the meantime," Mary agreed. "I'm alerting you that he will probably be after you about it from now on."

"Now that we know we will age slowly and gracefully

under the dome, I can tell you that the day for him to take over is a long time off. Besides, what about Michael? Doesn't he get a say in this?" Nick asked.

"He doesn't seem to share his brother's enthusiasm about it. Haven't you noticed? He's more into the management of the North Pole shops and entertaining the visitors than he is the delivery part of this," Mary answered. "He gets the biggest kick telling every new visitor that he is your son and seeing the shock on their faces."

Nick laughed and said, "Yeah, I've seen him do it."

Mary concluded saying, "This is discussion for the Smokies once we are settled. Nothing can be decided today on that score. We should call the boys and give them their new assignments."

Nick nodded and went for his phone.

At the other end of the North Pole Village, Forrest was inside Supersleigh securing cages and enclosures for the big trip south. He had already enclosed most of the animals he wanted to take down, with the exception of the polar bears and wolves. He would wait until the last moment for them.

The whole one side of the plane was makeshift stables for the reindeer and horses including Amerigo III, Santa's famous white steed that he used in Europe and the Netherlands around the Feast of St. Michael. Like Michael, Amerigo was a descendant from the original.

Forrest was about ready to begin loading the massive plane with its passengers. He had many elves and a couple talls standing by as he figured even under the safety of the dome, the animals would not care to be so confined for any long duration.

Except for the reindeer and other service animals, he would only take two of each species. He had been coaxing the alpha male and female wolf since he had been back along with a female polar bear that had given birth to two cubs each of the past four years and a beautiful and healthy male that came around quite often for salmon that Forrest kept on hand for him.

Dewey Antlerhorn walked into the plane and said to Forrest, "The bears and wolves have wandered into the zoo area. I fed them and they are eating in the enclosures we set up. How close are you?"

Forrest took one more quick look and pulled at a couple of the enclosures and said, "I'm ready, let's do this."

They left the plane and began moving toward different enclosures with Forrest heading to the bears and Dewey to the wolves. Forrest grabbed some fish and began leading the bears to the largest cages on the plane. They followed eagerly eating the fish bits as they went. Once in the enclosure, Forrest gave each one an entire fish to keep them busy.

Dewey was doing a similar trick with the wolves. And as Forrest had done, got them into the cages and closed them off. By the time they were done with that, the elves and talls that were standing by had assembled. Forrest took charge directing their activities as they carried each animal to the plane. Dewey loaded them into their cages on board the Supersleigh.

Inside of an hour the jet was warming up and the animals moving to the south were in their respective enclosures and ready for transport. Atlanta had been notified of their imminent arrival and was preparing to unload their charters into their new corrals and pens in the domed area Jim had built.

Many visitors, including Michael Kringle, took time off from their respective jobs to see the animals and the elves off to their temporary home. How often, they wondered, would they get to see an operation like this in progress? They wished Forrest and Dewey luck and told them they looked forward to seeing them in the Smokies. A few moments later the flying ark was lifting into the sky from its position between the petting zoo and the stables.

Michael was placed in charge of the Visiting Center at "Site B", which would include the new petting zoo. So he had a professional curiosity about the cargo, and what would be needed once the zoo and stables were established.

Kristopher was to head up the construction of the new Manufacturing and Training Center at "Site A". He was already packing and would take Firesleigh down with an army of workers and materials. Whitey and Jim were going with him, as was Ion Crosswire and George Mendez to build the first ever cold fusion plant in history.

Everyone was getting ready and packing up. There was great excitement especially since the announcement that nothing would radically change once under the new domes in terms of health or age of its residents, when it happened.

CHAPTER 49

DISASTER STRIKES

Rudy Clawhammer was going on the Thundersleigh with Kristopher and the others. He was anxious to begin work on the new Manufacturing and Training Center and had poured over some of the plans that Kelly, Susan and the others had been working on. It looked more impressive than anything they had now at the North Pole. Rudy was the lead carpenter for the center and was in charge of a vast network of carpenters.

He volunteered to help Forrest and Dewey as his plane wasn't scheduled to leave until the next day. Like some of the other elves around him, they were cleaning up and packing anything left behind such as bridles, tack and miscellaneous equipment that would be needed later at the new zoo and stable.

Rudy actually felt it before he heard it. It was like he suddenly lost his footing and fell to the ground. Except the ground was wet. He realized the ice was giving away beneath the stable and screamed for everyone to get out. Suddenly elves and talls were running in every direction and as Rudy tried to get to his feet the slippery ice underneath him refused to let him get a footing. He was in a location with no straw or bedding to help him and then he heard a crack.

He watched terrified as the entire wall on the west

side of the stable gave way and collapsed. The rest of
the stable began tilting toward the same direction, and
Rudy was sliding toward where the wall had fallen. A
group of elves formed a chain locking arm-in-arm,
desperately trying to reach their comrade. Even as each
elf joined the chain, Rudy slid further away from them
toward what was now an opening in the ice. The wall
had disappeared into the hole which was widening with
every moment.

Rudy grasped a wooden beam that marked the start
of another stall in the stable. He was hanging on as the
entire building continued its list toward the now gaping
hole a few feet from him. He heard a crack of timbers
and suddenly a support beam fell from the roof and
landed right where the elf was holding on and smashed
his fingers. Rudy howled in pain releasing his grip from
the frame.

He started to slide again, and the others trying to get
to him were now blocked by the fallen beam. Amazingly,
the only thing Rudy could think of at that moment was,
*Thank the good Lord, Forrest and his menagerie left
moments before, sparing us a true disaster.* Just then he
felt the frigid Arctic water at his feet.

He yelled for everyone to get back before everything
fell on top of them. This was followed by more cracking
and splitting above them. Rudy bellowed again for
everyone to get out and after another loud crack, about
half the roof caved in on top of him and the hole. It was
the last anyone ever saw of Rudy as the lumber floated
on top of the hole and there was no possibility of
reaching the opening without falling into the frigid

water themselves.

What Nick, Mary and the others feared the most had now happened. One of their own was lost to the melting of the glacier. Whitey closed off the Woodland Area once and for all. He surmised to Santa that it was probably the excess weight of the plane, in addition to the buildings themselves, that weakened the ice.

Losing an elf to natural causes happened rarely in the North Pole, and to anyone's knowledge no elf had ever been hurt seriously enough to succumb to their injuries. At least not since the construction and implementation of the dome. The shock and sadness that ran through the village was huge. Added to that, Rudy was liked by everyone who had come into contact with him.

What made things worse was that Nick had to postpone any type of service or remembrance of him until everyone was away from the pole. Otherwise Rudy might not be the only being they would be mourning.

Later on, the Council members decided the Elf Training Center would be named the Rudy Clawhammer Training Center in honor of their fallen compatriot. The elf that was hardest hit was Rory Whittlesee, the other head carpenter, who had worked with Rudy on so many projects. Things were made worse for him when he was asked to take over Rudy's responsibilities on the Manufacturing Area, as it was the highest priority for the new settlement.

Nick Kringle was determined to lose no more lives from this catastrophe, saying that losing buildings or structures was one thing, but losing lives was quite another. Nick and his friends were a week away from abandoning the North Pole entirely. He would make sure everyone was out by then and that no other accidents would occur no matter what it took.

Chapter 50

Starting Over

The day after the loss of Rudy, both Thundersleigh and Firesleigh took off from the North Pole with Thundersleigh heading directly for the first site and Firesleigh to Site B. As soon as they had arrived they were met by an assault team of trucks, materials, and manpower that had already been working on multiple buildings. They immediately began unloading the plane of its contents and putting materials into the staging area.

If anyone was surprised at how the North Pole was packed up and moved so quickly, the rebuilding of the new headquarters would astound them more, as it would be done in record time. Several teams were already laying the piping and electricity leading to the town and individual buildings. Many of the frames and walls were being hammered together by an army of people. The most unusual trait about them was that a great many of them carried a similar look and build to Santa Claus himself.

Cory walked up to Mary and Kristopher and said, "Not bad, huh? And many more are at the other locations with more arriving everyday."

Kristopher walked up to Cory and shook his hand.

After Mary hugged Cory and said hello she asked,

"How did you get everyone here?"

"We have buses that come and go every hour. They are also driven by Santa Ambassadors who double as truck drivers when we need them to be," Cory explained.

Kristopher said, "I can't believe how many foundations have been laid and the framing that's going on."

Cory chuckled. "Ella made it sound like Christmas would be canceled if we didn't have the village completed in a week."

"Have you had any outside interference since you've been here?" Mary asked cautiously.

"Only a couple people for the time being. That guy in charge of the dome, Jim, programmed the thing so it shows a giant rock blocking the path," said Cory. "It really goofs them up as they expect an open field, but so far they shrug it off and go around. Did you know this thing is soundproof, too?"

Mary smiled and nodded.

Two Santa look-a-likes walked up to Cory and the first said, "We finished the framing of the 'Big Bounce House' per Susan's plans, you can begin the electrical and plumbing. What do you need Santa Fred and I to do next?"

"Hold on and I'll check with the foreman. By the way, I would like to introduce you two very special people," grinned Cory, "Santa Jim, Santa Fred, I'd like you to meet, Mrs. Mary Kringle and her son Kristopher Kringle, the wife and son of our reigning Santa Claus."

"A great honor, Mrs. Claus and Kristopher," said

Santa Fred flustered.

"Forgive me," apologized Santa Jim, "I thought this young man here was a Santa wannabe like us, only a little young yet." He turned to Mary and said, "And I guessed you were another Mrs. Claus helping out, not THE Mrs. Claus. A great pleasure to meet you both." Santa Jim enthusiastically shook both their hands.

"The pleasure is ours," said Mary. "And we can't thank you enough for helping us rebuild the North Pole in the Smoky Mountains."

"It is more than our pleasure," said Santa Fred. "As Cory said when he recruited us, 'Imagine telling your grandkids how you helped Santa Claus relocate from the North Pole.' Of course we are sworn to secrecy as to the actual location. Besides, we sure cause a stir going to and from the hotel and walking around the towns we are in. That's worth coming here alone." Santa Fred laughed as he finished.

"Anyway, back to work," Santa Jim interrupted.

"Yes," said Cory. "Let's go find Nales Rooftop and ask him what building should be started next. Excuse us Miss Mary, Kristopher, we need to get back to it."

They both nodded and Kristopher said, "By all means." He turned to his mother and said, "It's time for me to get to my location too. Michael said he would be here later today and is arriving with Whitey."

She kissed her son goodbye and wished him success with the Manufacturing and Training Center. As he left, Mary sought out the 'headquarters' for the section and found Susan Fredrick amongst a stack of building plans and her husband, Bill, next to her talking to a couple other tallfolk and elves explaining the way the piping should run and where to place the sewer pipes leading out of the town.

They were both so engrossed with their work, that neither saw her walk up to them and when Mary picked up the plans for 'Santa's Friend Theodore' Susan stopped and said "Excuse me, I need that." She suddenly realized who she had barked at, and immediately softened her tone, "Oh, Miss Mary, I didn't see it was you. I'm sorry, I thought you were another worker helping themselves."

Mary smiled and squeezed Susan's arm saying, "I am another worker, and you may tell me where I can help out."

Susan was still shocked at her presence there and said, "Actually, we have a pretty great organization here, and I understand the same thing from Kelly at the MTA, and Whitey at the SCR. Everything seems to be coming together nicely. Everyone thinks it was a brilliant idea to split forces into three locations. We have a little good natured wager going on to see who will get their portion completed first. I think we are ahead."

"MTA? SCR?" Mary puzzled.

"Oh yes, the acronyms for Manufacturing and Training Center and the Smokies Christmas Resort, it is a little easier than that many syllables," Susan chuckled. "And this is the SVC for Santa's Visiting Center."

Bill walked up to retrieve some other drawings and said, "Susan is into acronyms, she'd shorten my name if it was physically possible. Good morning Mrs. Claus, nice to see you again." He grabbed the drawing he sought and walked back to the other group of people and started pointing to the plan.

"I'll tell you what," Susan said, "I was about ready to do a site tour and check the progress of some of the structures. If you can hang on a couple minutes, we can do this together and I can bring you up to speed."

Mary nodded and said that would be wonderful.

As Mary was waiting a rather burly looking elf walked up to her. His smile was brilliant against the permanently embedded coal dust around his face. "Hello, Miss Mary!" he said in a gravelly voice.

"Bless my soul, it's Ernie Whistlestop, my favorite train engineer! What have you learned?" asked Mary.

"Just as we predicted, this whole area is catacombed with track spurs and most tied into either the Norfolk-Southern or the CSX lines that go up, down and entirely around the area," answered Ernie. "I have found a bunch of coal spurs, and a few lumber spurs, located only a few miles from here. They are in various forms of disrepair, but nothing that can't be salvaged. I would say that with a modest crew, we could have a finished track up and running in a few weeks. Then it's a purely matter of building a roundhouse and a station here."

"So we can do a Great Smoky Mountains train to the Visiting Center?" asked Mary excitedly.

"Um, I'm afraid you will have to pick a different name, that one's being used already," corrected Ernie. "How about calling it the 'Sugarland Express'?"

"There was a really dark movie with that name," said Mary. "I don't want any negative connotations with our train."

They both thought for a couple minutes and then Ernie brightened. He said, "Since you don't want the name to give away where the passengers are going like before, why not name it after one of the founding elves of the last village and call it the 'Chekitwice Choo-Choo'?"

"Ooh, I like that," Mary said smiling. "Let me run it by Nick, but I bet he will like it, too. He has often said we should do something to honor some of the early founders like Carrow Chekitwice and Frederick Salsbury. That would be a great tribute to the old toymaker."

Mary thought for another moment and asked, "Can we run a line all the way to the McGee-Tyson Airport in Knoxville?"

"Technically it is in Alcoa, but I have followed freight tracks through Townsend and Maryville and many converge and go into Alcoa. Especially to the manufacturer there. So it won't be a problem once we get permission," answered Ernie.

"Maryville," Mary mused. "I like that. I'll have to do lots of shopping there."

"I need to get back as we are checking another spur line over in that direction, and I am meeting with the Regional Manager of CSX later today to find out what we need to get permission and set schedules to use their track lines down here," explained Ernie. "I'll give you a full report when I know something solid."

"Good luck in your negotiations," said Mary. "I know you will work everything out." And with that the brawny elf sauntered off with his train swagger of many years.

Susan walked up and asked if Mary was ready to tour her new SVC. Mary was still smiling from her visit with Ernie, and said enthusiastically, "I certainly am."

They began at the southern edge of the hamlet and Susan explained where each building was being erected and where they were putting the restaurants, and the new Reindeer Inn. The new inn would be the same size and shape as before as both Mary and Susan agreed that the North Pole version was always a grand edifice and little should be changed. The large footprint for the building had already been laid out and the foundation poured.

Mary commented that before in the North Pole, the only thing they had to do was scrape the ice level and build on top of it. Susan reminded her that is why they were moving today. Glaciers apparently were not forever.

Because they would not have two geologic levels like before, they had to spread out more and increase many of the building sizes or heights from their predecessors. Some one story combination shop/homes were now two-story and two-story were either larger or or had become three stories. 'Santa's Friend Theodore', the village's Teddy bear factory was reduced to three stories but was spread much wider to accommodate the manufacturing of the bears.

"Were we able to contain everything in the area we allotted?" asked Mary.

"We got a little creative, but yes, we fit it in," said Susan. "We had to reduce the distance between the shops, and some elves decided to share a structure and have both shops in one building, such as "Loomin' For A

Knit' joined with the 'Warmth of Faith' company."

They certainly seemed to fit together and Susan again gave a wry smile at the remembrance of her beloved ski suit that she, her husband and her families received many years ago from the North Pole and continued to hang in her closet.

"The toy soldier 'Sentry Shop' also joined with 'Crackin' Up', the nutcracker shop, as they both had a similar look," Susan continued and pointed to another larger building, "I made each one unique to keep their individuality."

Mary nodded and was enjoying the new changes. She felt that this new Visiting Center would have a more cozy, yet whimsical feel than before. She had seen some of the designs and color schemes that Susan and Kelly had planned before they left the North Pole. This was coming together exactly as she had envisioned it in her mind.

One of the things Mary liked more than anything about the old village was the train station. She loved how the train would pull into what was basically the middle of the Visiting Center allowing a shock and awe to its visitors especially coming out of the tunnel.

Bill had asked Ion about the cloaking devise and had designed a similar structure where the tracks would be laid before entering the village and created an illusion of mountain rock before reaching the station. This had a similar effect to the actual tunnel that the train went through previously.

Susan placed the train station at the exact center of town so that either side of the SVC could be seen by its passengers. She remembered vividly her own amazement the first time they pulled into the village and, like Mary, wanted to recreate that experience for the future visitors to Santa and Mrs. Claus.

After about an hour, Mary had congratulated Susan on an outstanding job. During the tour she had also run into many of the elves she knew and loved including several Council members like Freida Cutinglass, who was working on several stained glass pieces for the various shops.

Freida, instead of being overwhelmed by needing to provide so many works of art, was actually excited and smiling. Her fingers worked deftly with the metal and glass. She told Mary that so much of the old stain glass she had created was passe and she had wanted to redo many pieces and now it was finally time to accomplish this.

Keeney Eagleye was also there, working on the new Naughty and Nice Hall of Records that would also be placed in the SVC along with the new newspaper office, *The Polar Times*. Although its publisher, Alfie Newsworthy, determined a new name would be appropriate and decided to call the new publication *The Mountain Slate* which would carry both a traditional and digital copy of its offering.

Topo, Bilge, Ion, Jim, and George were split between the various developments working on the cold fusion plants. They were constantly running from one site to the other checking specs on each plant against George's modifications and layouts for each area. Mary spied Jim and Topo heading up to the new plant as she was walking with Susan.

When the two women were done, Mary told her again how pleased she was and that she was going to pop over to the SCR and see how Whitey was progressing with his team. Mary had arrived on the plane with Kristopher and the others but would now use the time continuum to jump from one construction zone to the next.

Before she had left, Nick asked her to not return to the North Pole, nor to let the boys come back. He told her if things went as he planned, he would join her sooner than later in the Smokies. They were finishing up the last of the packing, and the major machinery and most possessions were already away from the Pole.

She thought about where she wished to land at the SCR, as Susan termed it, and concentrated. She appeared in the middle of a structure that hadn't been there before and was surrounded by numerous Santa Ambassadors, many of whom called out in surprise at her sudden appearance.

One in particular by the name of Santa Walt came over and asked, "Can we help you little lady?" He was a huge man weighing over 325 pounds but affable. He said, "You gave us quite a start. May I assume you are not from around here?"

She laughed and said, "Actually, no, I'm from New York, then California, and finally the North Pole. I am Mary Kringle, better known as Mrs. Claus."

Several of the men and a couple women came over to meet her personally and welcome her to the Smoky Mountains and her new home. She was completely surrounded and questions were being fired left and right to her.

Finally a loud voice was heard over the din and some of the people stepped aside. Whitey Slipenfall walked into the center of the fray and said, "We have a great deal of work to be done, and not a lot of time to do it. I promise everyone will have a chance to meet Mrs. Claus and ask her some questions, but let's not bury the woman here and now."

They began to break apart, but there was an overriding curiosity about the real Santa's wife and what she was like. Mary understood and was hardly put off by the attention, but she knew Whitey was right and there would be a time and place for this later.

Britney Clearwater walked up a couple minutes later and joined the pair as Whitey was pouring them both a cup of coffee. "I'll take one, too, please," she said.

Whitey pulled out a third cup and filled it with the hot fluid and put sugar and cream in it the way Britney preferred. As he did this he said to Mary, "I apologize for that, I forgot to warn them that you and Santa may show up anytime or anywhere. It is obvious that Cory or Santa explained nothing about the time continuum to any of them."

"No, Nick always believed the less they knew about the actual delivery process the better," said Mary, "And many of them asked about it, but he felt it was better they figured out how in their own minds rather than give demonstrations. He made that clear with Cory and Katy from the start."

"And now they now have something completely new to contemplate," chuckled Whitey.

"I'll bet there are some interesting conversations this evening at the hotel," Britney joked.

"To be honest, I never gave it a thought," explained Mary. "I will have to use the continuum to get from area to area, but maybe I can find a particular spot to concentrate on away from the main goings-on so as not to create to big a disturbance."

Whitey thought for a second and said, "Oh what the heck, it might keep them on their toes if they know you and Santa can pop in anytime and any place you want." He began laughing. "In fact, I may begin doing the same thing."

Mary said, "Maybe not the best idea, we don't want to cause accidents. I think one of those guys almost sawed his thumb off he was so startled."

"Hmm, maybe not," Whitey thought and said "So would you like a tour?"

Mary asked to finish her coffee first and rest for a minute as she walked the entire Visiting Center with Susan.

"How are they coming?" asked Whitey.

"She says she's ahead of you," Mary said slyly,

"Oh, she thinks so does she," commented Britney, "I seriously doubt that."

"I don't know, they have quite a few buildings started and some framed," Mary cajoled.

Britney and Whitey smiled at each other and Whitey said, "We have something for you to see and you won't have to walk." He spoke into a two-way radio and told the person at the other end to bring the cart around.

A few moments later a large six passenger golf cart

pulled up to the plans area and Whitey told Mary to hop aboard. Mary asked where he had gotten it and Whitey said that one of the Ambassadors owned a golf course and loaned several carts to this project including this executive version.

She and Britney sat in the middle seat and Whitey got into the front with the driver. He turned sideways and began telling Mary some of the buildings they had started including the one she time jumped into, which would be the new spa and pool area.

Mary was looking around the area at not only the progress but more so the landscape around them. each area was gorgeous, this was the most beautiful of the three sites chosen. It was unanimous that this would make the best area for the recreation resort and would provide the most peaceful setting. She was more convinced of their decision now and was pleased how green and lovely everything was.

As they pulled around some trees, Mary couldn't believe what she was seeing. There stood an almost finished building of remarkable beauty.

"Say hello to the new Elven Resort," said Whitey.

"This is impossible," Mary said breathlessly, "How?"

Britney laughed and threw her head back saying, "It will be ready for visitors inside of a week."

"We decided that we wanted to get one building completed, so we put everyone on this at once," explained Whitey, "We have several elves working on the embellishments on the inside, there is full plumbing and electric and the appliances are due the day after tomorrow."

"We also have a couple other buildings framed and the electricity is in," Britney gloated. "Yeah, I don't think Susan is ahead of us."

Mary shook her head and said, "This is going to be an interesting contest."

After spending another half hour with Whitey and Britney, she decided to put off her tour of the Manufacturing Area for tomorrow as she was tired from her excursions. She knew where the hotel was and could easily use the continuum, but she thought it might be disconcerting to those in the hotel to suddenly 'appear' in the lobby.

She knew that a car was waiting for her at the Visiting Center. She thought about where her appearance might have the most negligible effect on others and concentrated. In a flash she was back at the rear of one of the framed buildings. This time there was no one around which she was glad about. She walked over to the headquarter pavilion.

Susan was off somewhere but she broke into a huge smile at the sight of two others there. She gave a big hug to her son Michael first, and then bent down to take her favorite elf into her arms. Denny Sweetooth returned the strength of the hug and said, "Oh Miss Mary, is this not the most beautiful spot on earth? So many elves have broken into tears over the beauty and peacefulness of this location."

"And wait until autumn," said Michael. "The pictures I have seen on the Internet are breathtaking. It will be nice to live in an area with four seasons."

"So are you here permanently?" she addressed Denny.

"I believe so," he said cheerfully. "There was really nothing left for me to do up north. I said my goodbyes and am ready for our next adventure."

"Good old Denny," Mary laughed out loud. "Only you could call this an adventure and be happy about it."

"Life is for the living, and after more than four hundred years, I am still enjoying it," he said with the permanent smile that seemed to grace his face.

"I actually returned here to pick up the car that was left for me, as I was going to the hotel," Mary explained.

"Before you go why not share a cup of cocoa at the canteen with us?" Denny pleaded.

"What canteen?" Mary said puzzled, as Susan didn't show her that.

"Folly me," Denny said teasing. He often used that phrase as he saw it once in a Frank Sinatra movie and loved it immediately.

They walked over to a new small building and inside there was Pierre Gastonlove working on giant pans of lasagna. Major appliances from the Reindeer Inn had been placed in the canteen and there were tables and chairs around the building. Pierre also hugged Mary and said in his thick French accent how pleased he was to be cooking for a crowd again.

Denny told her that they would set up two more eateries, one in each location, and would do a full meal for each one a couple times a week and rest on Sunday.

"But how did you get this set up so fast?" Mary said astonished.

"Remember, we miniaturized everything we could up north?" replied Denny. "It was now a matter of getting

electricity and restoring everything to its proper size.
These were on the plane that you came down in today."

Mary had almost forgot about the miniaturizing
process that made everything easier to pack and move
down south.

As they were sipping the cocoa Pierre had given
them, Michael started commenting how things were
going at the new center. "I asked Susan about one
building however, and she said that was none of my
concern and not to ask again about it."

"So let me guess, you're asking me about it?" Mary
asked sarcastically.

"Hey, if I am supposed to be overseeing this,
shouldn't I know what it is so I know if it is being done
correctly?" Michael asked in earnest.

"Weak, Michael, very weak," said Denny smugly.

Mary chuckled at both their comments and said,
"There are a few structures your father and I discussed
that we wish to keep to ourselves for the time being, and
we swore the various project managers to secrecy. I'm
sure the ones working on them probably don't know
what they are for, either. You will have to trust them
and us, and let them do what they are supposed to. Your
father and I will oversee those buildings."

"Denny, it is wonderful to see you, but I really am
getting tired and think I should get some rest," said a
tired Mrs. Claus.

"Of course, dear lady, let's get you on your way."
They picked up what was left of their cocoa and headed
back to the construction office.

Susan had returned and showed Mary the car that

Char had arranged for her. Mary said a quick goodbye and set up a time to meet tomorrow there and went on her way.

CHAPTER 51

THE LAST PLANE OUT

A few days later Nicholas Kristopher Kringle stood before the home he had been raised and lived in since the day he was born on September 16, 1854. He watched as first one side than the back began to break up and splinter. His eyes teared up as he watched the workshop where his father would later teach him about making toys instead of only playing with them. Where he would take over as Santa Claus from his dad.

This was the home he brought his bride, Mary. It was the place where both his boys were born, where they grew up and celebrated their graduations. It was the place he had always planned on leaving to the next Santa Claus.

When one of the three fireplaces toppled onto and through the roof, he couldn't watch anymore and he turned around and silently walked away. There was now truly no reason for him to stay in the North Pole, though there was the North Pole's Visiting Center house, which was originally built for his parents, Kris and Annie.

As of today, he still considered it their house, long after they left with Aeon Millennium for their "alternate reality" as Aeon called it.

Nick was anxious to be rejoined with Mary in their new village. And he already had heard about the impossible progress taking place there. He hadn't left the North Pole since they returned from that fateful trip together, and he was still picturing bare branch trees in his mind.

It was now the second week in May and Mary's birthday was in a few days on the 21st. He wanted to spend that day with her, though she had already sloughed it off saying it was no big deal this year. 'After you have reached a hundred, what's there to bother about?' she had kidded Nick.

But now the Woodland Area was gone, with a few sticks sticking out of the ice in various places. Since losing the stable and Rudy, they watched as one building after another fell before them. Some went a little at a time, and others just disappeared as the Woodworks plant had done.

The three of the planes were up at the top of the Manufacturing Area, between the Elven Resort and the Polar Power Plant. It seemed the most solid area, although Willie Movinmuch and the other two pilots stood by there craft in case. The last items and people had been filing into the three transporters and once gone, these would be the last flights from the North Pole.

The weather was steadily warming to the mid to upper 50's regularly, with the lows barely reaching freezing, if at all. They had dismantled the dome to use the nacelles for later. In a couple more weeks Nick guessed that many of the other houses might begin to break apart and sink, too.

If people from the outside discovered the settlement

now, it would only add to the mystique of the North Pole and Santa, and leave everyone wondering where they went. Nick allowed himself a smile at the thought.

In the new areas, he heard that a few 'outsiders' as they were now being called, had stumbled upon the new sites, but nothing untoward happened. Kristopher told him that one of the visitors walked right down the center of the Manufacturing and Training Center while work was going on all around him and didn't have a clue.

It had so surprised some of the Santa Ambassadors and tallfolk helpers, that they stopped what they were doing to watch the spectacle like watching fish through an aquarium. Many of them finally understood why the Village of the North Pole had never been found by anyone that the villagers didn't *want* to find it.

He received a call on his two-way radio, it was Willie. He said, "We are ready up here, Santa. Are you coming with us, or will you be using the continuum?"

Nick thought for a moment and said into the radio, "No, I'll be hitching a ride. I might wind up transporting right into a load of timber, since I haven't been to the new sites, yet."

"Roger that, we are ready to go when you are, Firesleigh out."

Firesleigh was heading to the Santa's Visiting Center and would be stationed there at least until everything had been relocated later this year. Supersleigh would be at the MTA and Thundersleigh at the SCR for the same duration. Each area had a hangar with a sliding roof, a couple hundred yards from their respective sites, and a road leading into the three areas making transportation simple. There were now many cloaking devises and mini-domes scattered around in each location making movement nearly impossible to detect. Ion, George and Jim had been alternately working on those and the cold fusion plants, which were now operational and functioning perfectly. Better than they had predicted.

There was now plenty of electricity and each plant individually could run the three areas, and a couple extra cities, taking up less room than a modest two-story house. There was also a good supply of water in the mountains and the ground water wells could suffice their needs for centuries. Nick guessed that long before they could ever run out, they would have another solution. In addition, except for cooking and drinking areas, Fred Wu had installed the new waterless showers in the bathrooms of each new dwelling to save on fresh water.

Mary insisted that their bathroom contain a traditional bathtub with running water. She insisted that nothing would ever replace some simple pleasures and that was hers. Although she allowed for the waterless shower to also be installed.

Nick knew he could have transported to the top, but he was thinking as he was walking. An entirely new area, a new life for the most part, and more new inventions and innovations then he had seen in the last twenty years. He thought of the saying 'the more things change, the more they stay the same' and he thought he could easily dispute this theory.

He looked around as he walked, taking in the abandoned houses and shops. He saw where he had first met and worked with Rory Mattle on the plans for Mattel, and the navigation shop where he spent endless hours with Sky Globetrotter working out the routes of the Christmas Eve flights. So many years, so many memories, all to wash away like the past.

He reached the plane and took one last look around. The other two planes had already left for the MTA and SCR, but Willie would wait the entire day if Santa asked him. Willie had been one of the original elves of the North Pole and was also one of the elves who escorted Nick's mother and father to this village.

"So this is it, the last flight out," Nick said to the elf.

Willie smiled and said, "It has been a good run and now we have a new place to begin a whole new run. Wait until you see your new villages. I believe you will be extremely pleased indeed."

Nick nodded and after a couple more moments turned to Willie and said in a forced enthusiastic tone, "So what are we waiting for? Let's go home."

"Will you copilot with me?" asked Willie. "I would be honored if you would."

Nick nodded and he and the elf walked through the length of the plane and Nick kidded with several of the passengers as the two of them made their way to the cockpit.

Nick strapped in after readjusting the seat and ran through the checklist with Willie. A few minutes later the beautifully decorated plane with its mural of elves running back and forth with their cargo and luggage left the the ground. Nick bid a fond and final farewell to the North Pole.

CHAPTER 52

A WHOLE NEW RUN

Nick was with Sky Globetrotter going over the preliminary routes for the next run. Now that they were working from a new base of operations, a whole new route would be established compared to leaving from the North Pole.

It was early November and everything was moving at full speed as it always did that time of year. He was at the Manufacturing and Training Center for now and he had a few more things to check on. He needed to return to Santa's Visiting Center by 3:00 pm so Mary, he and Michael could welcome the new group of visitors to the Reindeer Inn with Christel. They were certainly getting a bigger response than previously. Apparently everyone wanted to come to the Great Smoky Mountains, where before they were a lot more hesitant to make the trek to Fairbanks. *And why not,* Nick thought to himself, *I have heard nothing but praise about our new location ever since I arrived.*

He and Mary both were often stopped several times a day and told how beautiful and numerous other adjectives the new locations were. Most days they only used the dome to keep sightings from the outside from occurring, but they often matched the temperature and weather to the outside of the dome.

It had been a comfortable 63° day with mostly sunny

skies. Nick mused thinking about how the North Pole would be dark already and how they wouldn't see the natural sun for months right now. Nick and Mary and everyone concerned felt pleased with their choice.

Nick said goodbye to Sky and headed over to the Frederick Salsbury Manufacturing Building. He met Kristopher inside and they went over the latest requests for Christmas. As was normal, there would always be one or two toys that were the "hot" item that every child had to have. They reviewed where they were getting those, if they did not produce it themselves, and Kristopher explained that he would have to make another trip to California and meet with the manufacturer there for the boys' choice this year.

The new building was the same size as the previous one, but with so many things made outside with other companies, it worked out fine. Nick gave Kristopher his blessing and said to hurry back as there was much for him to oversee as the new Supreme Toy Maker.

Kristopher said slyly, "I could go and come back the same day if you would teach me the time continuum."

Nick ho, ho, ho'ed and said, "Soon enough my son. I promise next year we will begin your lessons. Just don't expect to be taking the reindeer reins for quite a time yet. Now that you are in charge of the MTA and Michael the SVC, your mother and I don't have nearly enough to keep us busy anymore."

"Oh come now, you both still oversee everything. And now that Whitey has assumed the lead elven role over the GSM villages, you both can do anything you want and begin truly enjoying your roles as Santa Claus and

CEO," Kristopher said.

It was true, after the first couple months of racing from one area to the next as the building was going at a lightning pace, he and Mary had enjoyed a type of Renaissance and were able to enjoy their time in the their new Smokies Resort Center and their new home there.

The elves had built a grand home as they did with Nick's parents, and in almost record time. It had been decided that since Kristopher would head up the MTA, and Michael the SVC, it would be better to place Nuck and Mary's home in the resort area instead. Nick and Mary were practically the first to permanently relocate to their new house.

Houses went up at a speed that would have made any general contractor jealous. Speed aside, every home was highly crafted and skilled artisans did the finishing touches utilizing their wood turning and artistry styles.

As before, each shop and dwelling was beautiful and eclectic in its appearance. There were as many different architectural styles as there had been in the North Pole, and a rainbow of colors. Often Nick felt a twinge of sorrow that the visitors that up to a few weeks ago couldn't see the true beauty around them. But he knew that was for the best, and there hadn't been a close call in all that time.

But that was made up when they received their invited visitors to the SVC. Everyone who came was awestruck upon their arrival. And though Christel, Fergie, and Gunther did their level best to convince the visitors that this was now the genuine home of Santa

and Mrs. Claus, it wasn't until they received their gifts
from Santa that they truly began to believe it. Some
acted like they fell into a dream and didn't wake until
they arrived home.

Ella and April were receiving requests almost daily
from elves wishing to leave their respective duties in the
various DC's to visit the new villages. And many asked
to return on a more permanent basis. They had to build
a second Santa's Rooming House to accommodate the
elf visitors in the SRC.

Mary had asked the Council if they could begin a
more aggressive rotation program to accommodate the
numerous requests. Nick said as long as it didn't
interfere with the efficiency of the DC's, it was fine with
him. It passed, of course, and a few elves were assigned
to set up schedules and stay durations. These elves
would be picked up and returned via the three jet sleighs
as they brought their cargo to the various centers for
staging for Christmas Eve.

Some minor changes were made, like the Warmth of
Faith Company was no longer sending ski parkas, suits
and gloves to potential visitors, but were now sending
jackets and extra clothing as an incentive. Loomin' For
A Knit had joined forces with them and sent sweaters
and sometimes children's outfits that were as soft as
down to the parents.

But much stayed the same. Christel no longer had to
warn off visitors away from the Manufacturing and
Training Center, and when asked where the toys were
made, the tour guides and elves said another secret
location, and that was the end of it. Balloon rides would

continue there as it was such a beautiful panorama to overlook the Great Smoky Mountains from so high up.

It was now a common occurrence for elves to go out among some of the tallfolk's towns and areas to explore their new world. They were always fairly treated by tallfolk of the area and because of this, along with the help that was received by the former visitors and Santa Ambassadors, the elves began to reduce their suspicions and wariness of tallfolk in general.

What everyone learned was that this truly was a center of Christian ideals and that with rare exception, people lived life according to God's law, not only man's. Of course it didn't hurt that more than 10 million people came to the area on vacation. So they were mostly in a great mood to begin with, but it was nice to see the elves really begin enjoying the people they were meeting around the area.

There had actually been no problems at any of the DC's over the years, and Nick was hoping that this would be the case in the new GSM locations. *So far, so good*, he thought.

After visiting with Kristopher and a couple other places he closed his eyes and appeared in the center of Santa's Visiting Center by the reindeer stable. He found Forrest and was talking about the reindeer games for that year and who looked the most promising.

"Sunburst has really come a long way this year and I am thinking of having her in the lead with Snowflake. I believe this is Strobe's year for the RN lead as his antlers are nearly perfect. Ginger and Nutmeg will probably make up the next set, followed by Comet and Prancer

and ending with Bullseye and Thunderbolt," Forrest
pointed at the reindeer as he spoke.

"Yes, Blitzen's grandson, I was hoping he'd be in
shape for this years run since we had to pull him from
the line up last year when he lost his antler," Nick said.

"I think they will both stay on this time, especially if
we keep him from tangling it up in the corral again."
Forrest said.

"How is everything working out in the zoo?" asked
Nick.

"Santa I really thought we might have a problem
when I moved those animals out of their environment,"
said Forrest shaking his head, "But when Dewey
Antlerhorn came up with the idea of a dome within the
dome and recreating their natural habitat, it seemed to
solve any issues that might have come from being here.
Further it kept other animals safe from the bigger ones.
If we ever need money, we could make a fortune selling
the dome to zoos around the world."

"I'm sure we could make a fortune with many of the
innovations we have, the cloaking devise, the dome, the
cold fusion plants, but we would have to live in the
world we created, and I don't think I am ready for that,
nor are most of these governments," said Nick sourly.

"When considering what the dome does for us and the
animals, maybe it could mellow them out some," Forrest
replied thoughtfully.

"Maybe someday." Nick ended with that thought,
"So is the zoo is ready for our visitors?"

"Just like always," brightened Forrest. "The wolf
whelps are really playful now and are developing their

own personalities. I see a future Alpha male in the pack, already."

After a few more minutes with Forrest, Santa went to Cocoa Nicenhot's Mug of Nog and ordered a Cafe mocha with extra chocolate. Cocoa laughed and said, "Yeah it's getting near that time, we need to chunk you up a few pounds."

Nick laughed and said, "Yes, if it were only true that I could." he looked around again at the new shop and said, "Cocoa, I really like the new look for this place. It is hard to believe, but to me it is more delightful than before."

Cocoa broke into a huge grin and said, "Yes Kelly Nightingale really captured what I wanted and did a great job with the plans."

"Hard to imagine where we would be without their help," Nick thought wistfully.

"Can't imagine, and don't want to," replied Cocoa.

Mary walked in and said, "I saw you walking in here. We got new pictures of Susan's baby. She's a month old yesterday! She really has changed in the last few weeks. Cocoa, may I have a black raspberry cocoa please, plenty of cream on top?"

"Right away, Miss Mary," the elf replied and went to work.

Mary placed the picture tablet down in front of Nick and they began looking at the photos. Mary started to tear up and said, "I can't believe they named their daughter after me."

"I always knew they had good taste," said Nick. "And it sure makes it easy to remember her name with me."

Mary punched him in the arm and said, "Yeah, like you could ever forget, after Susan practically had the baby here."

"Another few weeks and she would have," Nick chuckled. They had both watched Susan get bigger and bigger until she finally went home in September. "I'll bet if we wanted her to, she would have stayed right up past the delivery."

Cocoa brought the drink to Mary and they sat at a booth and talked of many things. Their son, Michael was busy seeing to final touches and room accoutrements in the Reindeer Inn with Christel. They now had a final list of families that boarded their respective planes and knew exactly who was coming.

Last minute wallpaper and decorations to make each person feel entirely welcome was being applied. After receiving the new arrivals, Michael would double check the new Visiting Center and make sure everything was stocked in the kitchen for his father while he was there.

Michael finally learned about the building that his mother said was no concern of his. At least not until she and his father presented a new house to him and told him that this was now his residence in the Visiting Center. "Oh? Kicking me out, are you?" he teased.

"Don't feel bad, we threw your brother out, too. Only he's in the Manufacturing Area, so we don't have to listen about you two going at it the whole day long." Nick returned the tease.

Their sons loved their new homes and each was tastefully done to match their personality. For instance, Michael had a gourmet kitchen like his parents.

Kristopher's had more convenience appliances and was often brought food from various elves and his brother, since he wouldn't cook much himself.

Nick and Mary knew that it would be Kristopher that would eventually take over for his father. He not only looked more like him everyday, but he was really into the delivery and its nuances. Michael loved being in the Visiting Center and was pushing his mother and Whitey for more visits from outside. He had found his niche in the hospitality sector, and the people loved him as much as Christel.

In so far as which center was completed the fastest, it pretty much had been a toss up, with both the SRC and MTA finishing a few days before the SVC. Everyone was in the spirit of competition, but each knew that the important thing was to get the village back up to speed, rather than who won.

Many of the shops and places sported new names besides the Chekitwice Choo-Choo, such as the Aeon Millennium Health Clinic, Rudy Clawhammer Training Center, and others. The Council decided that this would be the best way to remember those who had done so much to bring them here into the future.

After much of the construction had been completed, they had finally assembled the Council to hear and give progress reports. Since so many elves and folks were involved they had opened the august body to anyone who wished to sit in. Each section had gone up as fast or faster than they dared hope. Some thought dividing the village into three geographically different areas would cause hardship, but this proved untrue, and everyone adjusted easily to moving through the three locations.

During the Council meeting, Whitey had asked a question that every elf thought of at least once or twice. He asked the Council, "So now that we are officially here, what are we calling this place? We can't continue to call it the North Pole – South. That doesn't make sense."

The Council began the debate and names flew around the the room. Some ideas were more simple such as, 'The Smoky Village.' Other names were more bizarre like 'The Bald Pole' or 'The Villages of Tennessee and North Carolina'. Many just shook their heads and said something more simple but strong was needed. The name would need to eventually gain acceptance with everyone around the world.

"That's it!" exclaimed a voice from the back of the gallery.

"I'm sorry," said Denny Sweetooth. "What's it? And could you come forward so we may see you?"

Fergie Keepitneat stood and moved through the crowd. He came to the front of the room and as he looked at the Council with a big grin he said, "Look there are many buildings and such that have been dedicated to the many elves that have done so much for the village in the past. But we missed one, and it's a pretty major one in my book."

Santa looked at Fergie and said, "Okay I'm game, and I certainly am all in favor of your idea. Who do you suggest?"

Fergie smiled and said simply, "You."

Santa scoffed and sat back in his chair, "Don't be

daft!"

Fergie held his hand up and said, "Wait a minute! Who came up with this location? Who is the most beloved by the whole world? And who brought us here safely and has done what most would have thought impossible? Also, it would honor your father's legacy along with your own. Lastly, since we have three distinct parts of the village, what better name for the lot than Santa's World?"

"By God he is right!" exclaimed Whitey, "It truly was your inspiration and leadership that accomplished this, and your idea to get the rest of the tallfolk, excuse me, the populace to assist us. I agree and I make a motion to put that name to a vote right now."

A few moments later, it was officially recorded that the area would henceforth and forevermore be known as Santa's World.

At that same meeting Mary and Nick asked that the Council approve the idea that they would invite back most of those that had helped them make the transition to their new location. Everyone worked so hard and by the time they had finished their work they had to return to their own lives and never got to rest after their toil. Plus many of the workers never got to see the Visiting Center, as they were busy building in their own areas. And since Michael wanted more visitors anyway, the Council would gladly accommodate him.

At Ella's suggestion, they placed April in charge of figuring when people would be available to come up. Since they had nearly a thousand names on the list, they had already begun to consider several visits.

It was also decided to hold a festival every three years and bring as many Santa Ambassadors as they could reasonably house into the nearby towns. They would transport them via train to the Visiting Center for a day so they could see their handiwork and learn more about the the place where magic really happened. This would be available for every Ambassador that had put in at least three years of Santa service to families. Cory would maintain the list, and he and Katy would help put on the festival.

In regards to Cory, postings had disappeared from the various offending websites, and the school and they were left in peace. However, there were great tumults taking place among the various 'Santa' groups, with several suing one another over website names and slogans, and much ado about which group was the most authentic. It was a sad state of affairs, but luckily one that Cory and Santa's World could stay completely away from.

Reminiscing about recent events, the couple finished up their cocoas. Mary said, "I think it's time we headed over to the Inn. The train should be here in about twenty minutes and Michael wanted to go over your visitation schedule for the week."

Nick smiled and thought, *Perhaps it is true, the more things change, the more they stay the same.* He hugged Mary as they got up and said how happy he was. Then they walked off arm in arm to continue their service from Santa's World.

The End.

Read an excerpt from the 1st Book

in The Santa Claus Trilogyy

Believe Again,
The North Pole Chronicles

Believe Again

The North Pole Chronicles

1st in the Santa Claus Trilogy

Joe Moore

Chapter One

All the best things in the world can be found in the eyes of a child.

- Forrest Hedemup

The Beginning

Long before Santa Claus moved to the North Pole
and became world known, the North Pole began, and
was run, by the elves. They had come to the top of the
world after being treated poorly by bigger people. It was
not so much that they were beaten or kicked, though
occasionally that would happen, but because largely
they were just ignored or dismissed. People didn't take
them seriously, if they paid attention to them at all.
Tallfolk thought that since they were small, they
couldn't be very smart. Nothing could have been further
from the truth.

So they had come from many lands, each hearing the
promise of a better world. Elves came from every
continent, and like the tallfolk they lived among, these
elves were every shape, color, with pointed ears and
round, some short and others taller. Unlike tallfolk,
most of them were around four feet give or take a few
inches. They spoke different languages, they had
different stories and legends, and they brought various
hopes and ambitions with each one. When things had
become unbearable in the country where they lived,
those elves would pack up their belongings, and hoping
the stories they heard were all true, and the inner voices
were not false, they would make the arduous trek to the

frozen north.

Sincere speech needs to be spoken here, these elves were, and remain far smarter than the people they had lived amongst. And once they banded together, they discovered that together they exceeded genius levels. As anyone knows, two people are smarter than one, and four are smarter than two, and so on. But with the elves, as they increased their numbers, their collective smarts geometrically progressed and became nothing shy of brilliance.

In addition to being much brighter than tallfolk, they have a very peaceable nature to themselves. Rarely do they ever have a disagreeable day. Each one finds great joy in working with each other. They have a strong sense of accomplishment in everything they do together. On the rare occasion elves disagree on something, they work it through with compromises, or when in doubt, they bring in a couple more opinions from other elves, until an agreement on a particular course is resolved.

Because the North Pole was inhospitable to others, they were not only left in peace, but were able to build quite a large settlement. Elves advanced their discoveries much faster than the outside world, and they began constructing marvelous inventions and ways to accomplish things to tame their new land. The developments they came up with would have given any other country pause. Soon they were centuries ahead of any other civilization.

Being friendly and forgiving by nature, the elves not only did not hold a grudge against bigger people, but found tallfolk children wonderful in their overall innocence and curious nature. This was something that always had been particularly endearing to every elf. They enjoyed the fact that through play, many tallfolk children learned how to get along, and received good lessons from others. All of the elves wanted to encourage that playtime for children everywhere.

It was Carrow Chekitwice who first suggested that perhaps the elves might build some things for the children to play with and enjoy. Again, while the elves were genuinely not against tallfolk they still avoided them as much as possible. Of course even with their collective smarts, they had to deal with the tallfolk from time to time. They needed many goods and occasionally services from them, because even with all their advances, the North Pole could not provide all the raw materials that were sought after. But the elves had plenty to trade in order to get what was needed.

Not the least of these items were their wonderful toys that would often touch a heartstring of the tallfolk and cause them to remember, even if just for a moment, what it was like to be a child. And the tallfolk wanted to give these toys to their own children, which of course was what the elves wanted, too.

Because of their advances in tools, tallfolk often would be happy to trade for what the elves produced. Much of it had never been seen before, and often they were decades ahead of their own inventions and tools. Soon their products became in high demand. But problems developed as some of the inventions that were traded became used in ways that the elves had not intended.

Believe Again, The North Pole Chronicles by Joe Moore

Many products were constructed and used against other people and changed from their initial designs. Wars came about because of their advances to the tallfolk and their misuse. So the Council of Elves decided that they needed to carefully trade only the tools and advances that the tallfolk could handle during a particular time in their development. Many products and innovations would have to wait until the Council thought the tallfolk would not use them for destructive, rather than constructive purposes.

Meanwhile in the Arctic, their innovations kept being developed at a breakneck pace. They had not only learned how to tame their harsh landscape, but had developed a dome to help handle the often frigid blizzard conditions, and make the Pole not only livable, but enjoyable. They had become partial to cold weather, and liked the snow, although they preferred it in less amounts and more gently falling. Once under the dome, they were able to keep the inside around the freezing mark, and opted not to make it too much warmer. Elves would become sluggish and less inclined to get things done when it was too warm.

Of course they also developed a more seasonal climate including spring, summer and fall. Like the rest of the globe, they enjoy beautiful days and can control the sunlight artificially. Especially since the sun does not appear for six months in winter. But even more important than the climate, in developing the dome which is many miles across, they had constructed a barrier that became impervious to both outsiders and natural disasters, up to and including meteorites.

During their development they had also discovered an interesting side affect to living at the North Pole. They began living much longer than their tallfolk counterparts. And not just by a few years, but decades, and later, centuries. Each new generation lived longer and longer. It was believed that because of the strong magnetic properties of the North Pole, it resulted in elves eventually living hundreds of years instead as a normal lifetime elsewhere.

Since they were now so long-lived, they became master craftsman in nearly any activity they pursued, often spending several decades working and perfecting their craft before being considered journeymen or women. They eventually abandoned the traditional way of being named outside of the North Pole. Many forsook their old last name and took on new ones, often adopting something pointing to the craft they were particularly good at.

Before long, only first names were given to newborn elves, and they were allowed to pick their own surname when they felt the time was right. Few ever changed it once chosen, but some waited nearly a century or more before making their decision.

Occasionally some elves would want to make a change for a time and move back south for a while. Some wished for their old geography, and were allowed to work on behalf of the North Pole in other areas. These elves could return whenever they wished. The only requirement was that they could not disclose the elves culture, or location, to the tallfolk. They were especially not allowed to bring any of the tallfok to the North

Pole, and had to keep many of the advancements of the elves secret.

This continued for a great many years, and while elves kept abreast of what was happening in the other lands, they often just shook their heads and enjoyed their quiet peace in their secret habitat. Many of the elves that worked in other lands would load up a bag of toys after they visited and took them to the children of the area they returned to. Also, some elves would take a handful of toys and sweets to children of the tallfolk they traded with, and leave them quietly in various places where they would eventually be discovered.

As a matter of course, the elves would say nothing about the gifts and would just leave them secretly. Occasionally, a bag of toys would just appear in an area where children were known to gather and play.

Unknown to any elves at first, was one particular tallfolk doing the same thing. He had come from a lineage that began with a former bishop of early Christianity, originally from Turkey in Middle Asia. That bishop had been anointed to sainthood for his deeds and love of children. This good man, and then his ancestors, had already begun to have many tales told about them as they traveled throughout Asia and Europe.

The bishop of Turkey's sons spread into other European lands as did their influence. His ancestors had moved through Italy, France, Germany and the Netherlands. Each had begun many traditions in the lands they traveled, all culminating in events geared around the birth of the Christ child, just as their Bishop forefather had done. They had begun to be known by many names from each land they traveled like Papa Noel, Pere Noel, La Befana, Babbo Natalie, Sinterklaas and others.

Many of the toys the elves had left for children had been credited to this tallfolk. This never bothered them as it had taken the attention off the elves, and left them to distribute their gifts in peace. A couple times the elves were actually pointed to as the gift-givers. They just said nothing and walked away. The elves did not want the attention of the tallfolk for the gifts left behind.

Toward the close of the eighteenth century, one of the elves came up with the idea to approach the tallfolk gift giver and ask if he would help distribute the elves' toys to the children, as he seemed to be doing it anyway. Denny Sweetooth, one of the members of the Council of Elves, asked about enlisting the stranger for help. Immediately a great debate ensued over whether or not to break elven law and allow the stranger to visit the North Pole, and to witness the wonders of the elves and their land.

After all, he was a member of the tallfolk. Many argued that it was wrong to say that none of the tallfolk could ever be trusted. Others argued that dire consequences would take place if this was allowed to happen. In the end, and by a single vote, it was agreed that the elves would send a delegation to meet with the man. During this meeting, if the delegation agreed, they would invite him to the North Pole.

They had placed on this delegation some of their best and brightest including Carrow Chekitwice - who was

known for his leadership and careful ingenuity; Denny
Sweetooth – whose suggestion it was in the first place.
Also, though Denny was a baker and chef by trade, he
was known for his big heart and wise council; Forrest
Hedemup – who was in charge of all the animals and
training in the North Pole and a lover of all creatures;
Whitey Slippenfall – who was not only one of the
principle elves that made the North Pole habitable, but
was in charge of the defenses of the Pole, including its
protective dome, and finally, Ella Communacado – who
was the chief information elf in charge of
communicating with the elves outside of the North
Pole.

Carrow was an ancient elf who had helped design and
build the village in the beginning. He was slightly taller
and thinner than many of the elves with a beard that
ran all the way down to his knees. His face carried a lot
of wrinkles and the elves weren't sure if it was due more
to his age, or his stern nature. Carrow always seemed to
be frowning and studying things, whether village plans
or simple toys, with the same unending scrutiny.

At the opposite end of Carrow, Denny Sweetooth was
always smiling and jovial. He was as round as he was
tall, and looked like a dwarf even to other elves. Denny's
passion was food. Cooking it or eating it didn't matter.
He just loved being in a kitchen or near it. He also was
known to have the biggest heart in the North Pole and
was always offering counsel and help to others with their
many concerns.

Forrest Hedemup was chosen for his stamina and
strength. While no bigger than an average elf, he looked

like a ranch hand and was stronger than nearly any elf. He carried large bundles with no effort, and could handle himself with tallfolk if the need arose. He was chosen to help keep a protective eye on the delegation, and to assist with the animals they would need and their load. A good looking young man by elf standards, he was one of the few blond elves with deep blue eyes.

Whitey was aptly named, as he sported a full head of white hair that looked as white and big as a snow bank. He had piercing green eyes, and like Carrow, was taller than most of his village. Whitey was the protector of the North Pole. He handled the defenses and also the security within the Pole. Very rarely did anything untoward happen in the village, but if it did, Whitey was called to the scene. His keen senses were known throughout the village, and he had a great capacity for sensing what was right from wrong. It was for this reason, as much as any, that he was chosen for this important mission.

If Whitey was known for his intuition, Ella was known for being able to put thought into "sincere speech" as elves called complete truth. A pleasant looking woman with dark hair and dark mysterious hazel eyes to match, she was one of the more desirable ladies of the North Pole, and was often sought after by the single men of the village.

What made Ella important (and feared by less sincere men) was her ability to see through to the truth, or make sense of any garbled discussion, and put it into words that everyone could grasp. There are some that just have a difficult time talking with others. Ella could understand what they meant and spoke their thoughts in a concise manner. Just in case this tallfolk began saying things insincerely, or without clear meaning, Ella would be there to interpret.

When these intrepid five left the North Pole on their quest, it was an unusual time in history. As they headed for the Netherlands, Ella explained to the others that this was a time of turmoil in England. As they all knew, the English had colonies throughout the world, on every known continental land mass, but one of these colonies was rebelling against their home country and England was embroiled in a war with their own people.

Apparently 'Americans', as they were calling themselves, had decided they no longer wished to be ruled by England and wanted to be free and independent. The other elves felt an instant kinship to these people, as they had traveled to the North Pole for similar reasons, though elves would rather leave for places unknown than to create war on others for something as unimportant as land.

The troupe had spent most of the fall, and part of the winter, searching for their quarry through the Netherlands. He was known to be in Amsterdam for a time, but they were not sure he was still around. It seemed the man was anxious to avoid recognition and attention, just as the elves had done. Many times they were told that yes, someone had been by and left some food stuffs and toys, but he was gone before they could even thank him. They had been given a vague description of the man, but other then sporting a full white beard and mustache, and being of large and strong build, there was little else to distinguish him.

They finally caught up with the man they sought outside of Eindhoven in the south eastern part of the Netherlands around mid-December. They found him on the road heading out of town. He looked like a peddler and was carrying a large pack on his back. He had a long beard, hair and mustache.

But what the elves also saw was that his green eyes twinkled, and he had the reddest cheeks Ella had ever seen on a tallfolk. He called himself Kris Kringle, and he had a very pleasant demeanor about him. He was surprised when approached by the small band. While being of average height himself, he had not seen such a small group gathered together before. They said they would like to talk with him and invited him to dine with them at the local tavern.

Kris at first thanked the group, but told them he had to get his possessions to Tilburg, as he had children waiting for him. The elves pressed him further and said that what they had to say to him may help him reach a great many more children than just in Tilburg and Eindhoven. They also impressed upon that they had been seeking him for months and throughout the country. Kris finally agreed to have lunch with them and they all went to the tavern.

Once they sat down, it was an awkward beginning, as the elves didn't quite know where or how to start. They had spent so much time searching for the man, but never truly discussed how they would initiate the conversation once they found him. They were still apprehensive about sharing too much of their life in the North Pole, in case they decided against asking this stranger to join them, so they attempted to speak in generalities. Likewise, Kris wasn't sure what business they wanted with him, and while he was polite, he was a little impatient to continue on his way.

They found common ground when Ella asked Kris why he traveled around giving gifts to children and then watched as Kris' eyes lit up immediately. He explained that his ancestor had instructed as far back as 300 A.D., on how God so loved the world that he gave the greatest gift of all to the world. A child, a simple gift that would forever change much of the world and its beliefs. As Kris was the tenth descendant of the great St. Nicholas, he wanted children to know that they were still loved. So like his forefathers before him, he brought gifts to as many as he could, and especially during December to remind them of God's gift. He explained that between making, securing and delivering the gifts, his efforts filled the entire year. But it was around Christmas when he tried to have the biggest impact.

He said that many children lose their innocent nature too soon, and he wanted to help them keep a little joy even if just during his one visit each year. The elves and Kris got into a very animated and spirited discussion about children, and what made them the most special of all God's creatures. Forrest talked about how the best of any creature could be found in the eyes of a child. Denny regaled his stories about the joy of a child's expression in every sweet cake he gave them. Even Carrow who is normally of a stern nature, talked about the wonderment of a child as they handled one of the carefully constructed toys they were given.

The elves saw in Kris the virtues they had hoped; a strong and loving heart, a child's amazement of the earth and heavens, an innocence untarnished by the hardships of the world, and a vitality and enthusiasm that seemed boundless. With an indiscernible nod to each other, the elves began to talk in hushed tones about a wondrous land that was built almost entirely to serve children. They told Kris of their mission to find him and invite him to the North Pole.

Kris listened enraptured about the amazing things they were saying about their village and mission. Of course he had many misgivings about making such an argent journey to such a faraway place and during such an inhospitable time. Also, if he went he would need to bring his wife, and there were still the children in Tilburg that needed their toys, and what of Christmas coming? This time the elves were ready and met each of Kris' concerns with a solution.

It was finally agreed that first, they would assist Kris in delivering his toys to the children in Tilburg, then they would meet his wife and discuss the North Pole in more detail with both of them. Finally, if they both agreed, the elves would send another delegation to the Kringle's after Christmas, and they would all make the journey then. The elves promised that the journey wouldn't be as difficult as Kris envisioned, and they would bring very special clothing that would keep them both safe and warm during the trip.

After spending quite some time on the journey to Tilburg with Kris and then meeting Mrs. Kringle, the delegation was even more certain that they had made the right decision. Ann Marie Kringle was warm and enchanting with an easy smile and laugh, like her husband. Ann Marie was quite an attrative women. She was only about 5 feet tall with dark brown hair and soft hazel eyes.

They both seemed so very…jolly! They were comfortable to be around and they had an easy spirit wrapped in a blanket of endless faith. All had agreed to the plan as laid out by the elves, and set the date to begin right after the Epiphany, on January 7th of the New Year.

This accord would change history around the world for billions of children everywhere.

Read an excerpt from the 2nd Book

in The Santa Claus Trilogy

Faith, Hope & Reindeer

Faith, Hope & Reindeer

2nd in The Santa Claus Trilogy

Joe Moore

Chapter One

"This is so useless!" Jared Grady moaned. He stood up to his full 6'1" frame and rubbed his sandy brown hair with both hands. While he was only 42, he felt he had aged a good ten years this past year. He had rugged features, but he began to look more weathered in recent months.

Julie gave her husband of twenty years a sympathetic look, knowing his frustration all too well. "Something is out there for you," she said "It's only a matter of time. Now I need to go get the kids."

Julie jumped into her SUV and backed out of the driveway of their modest, but pretty, Cape Cod. She pulled up in front of the high school a few minutes later.

Her daughter, Susan, stood out front with some friends. Julie again admired her striking daughter, and was proud how she looked so much like she did at seventeen. Susan had the same shoulder-length auburn hair, high cheekbones and beautiful figure as Julie did. She had kept that good shape all her life and felt Susan would, too. Susan said a quick goodbye to her friends and hopped into the front seat. "Hi Mom."

"Where's Marshall?" asked Julie.

Susan replied, "He forgot his Chemistry book and since he has a test Friday, he thought it might be a good idea to study, so he went back to get it."

Marshall came jogging up to the car from the far building. "Sorry," he said scrambling into the back seat.

Faith, Hope & Reindeer by Joe Moore

"Hey Mom, did you remember to sign that release for the band concert on Saturday?"

Julie responded, "The paper is on the counter, now don't forget tomorrow, or they may not let you go."

Marshall smiled broadly. "Naw, they'd never think of leaving their best tenor sax behind!" Julie said, "You'd be surprised at the things they'd do in the name of school policy." She was proud of both her children and was pleased that Marshall's looks emulated her husbands, except like Susan, he had her soft green eyes and long fingers.

Both of the Grady kids were in great moods. This was that special time of year. They only had a couple more days, then no school for two whole weeks while everyone celebrated the holidays. Even final exams would be held later than usual and wouldn't begin until the latter half of January.

Marshall was more animated and he seemed to sense something particularly special about this upcoming break. Had you asked him, he couldn't say what – only a feeling deep down. Susan always loved the Christmas holiday, and knew this was her special time of year.

Neither of them could possibly guess what had arrived at their home as they got into the car.

 Chapter Two

Jared thought to himself, *This is going to be a very different Christmas indeed, but for an entirely different reason.*

As he walked away from the computer again considering their plight the doorbell rang. He opened the door to a FedEx envelope addressed to "The Gradys." Jared wondered if it might be an early Christmas present, but couldn't imagine from whom.

He retrieved the package and opened it. He scanned its contents and read and reread the cover letter. The return address stated "Alaska Authentication Department."

Julie and the kids returned to see Jared standing in the entryway reading and scratching his head.

Marshall eyed the FedEx envelope and asked "For me?"

His dad looked past Marshall at Julie and said, "Can I talk to you for a moment?" Julie feared bad news. They walked into the office and Jared closed the door.

"What's up?" asked Julie looking worried.

"Did you enter any contests or fill out any forms for prizes?"

Julie shook her head. "No, you know I don't believe in those, they exist to get people on their mailing lists and other marketing ploys."

Jared thought for a second. "What about the kids?"

"I suppose it's possible, but I've told them the same

thing and have discouraged them from doing it. Jared, what is this about?"

Jared handed her the contents of the FedEx envelope.

Julie read it and said, "This can't be right. Obviously this is in error or belongs to another Grady."

Jared shook his head. "Look at the cover letter and who it's addressed to."

Julie perused the cover letter. *Dear Jared, Julie, Susan & Marshall:* She was puzzled. "It still must be wrong. Let's ask the kids just in case?"

They left the office and called Susan and Marshall down from their rooms. Both said they heeded their mother's advice and didn't enter anything.

Then remembering something Marshall groaned. "Well I did sign up to win an iPod one time on the computer. Why, did I get one?" His parents were staring at the mysterious contents.

"What's this all about? Why the questions?" asked Susan.

This time Jared spoke. "It seems we've won a trip to Alaska. A one week, all-expense paid trip including airline and train tickets and we leave next week when your vacation starts and we'll be gone over Christmas."

"COOL!" "GREAT!" Both kids cried out.

"Now wait a minute," said Julie. "We don't know if this is legitimate or how we got this. It may be a scam or something."

Marshall took the letter from his father's hand and read it.

Dear Jared, Julie, Susan & Marshall:

Congratulations! You are invited on a special trip for the four of you to Alaska. Your tickets are enclosed. You will be traveling by Alaska Airlines to Fairbanks on December 19th then board an exclusive train following the directions below. This train will take you through some of the most rugged and spectacular terrain with the widest abundance of Alaska's wildlife you are ever likely to see.

You will stay at a magnificent five-star resort for six days and nights, where your every wish will be attended to and return December 26th via the route you came. All meals, lodging, tips and transportation are included. The only thing you'll need to bring is lots of warm clothing.

Please make certain you allow plenty of time to make your flight from Orange County's John Wayne Airport, as changing flight times or days cannot be allowed as it will affect the train schedule as well.

We know you will enjoy this trip of a lifetime and we wish you all a very Merry Christmas.

Sincerely,

Alaska Authentication Department

Faith, Hope & Reindeer by Joe Moore

"It must be for us!" Marshall said excitedly. "It has all our names on it. Cool. Are those the tickets?"

Julie stopped him in his tracks. "Now wait a minute young man, we can't go off to Alaska in the middle of winter on a whim, especially at Christmas."

Susan was now reading the letter and said, "You know it IS over the Christmas break, and it says everything's included." She looked at her father. "Dad, you did promise we would take a trip to Alaska before things went crazy with your job."

"Yeah but sweetheart, I was talking about a cruise or a summer trip to Denali, and not as Mom said 'in the middle of winter'!" He looked at the ticket information for the airline and train, again. It certainly seemed authentic. Then he said more to himself, "We aren't even sure this is real."

The next half hour consisted of a family debate. Susan reminded them (several times) how she would be going off to college next summer and how this might be the last 'family' vacation that they could all take together. Marshall's argument was centered on a more simple 'nothing ventured, nothing gained' attitude.

The final decision for that day was that Jared and Julie would look into this more carefully and at least verify the legitimacy of the "trip". Especially as to what strings might be attached. Then they would discuss this with them when all the details were available.

To this Marshall said, "Wow! I'm going to go see what kind of warm clothes I've got," and took off for his room.

Chapter Three

"I'm sorry sir, I cannot give that information over the phone," said the immovable Alaska Airlines representative.

Jared said, "Look, I'm trying to verify whether you have tickets in our name or not."

"I can verify that the flight number, day, time and destination are all accurate, but I cannot give you passenger details. If you wish, you may come to the Alaska counter with picture ID and we can verify any other information."

Trying to get the information about the train was even more nebulous. The only thing Jared could find out was that, yes, there is a Northern Express train, and yes, it left from somewhere in Fairbanks. But its route and schedule was some unusually strange secret, or at least not known by any normal line of inquiry.

Julie tried calling the Alaska Department of Tourism but got no further than Jared. No, they were not giving away trips, and yes, it was possible someone else was. No, they did not have an "Authentication Department". Yes, the cruise ships and trains generally stopped by September, but there are a few special promotions and companies that did do events over the holidays to get through the long quieter months of winter. It was suggested she search the Internet for more information on those.

Most of the next morning they tried to get whatever

information they could about the trip. The "resort" wasn't listed by name or address in the letter; the destination of the train left little to go on also.

Susan and Marshall had left in high spirits that morning and Jared and Julie were not pleased with the aspect of dashing their hopes when they came home. But it seemed like everything led to a dead end. They weren't very comfortable heading off to places unknown and unverified. Around 11:30 that morning the doorbell rang again.

Julie opened the door to a large box dropped off by UPS this time. When the Gradys opened the box they found four beautiful ski suits with matching gloves, each a different color and size. They were labeled for each of them. Jared's was a rich dark blue with light blue piping. Julie's white with red trim, Marshall's a dark forest green, and Susan's was also white but sported an eggplant trim. The enclosed card contained a hand written note, which said:

Hope this helps for the trip. We look forward to seeing you here.

The labels on the jackets read "The Warmth of Faith Company" of Alaska. Jared tried on the jacket over the sweatshirt he was wearing and it fit beautifully. He knew looking at the ski pants and gloves that they would fit equally as well.

Julie looked at him and shrugged. This was getting a little eerie. If someone was out to get them, they were going through a lot of expense and trouble to do so. The Warmth of Faith. Well they certainly would have warmth now, so she felt maybe they could supply the faith.

Faith, Hope & Reindeer by Joe Moore

When the kids came home Jared and Susan filled them in on the whole story about trying to research the tickets and destinations and expressed their concerns. They finally showed them the suits and gloves. Susan agreed with her mother that this was one of those times when they had to put faith before their cynicism. She reminded her Dad that often he reiterated what the Pastor at church said about how a little faith would go a long way.

Meanwhile, Marshall was already in his ski pants and putting on the jacket. In his mind, he was already halfway to the airport. Jared finally said that if the tickets on Alaska Airlines were good, they were going. If not, it would be the shortest vacation on record. All the same he might try going to the airport to at least get a secure answer for that part of the trip.

The kids weren't sorry about leaving over Christmas, and they would be home for the second half of vacation anyway. Everyone was suddenly in vacation mode, and for the first time in a long time, Jared wasn't transfixed on being unemployed.

Chapter Four

The next several days were spent tying up loose ends, going to Marshall's holiday concert, taking tests at school, getting vacation time for Julie's job approved and getting together with friends and exchanging what gifts they could before they left on Monday.

There was no time to shop for clothes and only time to restock essentials from the health and beauty departments. The Gradys were thankful for the new ski suits, and wondered how cold it would get. Jared looked on the Internet for weather and temperatures, but without an exact location, it was impossible to gauge. The weather varied widely throughout the state, from $-35°$ F with blizzard conditions to $42°$ F and sunny, with everything in between going on in that huge land mass. The nearest he could guess was their arrival in Fairbanks where it was a brisk $-10°$ F with snow on and off. What he did know was that they needed to pack anything they owned that was warm.

From quick trips on the Internet, Jared knew that Fairbanks was one of the best spots on earth to see the Northern Lights, and he hoped that the kids would get to see this most awesome display of nature. He was frustrated at not being able to plan properly for the trip and felt that he didn't have much control, which of course was correct.

But then again, it was rather exhilarating to not have to worry about the details and to go "sight unseen" into this vacation. He did try to locate rail lines and such around Fairbanks, to no avail. He hit a whiteout trying to gain any new information. He also never got to the airport, and figured if everyone else could muster up some trust, he would too. Besides, the worst that could happen is that the tickets weren't real, but for some reason he didn't believe it.

Faith is a marvelous thing.

If you would like to purchase the Trilogy books or any other books written by Joe Moore, you may buy his books at bookstores or Amazon.
You can also purchase autographed books through our website at

www.thenorthpolepress.com

or scan the QR code

About The Author

Joe Moore has written millions of words over his lifetime. A graduate from California State University, Northridge, Joe is a former publisher, editor, advertising, marketing and sales executive. He worked on hundreds of campaigns and articles with thousands of proposals and stories for everything from fishing equipment to business magazines. This may help explain why he is able to write in so many genres.

Moore is a former feature writer for several Southern California periodicals. He has three books published in his Santa Claus Trilogy – *Believe Again, The North Pole Chronicles and Faith, Hope & Reindeer and Glaciers Melt & Mountains Smoke.* He is very excited to have his first three children's books published. *Santa's World Introducing Santa's Elf Series, Jamie Hardrock, Chief Mining Elf and Shelley Wrapitup, Master Design Elf* in the newly created Santa's Elf Series©. These books are produced for early readers, written in rhyme, and illustrated by Moore's wife, Mary. Moore has written a total of 25 children's stories for the Santa's Elf Series that will be published at the rate of about two per year.

Moore is also venturing into new genre's of suspense/horror with *Return of the Birds* and is currently working on a ghost series.

Moore has been seen and interviewed on nearly every news program, such as Good Morning America, Fox News, ABC/NBC/CBS News and in numerous radio programs and newspapers. He also appeared on Disney Surfers, Nickelodeon, in numerous parades, on billboards and he and his wife were featured guests on

Wealth TV with the late Charlie Jones (NFL Media Hall of Fame announcer). As a professional Santa Claus, he works with daycare centers, visits dozens of homes and corporations, and spreads his goodwill and joy with Mrs. Claus everywhere they travel.

Joe and Mary Moore, (as Santa and Mrs. Claus) also give of themselves, having contributed countless hours (and toys) to worthy charities including, the American Cancer Society, Children's Hospitals, Military families, Domestic abuse shelters, Community projects for schools, "Angel" programs, Hospice centers, Meals on Wheels and more. Both Joe & Mary feel truly blessed by God to be able to bring such joy and happiness to others.

Moore's other passion is cooking! He enjoys creating spectacular meals for Mary and his friends. He also enjoys fishing, even though he admits his wife can always out fish him!

The Moores reside in the beautiful Smoky Mountains of East Tennessee.

www.ingramcontent.com/pod-product-compliance
Lightning Source LLC
Chambersburg PA
CBHW071145020726
47502CB00002B/279